Yours Temporarily

The Office Heartthrobs Book 1

Rose Fresquez

Rose Fresquez Books

ISBN: 978-1-961159-20-4

Yours Temporarily is a work of fiction. Names, characters, places, and incidents are either the product of the author's imagination or are used fictitiously, and any resemblance to actual persons, living or dead, business establishments, events or locales is entirely coincidental.

Editing by Deirdre Lockhart.

ACKNOWLEDGEMENTS

I want to thank the Lord, my Savior. Without you, Father, there's no point in trying to do anything at all. It's my prayer that I can honor you with my words. I thank you for connecting me with an amazing group of people who helped support me in accomplishing this novel.

To my husband Joel, who works so hard to provide for our family, so that I can stay home and take care of the kids. I'm so blessed that we get to journey through life together.

To my children Isaiah, Caleb, Abigail and Micah, you fill my heart with joy. Thanks for the giggles, laughter and encouragement.

To my editor, Deirdre Lockhart. You're a true blessing from God. Your insights and wisdom have helped shape this story.

And to GOD, Who makes everything possible. Without God's wisdom and creativity, this story wouldn't be in existence.

To my insider team, thanks for always suggesting the coolest ideas.

To my Street Team. Thank you from the bottom of my heart.

CHAPTER 1

Jeremy

"What do you mean—you're not so sure?" Shifting in my black leather chair, I press cold fingertips against my temples and try to massage away the day's tension. "The purpose of this meeting is to go over the projections you sent."

Screen silence? Seriously? Why's he so bent over a minor issue rather than the sloppy reports?

I clear my throat. "You're a branch manager, and I expect you to handle whatever program you prefer. Should you think I wouldn't approve, that should've been an earlier question before this meeting." My face reflects at me. The glow from the computer screen casts me in a harsh light, highlighting the exhaustion etched into my features. As COO of one of the nation's top financial firms, I must maintain a firm persona as part of the job. Now, I bounce my knee under the table, my role being tested.

A silence passes before Kahale's face pops to the corner of my monitor, and a spreadsheet occupies the rest of the screen.

"I'm sure you already saw this. What do you think?" His voice cuts through the monitor. His grin wide, he's oblivious to my simmering impatience. This virtual meeting with the Hawaiian branch has dragged on far too long.

"If this is the copy you emailed, these projections won't work." I lean forward, giving the spreadsheet a cursory glance before I refocus on the man's tan face in the pop-up. "I need them revised and resubmitted by the end of the day Tuesday."

Surely, he can hear my urgency. He has an entire weekend, plus Monday and Tuesday. More than enough time to get the job done. These aren't mere numbers on a spreadsheet. They're the compass by which we'll navigate this fiscal year. Now, nearly halfway through January, the delay is more than a hiccup—it's a threat to our strategic posture. I'm only letting him off the hook because he wasn't the branch manager last January and he's yet to learn my expectations.

"I'll resubmit it by the end of Monday."

A day sooner is even better.

"Thank you." Given the circumstances, I try for the positive reinforcement I use for those who get their jobs done.

After the call, the silence in my office feels more profound. I drum my fingers on the desk, the noise set against the hum of the small fridge by the bookshelf and the faint sounds of the city below. The diminishing light casts the San Francisco skyline in subdued hues, signaling time's passage in the world beyond this glass building.

The city's building lights begin to sparkle like far-off stars, breathing life into the evening as the day's commotion subsides. From my vantage point on the fifty-eighth floor, it appears as though life itself is drifting by.

I stifle a yawn. My fingers brushing against heavy eyelids, I battle a relentless fatigue that's become my unwelcome shadow. My gaze drifts to the table nestled among the sofas, the spot where my assistant lately insists I sit for my lunch break.

My stomach sends a plaintive rumble at the sight of the covered container Jill brought earlier. But a single email spiraled into a phone call, and then the afternoon was a blur of back-to-back commitments. With my many office hours of sitting still, the twice-daily escape to the penthouse gym is a necessity to my routine.

My phone buzzes from beside the computer. It's probably my mother again. Whatever she has to say can wait. I still need to recover from her unsettling call earlier today, which disrupted my composure and left me wary of any further calls from my cell phone for the day.

My jaw tightens. Just the memory of our conversation sends me off track once again. I reach for my pen from the blue sticky notepad next to my keyboard. Sitting up straighter, I tap the pen on my jaw. The metal is cool against my flesh as I ponder the story I had concocted—a lie that's still gnawing at me.

At thirty-one, I'm my own man, answerable to no one. Yet, every conversation with my mother resurrects my inherent timidity. She was overenthusiastic about my brother's impending wedding, or rather, more excited about reuniting me with Sonya at the upcoming ceremony. The moment she laid out plans for accommodations, ensuring my ex and I would be under the same roof, my tongue slipped.

Now, the task looms over me. I need a girlfriend before the end of March—no, earlier. I'll need to familiarize her with my world and shield her from becoming my mother's new project during the one-week visit.

For many, navigating dates comes naturally, but for me, it's almost a Herculean task. Social engagements are not my forte, except with my friends, so I avoid such interactions like a bad investment. I tap the pen against my lips, my thoughts drifting to the last woman I interacted with. Clarissa. Undeniably beautiful, she displayed a clinginess right from the start. Our first lunch outing felt less like a date and more like an obligation. Nothing could compel me to call her back.

Until now.

A knock interrupts my thoughts. Before I can respond, the door swings open.

"Damien Blackwood." I adjust my shirtsleeves as he enters.

"Jeremy Kress," he responds with a curt nod, his darker skin tone, unlike mine, seems to hide the tiredness of his eyes. I gesture for him to take a seat across from my desk.

A palpable skepticism adds tension to his posture as he sits, likely stemming from our heated discussion yesterday about the promotion he expected but didn't get. His eagerness to excel reminds me of my early days as a stockbroker. He's one of the few team leaders who consistently meets his objectives without needing reminders.

"Do you have a moment?" His bright eyes scan me intently.

"I wouldn't have offered you a seat otherwise, would I?"

Damien exhales. "I hear Smith's retiring at the end of the year."

Wow. How quickly the rumors spread about our financial-planning analyst.

I lean back, appraising him. His ambition is clear, but he's more suited for other roles. "The position you're talking about is a senior management role."

"I can oversee financial planning and analysis functions just fine."

My brow rises. No doubt, he knows what the job title entails and can handle it. I still have to state some reasons why this position might not be a good fit for him. "Don't forget strategic planning and significant contributions to high-level decision-making processes."

"I can handle it." He squares his shoulders beneath a blue button-down.

I tap the pen on my chin, considering his potential. With intense training, he *can* handle it. However, I need his help to keep all the other branches from slacking—it's an upcoming opening that might suit him better, unknown to the rest of the team. But I can't tell him yet, in case Mary Walsh changes her mind and extends her retirement for another two years or so.

"Damien, it's past office hours." Usually, no one other than the cleaners and me are still in the building on a Friday night. I swivel in my chair, rolling it forward as I try to soften my tone. My assistant, Jill, suggested I was rather curt with him yesterday and reminded me of my New Year's resolution to be more approachable this year. "We have a whole year ahead for you to demonstrate your capabilities for such a role."

He nods, his expression clouded before he replaces it with a half smile. "Of course."

"I don't make the final hiring decisions, you know," I remind him, although I have significant influence in the selection process, especially for key positions.

"I usually don't stay this late at work." He adjusts his loose tie, clearly uncomfortable about whatever he's about to say. "I started driving home and then had to drive back. You're invited to a small staff get-together at my place tomorrow."

"You're inviting me to your house?"

My eyes bulge, probably almost comically so. Invitations like this from subordinates are a rarity.

"I know you're a busy man." He nods, standing, seeming to conclude what my response will be. "I knew you wouldn't come, but my sister insisted I ask. She wants to record or practice her recipes—"

"Time and place," I say, decisively.

Damien's eyes now mirror my earlier reaction, clearly taken aback. I can almost see him recalibrating his expectations. I might regret attending a party with the employees he's invited, all of whom I seldom interact with. Yet, as their boss, I can't appear disinterested in their lives, especially when we're promoting a healthy work-life balance after an employee passed out last year from stress, which was more family-related than work.

The silence between us stretches, almost tangible, before I nod. "All right, Blackwood."

He clears his throat, then adjusts his already tucked-in shirt into his khakis. "I'll…" He lifts his hand, obviously struggling to regain his composure.

My chest swells, and I tap the pen in my hand. Damien hadn't expected me to accept his invitation, and that, in itself, is an intriguing development.

He leaves with a promise to text me the address and time, scheduled late tomorrow. Saturdays I usually reserve for work with no interruptions from the staff. Sunday afternoons are my social days for weekly rounds of golf with my friends and fellow executives. Attending this gathering will be a step outside my routine.

***

Navigating the unfamiliar outskirts of the Bay Area on a Saturday evening, I find myself in the Mission District. Its quaint streets are a reprieve from the usual hustle of the places I frequent. My Tesla runs silently and smoothly against the pavement, contrasting with the odd fluttering in my stomach. The car's navigation system cuts through the silence, announcing my arrival outside a vibrant two-story house. A warm embrace of fairy lights illuminates its bright-red door.

After parking on the street, I retrieve a brown bag with two boxes of chocolates—my contribution to the gathering. My leather shoes pad against the walkway to the steps, the bag in my hand crinkling and punctuating the quiet evening.

Beyond the front door, muffled activity, pots and pans clanging in preparation, greets me. I suck in a deep breath to steady my nerves, then straighten my collar before pressing the doorbell. Chimes. Hmm, homey, like Granny's house.

I wait alongside potted calla lilies basking in the warm light as streetlights glow amid the neighborhood's eclectic brick, Victorian, and Edwardian homes, each with a unique charm. However, this particular house stands out with its stone porch and stark-white shutters. If there's a party, though, there's not a single car in the driveway or on the street. I pull out my phone to check if I'm at the right house, then wince when my eyes glaze over the phone screen. I'm an hour early. Snap!

Each time I look at the phone to check one thing, something else always snags my attention. Right now, it's my brother's text. I can't ignore it, and I feel my face split in half as I read the capitalized text.

Gavin: FIANCÉE? I KNOW IT'S FAR FROM THE TRUTH. CALL ASAP.

I stagger when a door jerks violently and slams my forehead. An "ouch!" escapes as the phone slips from my grasp. A woman scoops it up and rushes over with a stream of apologies.

"I'm so sorry." Her vibrant energy belies the situation. Handing back my device, she takes the bag of chocolates from my other hand. "This door is sticky."

Slightly dazed, I rub my forehead. A door slam shouldn't be this painful.

Her eyes, lively and warm, shine in the porch light. Her skin is a flawless shade of brown, with dark curls framing her oval face and dangling just above her shoulders. In an orange long-sleeve dress with a vivid print, she gives a sunny vibe. She's shorter than the average woman, yet every inch of her is a presence that can't be ignored.

"This cheap door." She winces. "Damien has been meaning to fix it, but well... Come in. Let's get some ice on that forehead."

I'm an hour early, so I wave back toward my car and suggest waiting in it.

But she shakes her head, her curls bouncing. "Please stay. I'm Zuri."

"Jeremy." The tension in my shoulders drains. Is that a hint of ease I'm sensing in her presence?

"Oh, Jeremy, I'm so glad you came." She arches well-sculpted brows, her mock astonishment charming. "Damien didn't think you'd show."

"I'm a man of my word." I close the door behind us and follow her. Despite the striking contrast between them, this must be Damien's sister. But again, I don't know him well because we only talk about work. Clearly, he's talked about me to her. I can only hope whatever he's said was good.

As we cross hardwood floors through a room where pleasant sage walls host a lifetime of pictures, tantalizing scents beckon us to the kitchen. "Thanks for inviting me. I know your brother only did so because you were the initiator."

"Damien talks about me?" She pulls out a barstool and pats it for me, her movements fluid, natural.

"Yesterday, I learned he has a sister." Yep, that's how little I know the employees. "Apparently, I'm here thanks to you."

I slide onto the offered stool. Food trays line the marbled counters. Most are in foil pans with burners beneath them, likely keeping the food warm. "How many people are you expecting?"

"About twenty or so."

Just a tenth of the staff, but it's a fair amount. I'm lucky to be included in this party then. Damien mentioned something about his sister wanting to try out recipes. "You prepared all this food?"

She nods. "I'll get you some ice first." With a wave, she dismisses my protests, moves to the counter, and sets the bag of chocolates in the one open space. She then returns to the stainless fridge and pulls out a bag of frozen peas. "You're the first one here, so you get to be my taste tester."

My stomach responds with a timely rumble, eliciting her giggles. "Your fault for mentioning food tasting," I quip and shift on the stool. More dishes await on the dining table connecting the kitchen. "So, you're a chef, huh?"

"Something like that." She applies the bag to my forehead, and I grimace at the coldness. Our hands brush as I reach to hold the bag. Her care is natural, so I have no reason to assume whatever Damien said about me was negative.

As Zuri glides to the counter, opening and closing the maple cabinets, I set the cold bag on the marble island, no longer willing to endure its biting chill against my skin. Rolling up my sleeves—part habit, part testament to my increasing ease in her company—I watch her stir a pot on the stove, steam rising in curls. Anticipation builds within me as she works. And as I further relax, I almost imagine she's working more than culinary magic.

CHAPTER 2

Zuri

Wow, Damien's boss! Jeremy ain't nothing like the dreary, uptight image Damien painted. I pride myself on gauging people's traits from their looks, and Jeremy, with his neatly styled, side-parted hair, strong jawline, and well-groomed beard, screams meticulousness. He's the punctual sort, no doubt the kind who insists on precision and order in everything.

"I'm so sorry again." I return and set a glass of ice water before him. In the rush of preparing for the evening, we neglected the drinks. Damien and my two best friends ran out to fetch ice and sodas, leaving me to finalize my meal preparations.

"It's not a big deal." His startling blue eyes catch the light, accentuated by the blue shirt he's wearing. He seems at ease, sleeves rolled to his elbows, revealing a fancy watch and toned forearms.

"You should keep icing that." I gesture toward the abandoned bag of frozen peas, then his slightly swollen forehead. His fair skin looks like it might bruise easily.

"My mouth is watering for the food tasting you mentioned." Apparently, he's uninterested in icing his sore spot. He rubs his hands together in anticipation before standing. "Can I wash my hands, please?"

"Of course." I guide him to the sink and reach for a towel from the cabinet. The water hisses as he turns on the faucet. From my vantage point, I admire his stature. He towers over my modestly five-two frame by almost fourteen inches. Broad shoulders stretch out his shirt, and tidy stubble frames a chiseled jaw similar to what I'd see in ads for cologne or expensive watches.

His blue eyes are like a snippet of the ocean itself. He washes his large hands, rubbing them together with deliberate precision. Then he turns off the water, and I compose myself enough to offer him the towel and act as if I hadn't been stealing glances.

"Such great service you have here," he comments.

My pulse picks up, and so does the flip of my stomach. But that won't do. Nope. No way! No heart racing or somersaulting of any sort. Fleeting romances ain't on my agenda, and even if they were, Jeremy is off-limits—he's my brother's boss, the grump Damien can't stand.

My gaze drifts to the basil plant on the counter as I throw a pitch for my business. "That's the kind of service you'll get at Zuri's Daylight Café."

"Where's Zuri's Daylight Café?"

His genuine interest sparks a flicker of hope in me.

"I'll be opening it soon." I skirt around the specifics. I need funds to renovate before opening, but if he's gonna be a potential customer, I can't risk him seeing the place in its current state—still cloaked in the shadows of its previous owner.

"I like that entrepreneurial spirit." He nods, and sincerity gleams in those eyes. He takes his time to wipe his hands and doesn't press for details, instead folding up the towel, which isn't something we take the time to do around here. "Where should I put this?"

I take it from him, grateful for the distraction. With Damien and my friends out, I've gotten this unexpected chance to peel back the layers of Jeremy's persona, laying the groundwork for future conversations about my brother.

As Jeremy sits back down, I mention the kombucha tea I've made. It's a hit-or-miss beverage, and I doubt it's his cup of tea. But he surprises me, claiming a love for the fermented drink.

Maybe there's more to Jeremy than the corporate shell he wears.

"This is good." He salutes me with the cup after taking a sip. "Will you have this on the menu?"

I stand taller. No reason to squelch a swell of pride. "Maybe on special orders." It takes extra effort, but his genuine interest sparks a bit of my excitement, especially when he asks about the café's location.

"In your office building. The former Carol's Café." The words blurt out against my earlier reservation to keep the café's whereabouts a secret. He'll find out sooner or later anyway. As his immaculate brows rise, I affirm, "I'm the new owner."

"That's the best kombucha I've ever had."

I bask in his praise, but unsure how to handle compliments from an attractive man, I need a diversion.

"Come. Let's check out the snacks." I lead him to the array of dishes. The kitchen is fragrant with garlic, bacon, and basil among so many other flavors. With the clear wrap over the foil pans, the snacks are visible. I point out the bacon-wrapped dates first. "These have no spice." I explain before moving to the spicy chicken bites, then the jalapeno poppers, and the two slow cookers radiating warmth in the house. "Chicken and beef for the wraps."

"I love spicy food." His eyes light up at the chicken bites. "I don't get to eat it often."

Handing him a gold disposable plate, I encourage him to start with the jalapeno poppers, the spiciest appetizer I made. "The chicken is spicy too, actually."

He takes the serving spoon from a plate between the foil containers, and I open the poppers. Steam rises, and I'm pleased the small candles beneath the foil stands are doing their job to keep the snacks warm.

"I'm going to try one of everything first."

I laugh. "That's what taste testing is for."

When we return to the marble island, I sit across from him about to suggest saying grace. However, he's already diving in, pure enjoyment lighting his face.

"What did you call this with jalapenos?" he asks between bites, blowing out his tongue more so from the still-hot food.

"Jalapeno poppers." Amused by his enthusiasm, I hand him a napkin from the stack on the island, and he wipes his mouth with it.

"I can't believe I'm just meeting Damien's chef sister today."

"I've only been here four months." Not that he needs an explanation, but Mama always taught us to speak in full sentences, so that's how I roll. "I'd ventured out to Florida. Then my roommate got a job with your company, and it felt like the right time to move back." I mention my friend Lexi, Stone Financial Enterprises' new graphic designer, and Olivia, who works with Damien.

"I know Olivia. She and Damien have a good working relationship. They're the top analysts on my team."

Wow. What a genuine compliment. Too bad, I couldn't record that for Damien because it doesn't seem like Jeremy ever compliments him.

"It helps that they're best friends and all live here." I wiggle on my stool. "Often Damien and my friends discuss work and make me feel like the odd one out."

He winks. "I'm sure you could distract them from work with your cooking."

I shrug. "We cook dinner together." I tell him about our playful food wars in the kitchen, and his infectious laughter resonates deep and warm.

As the hour progresses, I find myself refilling his tea and getting more appetizers. He's curious about my current occupation, and I'm almost embarrassed to declare "food blogger" as a career. "I've never had a 'real' career." I rock my stool side to side. "I've published a couple of cookbooks, though." I've always feared being a chef in a real gourmet kitchen and having a boss with rules, but I've never felt this odd need to defend my passion. Maybe because he's so successful and pushes Damien so hard. He's gotta be looking down on me now, right? "I kind of like to do my own thing, but it's time for me to give back to the organization that funded my culinary school. It would be hard to do if I'm working for someone else."

"What organization?" His gaze narrows, and the full force of his attention makes me squirm, despite the sincerity brimming in his blue eyes.

"I still volunteer at Crina Medical once a week and help with their monthly mental-patient dinner program. Patients with mental challenges meet to cook, eat, and share their stories in a supportive environment." It was then that my passion for cooking came to life. "I was amazed by how they opened up and fostered connections as we cooked and dined together. I started volunteering after high school, and one of the founders told me they had scholarship programs I could apply for. Little did I know it was a full ride."

But I plan to give back to the organization. "If my café pans out, I'll use the space and my talent to host that program and perhaps give financially too. For now, I can only give back in time, and I try to do that as much as I can."

"I like that you're passionate about giving back." A thoughtful nod dips his chin. "But don't underestimate the real commitment you'll have to run a café."

He points out the demands of running a business, and I agree, sharing my fears. "I took a chance with the café, using all my book-sales funds. I'll be thirty in a year, and I wanted something to show for it."

It's strange, opening up like this to Jeremy, a man I've just met. Perhaps it's the ease of talking to someone not entwined in my daily life. I find myself leaning in, resting my chin on my hand, spilling fears and hopes I haven't even shared with Damien or my friends. An unexpected understanding about him makes it easy to share. Plus, I might never see him after tonight, unless I glimpse him when and if he stops at my café after it opens the last week in April. "Being my first time..."

I catch myself rambling. When I quiet down, Jeremy's head is tilted to one side, his gaze thoughtful and his hands resting on the island top.

"I said too much, didn't I?" I swipe my curls back from my face, self-conscious.

"Give yourself some credit," he says, his tone reflective. "You took a big break to find yourself."

I fiddle with a curl, twisting it tight around my finger. "No one needs more than five years to find themselves."

"You should be proud. You've been doing what you love. You started a blog, shared your recipes with the world, and wrote two books before thirty." He shrugs. "More than five years in the making, you have something to show for those years too."

His words ignite a warmth in me, a burgeoning respect for this man who was just a name to me until tonight. As he talks about strategy and business planning, an unexpected connection builds. "If you have any funds, even a hundred dollars, that's a start."

"For buying kombucha supplies?" I quip, shaking a finger at him.

"That's enough kombucha for me." He places a hand on his chest. "Who cares about anyone else as long as I'm sorted?"

His humor, a delightful surprise, draws me to his intellect and charm. We discuss my financial strategies for the café, and his reminder to focus on essentials resonates. "But I want to do it right." I still fear embarrassing myself should I fail at running this small lunch café.

"I get that. Doing it right is important." His lightheartedness eases my worries as he leans in. "Forget the furniture. Let people stand and eat. You've got a fridge for our kombucha and a stove. The rest will work out."

Again, his laughter is infectious, and I join in, feeling a familiar warmth. But the front door bursts open. Damien and the girls return, laden with supplies.

Jeremy rises, his smile vanishes, and his demeanor shifts as he meets my brother. Damien, two years my senior and a shade darker than me, stands tall. I always joke that God shaved off my height and added it to my brother, but Jeremy still overshadows him.

"Kress?" Damien's frown deepens as he sets two bags of ice on the counter. His gaze moves between us and narrows with the protectiveness he always has when he meets a guy he assumes might like me. "I see you've met my sister."

"She's great." Jeremy shoots me a warm glance. "Need help with the groceries or whatever?"

"Er..." Damien blinks, then hesitates. "No." His frown relaxes while he puts out his hand, and Jeremy winces as he looks at his right hand, then the plate with our forgotten appetizers. Damien gets the message that Jeremy's hand is greasy and acknowledges it with a nod.

"Welcome, Kress." Olivia bounces over, her blonde-highlighted ponytail shining under the light.

"Thanks for having me." He half waves, half salutes her.

Lexi chimes in, introducing herself and reminding him of her new position in marketing as a graphic designer at Stone Financial. "Marino is my boss."

"Nico." He smiles, evidently familiar with the man.

The dynamic in the room has shifted, and with it, the urgency to load drinks in the cooler and ice them. I draw in a slow breath to ease the odd constriction in my chest as my time with Jeremy ends.

The party soon fills up, and mild shock contorts some faces as they greet him. But a few women steal admiring glances at him—not that I can blame them. His good looks *are* hard to ignore, and he apparently has secret admirers at work, even if he keeps to himself. Damien, never one to miss any tunes for a gathering, realizes what I had forgotten and turns on soft music to set the mood. I'm grateful Jeremy arrived before anyone else.

With twenty-eight people, including my roommates and me, the seating is limited. But it doesn't seem to bother anyone. They're content to mingle, chatting and laughing in small groups while nibbling my appetizers. Lexi's photography skills, which have been a blessing for my blog, are on full display as she weaves through the crowd, snapping away.

Jeremy tries to blend in, but he soon finds his way back to his seat at the island. Snippets of his conversation with Damien drift my way while I pull out the southwest wraps I'd kept in the oven at a low temperature. There must be a gap in their relationship if they're discussing the weather—something about the fog outside. Damien's definitely holding onto a misconception due to the recent promotions he missed and blames Jeremy for.

After setting the southwest wraps on the dining table next to the chips and dips, I move to the living room for my water. I answer questions as people rave about my food and ask when my café opens.

"In April," Lexi boasts, snapping pictures as I stand outside of a loose circle. Dressed in white leggings and a black top, she appears casually comfortable. Her short brown hair shines vibrantly under the recessed lighting.

I shift my foot, uncap my water bottle, and sip at it, unsure how to act normal with all the praise.

A woman almost as petite as I am, whose name I can't remember, brings a tray of bacon-wrapped dates. "You guys have to taste these."

With everyone's attention turned to the food, my gaze finds Jeremy as Damien leaves him and joins the guys by the dining table. Their deep laughter rumbles through the room. But Jeremy sits alone, excluded, and my heart squeezes. He's not the stern boss I expected, and he's been nothing but warm and engaging with me. Determined to brighten his evening, I return to the kitchen, grab one of the boxes of chocolates he brought, and sit across from him.

"Are you glad you came tonight?" I try not to stare at the bruising I created on his forehead.

"Thanks for having me." He smiles. "The appetizers were a highlight. Sorry I didn't have room to try the main course." He opens the chocolate box and studies it before offering it to me. "Take your pick."

I choose mint, which prompts his playful reaction. We then turn it into a game, randomly selecting chocolates, some of them hitting the mark, others not so much. Like the one I bit into without reading what it was. I wince and pass the other half of it to him. "This is a very mysterious piece of chocolate."

"I love mysteries, by the way." He takes the piece from me and lifts it to his mouth, biting into it as I await his reaction.

"You love mysteries?" My voice rises as his face scrunches before he forces a swallow. I cover my mouth with my hand, stifling a laugh at his expression. "And you *still* love mysteries?"

"You're not being nice, laughing at me." He reaches for the water glass and lifts it to his mouth, guzzling the rest to clear the distaste.

"Your expression was priceless."

We talk more about the flavors we've tasted, our favorite desserts and treats. Our conversation wanders, and the other chatter in the house fades while we discuss movies, critiquing characters and scenes, laughing freely. It feels easy, natural—a side of me that's rarely brought out, especially by someone I've just met. I must say, Jeremy isn't the gruff boss my brother complains about. He's just Jeremy, someone who appreciates good food, laughs at my jokes, and shares a love for mysteries.

As the party chatter continues around us, my mind races. I don't normally overthink things, but I can't shake this feeling. I believe God orchestrates every encounter, and Jeremy's presence tonight feels like divine intervention—okay, I invited him, but Damien didn't think he was one for social engagements. Considering the bump I gave Jeremy, making amends seems right. What better way to apologize than by preparing one of his favorite dishes! Wouldn't that be a perfect gesture after our initially awkward and now-enjoyable encounter?

CHAPTER 3

Jeremy

The early morning San Francisco fog weaves ethereal tendrils around Stone Financial's towering glass building as I make my way inside. My polished shoes click against the pristine marble lobby floor.

Stationed behind one of the three reception desks, Naina looks up as I pass by. A fresh bouquet of pink roses on her desk adds a splash of vibrant color against the silver company logo sculpture towering over it. She voices a polite "good morning," and I respond. Her professional demeanor and work ethic are why, in her late twenties, she's the leader of the Stone office administration team.

Moving past the computer stands, coffee cup warm and firm in my hand, I head for the elevators. I greet Lopez, one of our guards, standing on the other end of the elevators, just as the nearest one slides open. Inside, I'm enveloped in the hushed, reflective space, my mind already racing to the tasks awaiting me.

Besides the security team, I'm usually the first one in the building, but I had a somewhat bigger excuse to pick up a latte for my assistant.

My heart feels uncharacteristically light today. The reason? A potential wedding date. Of course, this hinges on whether I can find time to navigate a few lunch meetings to get to know her better. The wedding is three months away. Still, not only do I like to plan ahead but also I need to get this fake fiancée squared away so I can focus on work.

Yesterday, I summoned the courage to call Clarissa, offering an apology for not reaching out sooner about another date. I met her six months ago at a financial conference where my boss was the keynote speaker. During that event, I led the analytics reports clinic, which Clarissa was attending for her company.

"I wanted to talk to you about something." I told her when I ventured to call last night. It had been three months since our last interaction, but to my relief, she expressed a keen interest in meeting up. Her schedule was open for lunch today, but Mondays being pivotal for setting the tone for my workweek, I hesitated.

Then Clarissa said she'd drop by my office, citing some business in the Bay Area. Meeting at the office seemed ideal, especially considering I don't want it to be a reunion of some sort. I'd rather keep things somewhat casual.

While I have a grand plan to ask her to be my fake fiancée for a week, Clarissa has no idea why I called her. As the elevator ascends, I shift my stance, less sure of my intent. Will it be too forward to suggest a temporary arrangement, just for the wedding? This meeting with Clarissa feels more like an intrusion than a convenience. Yet, facing Sonya with Clarissa by my side beats giving her the impression I've been unable to move on since she broke my heart four years ago. This requires a careful approach. But the first step is gauging Clarissa's response to my invitation.

When the elevator deposits me on the fifty-eighth floor, Jill stands hunched as if she has an important detail to add to a calendar. Her hands dance over the keyboard, the rhythmic tapping a familiar soundtrack in our high-paced environment. She glances up, her unflappable demeanor faltering as she frowns at my forehead. "Tough weekend?"

"I went to Damien's party." Zuri comes to mind, and I smile, handing over Jill's beverage. I have to bring her an offering when I give her tasks unrelated to work. Before she can get the idea of my intentions, I ask about her weekend. "How was the visit with your in-laws?"

"Wait, wait." She drawls, her voice tinged with a southern lilt. She blinks and hefts her coffee cup to emphasize her surprise. The way her dark bob swings, framing her features, conjures images of my aunt—though she favors brown suits with a consistency unlike Jill, who reserves her brown attire for sporadic appearances. "You went to Damien's party? How did that happen?"

I shrug. "He invited me. Shame you weren't there." Jill must've also been invited but couldn't attend due to her family commitments. "Everyone kept their distance from me." Except for Zuri, the only reason I didn't leave the party before it even began.

"If everyone kept their distance"—Jill's eyes crinkle—"how'd you get the bruise?"

"Not everyone kept their distance." I tinker with a coat button. My smile broadens as I reminisce about my time with Zuri—her effortless warmth, her exquisite food, and our easy conversation. I even recall her favorite color, a puzzling detail. Never before have I felt so at ease with someone I just met.

"Does that smile have anything to do with the latte bribe?" Calling me out, Jill takes a sip of the coffee.

"I bring you lattes sometimes." I glance at the lollipop bowl next to the framed picture of her and her husband with their two teen daughters.

"Aha." She wags her eyebrows, clearly not believing me.

"It's a busy day." I lean in closer to her desk and rest my hands on the tall, smooth surface, cool under my fingertips. "Virtual calls, meetings, tasks, the usual Monday drill."

She deadpans me. She knows my schedule. She puts it together.

"Only one person is permitted to interrupt me today. Around lunchtime." Everyone has a different lunchtime, and Clarissa wasn't specific when she said lunchtime.

Jill waves her cup at me, her expression playful. "Oh, look at you, social butterfly. Since when do you attend parties and allow interruptions at work?"

I lower my voice as the elevator dings open, revealing an empty space. I'd best describe Clarissa, though I'm not good at painting pictures with words. "She's strikingly beautiful, poised, and stands out. You'll recognize her immediately."

Jill shakes her head, lifts her drink to her mouth, and sips it. "All right, Mr. Mysterious. How long have you known each other?"

I ignore her question to stress one more instruction. I can't afford to slack off on a Monday. Otherwise, the rest of the week will get backlogged. "Just check the camera when Naina buzzes up for anyone looking for me."

Jill nods, still chuckling. "Must be someone very unusual for you to invite her here."

I wave her off and head toward my office. Nature-inspired art adorns the walls above a seating area outfitted with white linen sofas and a glass table. The mountain landscapes evoke memories of my childhood home. Adjacent to the seating area, a bookshelf houses my research materials alongside frames showcasing the awards and medals I've accumulated over my eight years at Stone Financial. This space is more than just an office. It's a reflection of my journey and motivating passions.

The city skyline, buried in fog, stretches out beyond the panoramic windows. Fog or sunshine, the view never gets old.

I settle into my chair and boot up my computer. Entering my password brings up today's updated agenda by Jill. She cheekily added "Jeremy's date between 11–12:30." She even highlighted it in yellow and added a tongue-sticking-out emoji. The agenda also includes virtual meetings with branch managers across the country and at several international branches. While I don't plan to tackle all these calls in one day, I have a virtual meeting with executives at eight—just thirty minutes away. This leaves me ample time to review the agenda once more.

***

The morning vanishes in a flurry of activities, including two scheduled meetings and two unexpected calls. One call is from a vendor seeking to renegotiate their contract terms. The other is from a new, demanding investor eager for updates on our strategies for the upcoming year's company performance.

I catch a break as I scan the list of the project steering committee, determining which branch needs my immediate contact.

Then Jill's voice cuts through the intercom. "Your lunch guest is here."

It's eleven fifty-five.

"Send her in." I shift in my chair, now second-guessing this engagement.

My heartbeat accelerates when a soft knock sounds at the half-open frosted-glass door. I clear my throat, then call out. "Come in."

The door swings open, but it's not Clarissa.

"Zuri." I stand from my swivel chair. My heart kicks up another beat as she meets me with a sheepish smile. "Hello."

In a navy-and-white-print maxi dress, she's even more striking than Saturday night. The daylight streaming through the windows enhances her natural beauty, catching her curves and the glossy spirals of her curls. She looks taller today. Apparently, those heels peeking out beneath her hem are adding to her height. Her hoop earrings dance against her cheeks, and her eyes sparkle with guilty mischief.

"I thought I'd stop by." She hefts the bags in her hand, and an unmistakably savory aroma wafts my way. "I, uh, brought you some food. Felt terrible about the door incident. I hope this makes up for it."

Frozen in place with no idea what to do or say, I clear my throat and grip the back of my neck. Why are my palms sweating? I wipe them on my pants and move around the desk.

"If food is what it gets me, then I'm glad you slammed a door into my head." Besides the bruise, I can barely feel the pain. "What do you have there?"

Zuri saunters toward my desk—her skirt swishing with her languid movements and drawing my attention to places I shouldn't be looking. Then she unloads containers from the insulated bags. "You said you love spring rolls, so I got carried away and made some dishes to accompany them. I had to throw in a salad and jalapeno poppers for good measure."

My stomach rumbles. I move close and lift the lid off one container. "This is quite a salad." meat, greens, peppers, and an array of colorful vegetables form a visual masterpiece. Also, enough to feed at least four people. "An apology feast? I won't say no to that."

I carry the salad and another container, slightly warm in my hand. "I hope you're staying to feast with me," I say without hidden intentions because I enjoyed her company. "I'm not eating all this food alone."

"I'd hate to interfere with your work. I've already interrupted when I made this surprise visit." She carries two other containers and joins me in the seating area. "I won't stay long."

"You got blog posts to upload?" I shift further into the chair.

She sits on the loveseat across from me, smooths her dress, then eases her red handbag to the empty white cushion next to her. She hands me a fork from the tote bag, a real one, not disposable.

"I'm only posting one recipe a week, rather than daily." She pulls a spoon from the tote bag. "I'll use a spoon."

I offer her the fork since it's all we have, but she refuses. "This is your food, and I wasn't supposed to eat it."

"All right, all right." Remembering to wash my hands, I excuse myself to head to the bathroom.

When I return, she wiggles fingers clear of nail polish. "My hands are clean."

"I'm not making any judgments." I spring my arms free from my blazer and drape it behind the chair.

She points at me. "I've seen how detailed you get into handwashing. It's like a ritual."

"With your feasts, there's a chance I'll be using my hands." When I fork the salad and lift the first bite, my mouth waters at an explosion of flavors, rich and balanced. Oh man, I was starving. "This is incredible."

She has her eyes closed, clearly praying. Something I've never done—unless going to church for weddings or the two times I attended church camp count. My brother prays. He became spiritual during his yearlong visit to Africa.

I open another container and fork a bite of the spring rolls, the outside crispy, the inside juicy. "These are the best." And I'm not kidding, because they beat Bamboo Gardens, supposedly the best spring rolls in San Francisco. "I haven't even dug into the poppers yet."

Her smile widens, a visible relief sheening her eyes. "I'm glad you like it. It wasn't hard to prepare." She reaches out with her spoon and scoops steak from the salad platter.

"I'd better invite Jill to join us at the feast." After all, we can't let all this good food go to waste.

Zuri dismisses me with a wave of her spoon. "I'd brought extra spring rolls and gave her a container. I also gave some to Naina at the front desk downstairs." She smirks. "I guess I planned to bribe my way in."

Wow. She's pretty good at remembering the names of people she'd just met—unless she met them before. "How long have you known Jill and Naina?"

"I met Naina when I came to look at the café three months ago. I just met Jill today." She snatches a napkin from the bag and reaches for one of the bacon-wrapped poppers. "Jill's really nice."

"Not to me." I scoop another bite, lighthearted. Zuri must have an incredible way of making everyone she meets feel like they've been friends forever.

I seldom get women visiting me. Today, of course, I have two of them. Zuri *is* beautiful, though not in a screaming sort of way, so little wonder Jill mistook her for Clarissa.

I want to know more about Zuri, including how she made this food. I fork the salad again and try to keep an even balance of all the dishes. Everything is scrumptious, but clearly, I'm not the reason she made all this food. Which leads me to my next question.

"Did you come by here after dropping off food for your brother?"

"I made this specifically for you." She tilts her head to the side. "Damien prefers sandwiches for lunch. He doesn't even know I'm here."

"And if he knew you were here, would it be a problem?" Now why did I ask such an uncalled-for question? Maybe because Damien made those sudden appearances in my office last week. "Afraid he'll tell your boyfriend?"

"I don't have a boyfriend. I don't need distractions right now." She waves her spoon in the air. "As for Damien, it would shock him to find me having lunch with you, considering we just met. He can be kind of protective."

She'd mentioned living with her brother at the party. I almost delve into that topic, but she reaches for a spring roll and steers the conversation back to food, her passion evident. "My priority is Zuri's Daylight Café. I'm not sure I'll have spring rolls on the menu."

"If you do, they'll be a hit." I test another bite. "How do you prepare them?"

"I start with fresh vegetables, thinly sliced." Her eyes alight, she launches into an animated explanation of how she makes her spring rolls, and her delicate hands help her express herself. "Then I sauté them with garlic and Asian spices. The key is to keep them crunchy. For the dipping sauce, I use soy sauce with a hint of honey and sprinkle in some chili flakes to add a bit of a kick."

I've forgotten to eat. Her enthusiasm leaves me enrapt.

"When I open my café, maybe your staff could come for an interactive cooking day." Her eyes sparkle. "I hear you have staff team-building days. The kitchen is a perfect place to connect." Her expression falters, a shadow dimming her features while she scowls at her black flats. "Of course, that depends on if my café launches successfully."

Right, she shared her financial constraints at their party.

With this familiar feeling between us, I'm surprisingly at ease, more so than I would've been with Clarissa. "I might have a solution for your business."

The words escape before I second-guess them. I'm already reconsidering my plans with Clarissa. Asking Zuri is a better decision.

"I'm listening." She leans forward as she takes another bite of the spring roll.

I set my fork on the folded napkin. "I'll cover your café's initial costs." On Saturday, she mentioned how much she needed when she opened up about the financial strain for start-ups. "I mean..." My throat closes, and I falter, unexpectedly vulnerable. But it's too late now. I might as well finish what I'm supposed to say. "In return, would you... be my fake date at a wedding in Colorado?"

Zuri blinks as if she didn't hear what I said. She's not smiling, but she's not frowning either. Is she surprised or shocked? Maybe something between those lines. "That's quite a request. Why a fake date?"

"I'm not looking for a relationship or anything. Been there, done that." I wave in the air, giving in to the need to explain myself. More than anything, I fear getting rejected. "It's to stop my mother's matchmaking. She wants me back with my ex."

Why am I telling her all these details? Well, she needs to understand this is temporary. "We go back to our normal routine as soon as the wedding is over." I square my shoulders and meet her gaze.

She bites her lower lip, seemingly weighing my proposition. But it's adorable, and my gaze fixes on her round lips longer than necessary—unintentionally, of course.

My unconventional proposal seems to clog the room. Zuri nods as she scuffs one foot back and forth on the white area rug over my marble flooring. "This is an interesting twist to our... collision. Let me think about it." She falls silent, drawing a line with the toe of her shoe, then smoothing it out. Meanwhile, I fork a jalapeño popper and lift it to my mouth to occupy my hands.

"Your request isn't the oddest I've ever encountered." She breaks the brief lull, a lightness in her voice.

"It's not?" I wipe my mouth with a napkin, my curiosity piqued now that we don't have to focus on the awkwardness I created.

"Well... One time I entered a couple's baking contest by myself. I was so desperate not to miss it that I convinced a guy waiting in line at the coffee shop to be my 'husband' for the day." I'm not sure why I get a sudden discomfort when she talks about this guy. "We ended up winning third place for a cake more lopsided than a sinking ship. He still texts me every year on the 'anniversary' of our victory."

"Now that was a bold move on your end—"

She holds up a hand, silencing me. "You might find this even more odd." Her eyes dance in the vibrant light through the windows, her hands moving as she talks. "One time, I was walking my neighbor's dog at the dog park, and I ran into this guy who believed his pet could tell if someone was 'the one' for him. Apparently, he was looking for a female dog owner and considered it a sign based on whether the dogs got along. And I'll spare you the details of my first time in a couples-only salsa dancing." Her hand covers her mouth, stifling another fit of giggles.

By the time Zuri leaves my office and I get back to my computer, she'd stayed well over an hour, though it barely felt like thirty minutes. Her presence seems to warp time, making it pass unnoticed.

My gaze flits to the now-closed frosted door. I'm half-expecting Zuri to walk back in and accept my proposal. As crazy as the idea might be, it's a necessary strategy to deal with my mother's relentless matchmaking with my ex-girlfriend. If you're going to fake dating, why not with someone whose company you enjoy?

Zuri would be the perfect fake date—fiancée actually since I told Mom I'm engaged. My phone buzzes, and a message from Clarissa flashes on-screen. A frown creases my forehead as I swipe to read her text.

> Clarissa: You could've just told me you were busy before I wasted my time coming by. Let me know if you want to catch dinner tonight.

Dinner? Yikes. Clarissa might've come by while Zuri was in my office. I stand, and my swivel chair rolls further to the cupboards. What happened? Why did Clarissa leave without seeing me?

Jill's by the watercooler next to the long conference table, deep in conversation with Emma, my boss Logan Stone's assistant. Emma works on the fifty-ninth floor but sometimes takes the stairs to come down for her breaks so she can exercise throughout the day.

Sucking on a lollipop, Jill stands there, listening to whatever Emma is saying—funny for a woman in her forties to love that kind of candy. As I approach, the women glance at me, and when I say hello to Emma, she lifts her water cup. "I'd better head back upstairs."

"Hello, Mr. Kress," Jill singsongs, her knowing grin slightly hidden as she sucks on the red lollipop before walking back to her desk. She believes that, whenever I come to her, she needs to be behind her computer. This is usually true since I often need her to jot something down in the schedule if I haven't emailed her about it.

"Mr. Kress, really?" I follow her. She calls me Jeremy unless she's up to some mischief. When she steps behind her tall desk, I lean against it. "Did someone else come by today?" If I were in Clarissa's situation, I'd be furious about the wasted time.

Jill settles her lollipop on a napkin. "You said to look out for a gorgeous woman. I sent one who wasn't gorgeous back, told her you were busy."

I wince against a twinge of guilt. "And Zuri? Who arrived first?"

"The other lady came first. But I have to say, Zuri's quite a doll, right?" Her eyes twinkle as she tilts her head. "Isn't Zuri prettier than, well, whoever her name is? Plus, Zuri brought food. A way to a man's stomach." She smiles, patting her stomach, then pulls over her chair, and climbs into it. It's always hard to tell whether she is sitting or standing behind that tall desk.

Zuri's beauty is subtle, but after spending time in her company, I find her far more attractive beyond her outward appearance. She's captivating.

I pinch the bridge of my nose, thrown off-balance. And now Clarissa thinks I stood her up again. "I didn't know Zuri was coming."

Jill picks up her lollipop and points at me with it. "Jeremy, you never talk about any woman, and now you've got two in one day?"

As she laughs at me, I grin. Yep. What a mess I've created.

I return to my office, and my phone buzzes again with a text from an unknown number. I read the message, curiosity coursing through me.

> Unknown: I snatched your business card on my way out, called Jill, and got your number. Can we meet at the café downstairs tomorrow at five? Rumor has it you like to work until seven, but I'll bring dinner. We can discuss more about this "fake dating" of ours.

"Of ours." Does that mean she's in?

Excitement tingles through me as my thumb hovers over the phone screen. I haven't clarified my need for her to pose as my fiancée, not merely as a date. This arrangement must be convincing enough to derail my mother's plans. As I begin to type a response, my mind races with the implications. *Goodbye, Clarissa. Welcome, Zuri.*

CHAPTER 4

Zuri

I pace the café's tiled floor. Each step echoes in the space with chipped chairs upturned on the wobbly tables. I don't need to walk around the wall to know the other half of the café is set up the same way. Ten tables, each with four to six chairs. Yep, not quite what I envisioned for my plan. And settling for less isn't how I want to start a business.

But that's the least of my problems. Jeremy will be here soon. With the way he keeps time, he might be twenty or thirty minutes early.

I rub my eyes, not proud of how I'm going about this. Relying on his financial assistance feels like an odd compromise. I've always dreamed of visiting Colorado, and under different circumstances, attending a wedding with Jeremy wouldn't require such a trade. But the harsh reality is my café needs this money.

A steely cold tightens its grip around my stomach, and I press my hands against the clamping pain. More than the café's future unsettles me. Confidence prompted me to text, but was I wrong to meet here after work hours and disrupt his schedule?

As I glance toward the kitchen, at the cash register where bags of our dinner supplies await, a soft knock at the half-open door jolts me back to reality. Jeremy emerges, handsome as if he just stepped out of a glossy magazine. His brown hair, sleek and well combed, shines under the recessed lighting. His broad shoulders stretch out the crisp white button-down, neatly tucked into navy dress pants.

My heart lurches to a stop, misses a beat, and then starts to thump. How misguided my grand plan for this meeting was! With his sophisticated air and polished appearance, he's out of place in my work-in-progress café. He's too refined for a self-prepared dinner here. As for my fantasies about him since the day we met, they're just dreams. The last time I dated someone in my brother's circle, I ended up messing up his friendship. If I fall for Jeremy and things don't work out, Damien might have to find another job. But that won't be a problem because I'm not Jeremy's type. Well, I'd thought I was Mike's type, but he didn't find me attractive enough to stick with me. So, I have no idea whose type I am. With each step Jeremy makes forward, my confidence wavers and morphs into a growing sense of inadequacy. I feel every bit too unsettled, too short not to be overlooked.

"Hello."

I shake my head and work to breathe normally. His approach, weaving through the haphazardly pushed-aside tables and chairs, seems almost tentative. The soft padding of his leather dress shoes against the beige tile floor marks his progress.

Clearing my throat, I straighten up and muster a smile that better conceal my nerves. "I hope you don't mind meeting here." Good. I sound more confident than I feel.

"Not at all." He pauses to sit on the edge of a table and scans the space. "It's been a while since I've been here."

"Three months is a long time for a restaurant to be closed. I got a good deal on the lease because it had sat so long."

He scratches his stubbled jaw. "I haven't been here in a year. Most times, I eat at my desk. Jill arranges my food delivery."

And here's an opportunity to share my vision. "That's why I need this café. To convince people like you to step away from your desk when it's mealtime."

"Is that so?" His well-sculpted mouth curves into such a charming smile I can't maintain eye contact, so I start walking and beckon him to follow.

"As you can see, changes are necessary." I gesture around the room, my fingers brushing over the vacant tables and chairs. "I want this place to be a haven for conversations, an escape from the office routine." I pause to face him. "You know what I mean?"

Jeremy shakes his head, his gaze shifting from the dark-gray walls back to me. His warm blue eyes seem to absorb every detail. "You sound like you've done this before."

A nervous chuckle jitters free, and I wring my hands. "No, far from it. My blog was my focus, but it never paid the bills." But he doesn't have time to listen to me ramble, so I steer the conversation elsewhere and guide him to the wall bisecting the café. "I'm not sure who designed this layout, but I spoke with your company's architect. This isn't a support wall, so it can be torn down. It's less than inviting now."

He holds up a hand, stilling me. "By less inviting, you mean?"

"Closed off." I fumble with my sleeve. "An open space feels warmer, more communal. People can see each other, maybe even interact over their meals." More than anything, I believe in the power of food to bring people together. "Food has a unique way of opening people up and fostering connections. It's a powerful tool in combating loneliness."

"That's a concept I've never encountered before."

Pointing at him, I grin. "You will soon." Especially since I'm hoping to cook with him and discuss this whole fake-date arrangement. My plan now seems tangible with him standing here, though it still feels like a leap into the unknown. At least, this is the perfect setting to ease my nerves.

"I want to show you something." I beckon him toward the kitchen. The small functioning fridge's familiar hum fills the otherwise silent space, a stark reminder of the broken commercial fridge, a dormant giant needing replacement. The freezer, too, might need a fix. These are just a few of the many expenses looming over my start-up dream. In the meantime, I'm paying the lease without turning any profit. I try not to think about that.

I grab the red apron hanging by the kitchen entrance and toss it to him. He catches it, eyeing its carrot and herb decorations. Slipping mine with its puff-print cupcakes over my head, I tie it at the back.

"What do you want me to do with this?" He waves it at me.

"We're going to cook our dinner." I stifle a laugh at what could be a challenge to him. His eyes widen. I know full well his hectic work schedule probably means a late-night dinner. "You haven't eaten yet, right?"

"I usually order takeout." He shrugs and slips on the apron.

"I figured as much." Damien often mentions Jeremy's long office hours. "I thought it'd be a good idea to discuss your brother's wedding and the whole fake-date situation while we cook."

"Okay." He moves to the sink and rolls his shirtsleeves higher. Then he fumbles with the apron strings, and I laugh, step close, and show him how to tie it properly. But he's grumbling. "For your information, the only reason I'm wearing an apron for the first time is that I know you're taking charge of whatever we're cooking."

"And I'm ever so grateful you're here." My whole body feels light as I finish tying his apron strings. There's a sophisticated scent coming off him, subtle yet captivating.

As he meticulously washes his hands, I struggle not to look at him. Still, I watch the movement of his strong forearms, and my mouth dries. Wait—am I *drooling*?

Get a grip, girl! Clicking my tongue at myself, I move to the empty sink beside him and turn on the faucet. I lather the soap to wash my hands, though not with his thoroughness. After drying my hands with a paper towel, I cross to the long counter to gather the necessary supplies and ingredients for our first baking adventure together.

"What are we making?" He wipes his hands and cocks his head, leaning in behind me.

"Shortbread cookies." I peep over my shoulder to check his reaction.

"Did I happen to tell you they're my favorite?"

"I had to go with some favorites if we're diving into deep matters." My chest warms, a connection already forming in this shared activity. The night we met, I learned all the basics about him.

He steps closer, his presence dominating the space. "What do you want me to do?"

"There's a mixer in that bag." I point to the red tote. "If you don't mind getting it, that would be great."

When he retrieves the hand mixer, I open the sugar bag and pass him the measuring cup. "Pour two-third cups of sugar into the mixing bowl," I instruct. As he delicately pours the sugar, almost as if fearing his arm might break, I cut in butter, splash vanilla, and sprinkle salt into the same bowl. Once we've creamed that, I set him to open the flour. "While the cookies bake, we'll start on dinner."

"What's for dinner?" He dips the cup into the flour. Is he *that* meticulous by nature or just trying to avoid making a mess?

"Steak fajitas and veggies." At his precision movements, a mischievous thought teases me. Imagining his neatly trimmed beard or face smeared with a bit of a mess, I struggle to suppress a cackle.

"What's so funny?" He eyes me, his eyebrows rising.

"Remember how I talked about food wars in our home kitchen?"

"Uh-oh. What exactly are food wars again?"

I dig my hand into the flour, scoop a handful, and step on tiptoes to smudge it on his cheek. He gasps followed by a comically exaggerated frown.

"That's a food war." I flick the rest at his apron.

Jeremy swats flour off the now-dusty red apron. Then, his grin mischievous, he reaches for the flour bag. "Ah, a food fight. Well, now you're going to get it!"

"No, don't!" I shield myself with my hand and scoot further away. He thrusts his hand into the bag, and I dash off, my laughter echoing around the kitchen.

"You're not getting away with this, Zuri."

Uh-oh. I *love* the way my name slips off his tongue. Could be why I stop running and he catches up to smear my left cheek with flour and then my right.

"Not fair." I protest as we engage in a playful tussle of me trying to get the bag from him, which is ridiculous when he simply holds it over our heads. To reach, I'd have to climb him like a monkey to a tree. Unless... I tickle his side, and the bag comes down. As I scoop it, our laughter floats with the flour now flying everywhere until we're both dusted as white as powder sugar doughnuts.

While we catch our breath, he brushes some flour from my face, tracing the curve of my cheek. I can scarcely breathe as his fingers trail slowly, lingering, edging toward my mouth. It might be intentional. It takes willpower not to nip his flour-coated fingertip as he locks his eyes with mine. In that instant, time seems to pause as if we've forgotten the world outside, and awareness simmers between us. Thick and unmistakable.

I look away, clearing my throat. "We, uh, made quite a mess." My voice sounds ridiculously strange! And now I'm afraid to look at him. I survey the kitchen floor coated in a fine layer of flour.

"Worth it." At his chuckle, I manage to look into blue eyes still atwinkle. My cheeks warm, but my smile stretches wide.

"Now we got carried away and used up all the flour." I crouch to pick up the bag. "That means no cookies."

"There's not enough for too many cookies, but there's enough for our dinner." He points to the mixing bowl.

Our impromptu flour fight confirms he's slipped into my world, turning an ordinary evening into something delightful. Cooking dinner together feels just right.

"You better show me what to do next if those cookies are going to get baked."

Right. I dust the floor off my apron.

"Good thing I have a change of clothes in my office." He keeps dusting off more remnants of flour from himself.

"You don't need to change." Careful not to slip on the floury floor, I move to the fridge for eggs. From what I've been told, all the executive offices have showers, which is probably why he isn't stressed about the mess I made of him.

Our hands brush as he takes the salt from me, and a little zap sizzles through my veins.

Jeremy's cautious yet willing participation in this wraps me up in warmth. Is it possible we might be cooking up something more than a fake-date arrangement?

***

The aroma of sizzling steak and freshly baking cookies fills the kitchen, while the rhythmic chopping of vegetables and the steady hum of the refrigerator provide a comforting backdrop. Jeremy and I move in sync, and our easy conversation flows.

Taking advantage of the moment, I broach the subject of our gathering. It had better not be a sensitive topic. "I get the feeling your mom likes to be in control of things?"

He pauses his chopping, the green pepper forgotten. "What?"

"I mean, considering you feel the need to lie to her about your wedding date."

His oh-so-well-formed lips curve, and his eyes gleam. "'In control of things' is putting it lightly. Spend two minutes with my mom, and you'll see how much she loves micromanaging. If she could, even flies would be camping out in roses by her command."

I laugh at his statement. "About your wedding proposition..." I stir the meat sizzling in the pan. "I've given it some thought, and I'm willing to do it." Of course, I am! My heart races at the mere thought. He is undeniably handsome. What girl wouldn't want to be his date, even if it's just pretend?

He sets down his knife. "You're agreeing to be my fake fiancée?"

Wait. Fiancée? "I thought it was just a fake date."

"If we're going to convince my mother of our relationship, a ring would make it more believable."

I touch my naked ring finger. A fake proposal is far from the dream I've always harbored.

"I'll buy the ring, of course," he adds, seeming to notice my hesitation. "I know wearing a ring might be a step too far—"

"No, I'll do it." I shouldn't have any second-guessing, really. "When is the wedding?"

"The first weekend in April, despite the unpredictable Colorado weather."

"I've always wanted to visit Colorado." I try not to focus on my financial needs. "Going there could be a trade enough in itself."

He holds up a palm in the universal stop signal. "You need funds for your café, and that was our agreement."

So he's a man of his word. Even though I want to tell him to loan me the money instead, I'll discuss that later. "This wasn't the way I dreamed of a proposal."

"No?"

I shake my head.

"What idea of a proposal did you have in mind?" With his tone light and carefree, he keeps his full focus on me. The knife now rests on the cutting board, and he seems interested in what I have to say rather than the task I assigned him. Might as well tell him since he's becoming a friend, sort of.

"It's silly, but I like it simple. Thoughtful proposals, nothing overly fancy, but something unusual." I flip the steak strips, thinking of the different engagements I see in movie scenes. "A proposal in the rain or on a hike. Something not too planned."

"Quite a romantic, huh?"

"Takes a romantic to know one." I snatch the garlic bulbs on the plate, put them in the press, then squeeze garlic into the meat, and add salt and pepper. "I've never played a fake fiancée before, but I guess we'll need some practice runs if we have to convince your mom."

"Trust me, where my mother is concerned, we need to be very convincing. She'll watch you like a hawk." His jaw clenches when he mentions the length of his mom's effort to reunite him with his ex. "That's why we need at least two months to get our facts straight."

"Hence, the need for practice." Which may be harder than I anticipated. Especially if he often looks this endearing with a dusting of flour on his chin.

The timer goes off. Using a kitchen towel, I pull the cookies out of the oven.

"Taste test?" He edges in closer.

"They'll burn your mouth."

"My mouth is already watering, so burning is not a threat."

I laugh at his lightheartedness and use a butter knife to scoop a drop cookie. After all, I didn't have time to refrigerate and cut the dough. He takes it and breaks it in half, sharing it with me. As we each bite into it, I'm reminded of the innocent photo Lexi took of us. The natural ease between us while we ate chocolate felt almost like a rediscovery of something long lost. There's an undeniable comfort in Jeremy's presence, a comforting and intriguing familiarity.

Minutes later, the same warmth still envelops us as we sit at one of the tables, our laughter and conversation filling the space. A curious thought nudges me, and I speak before I can caution myself against treading into more personal territory. "What's your fiancée back home like?"

Are any feelings lingering there?

"Ex-fiancée," he corrects, his jaw tensing.

Okay, so this is a sensitive subject. I pivot to lighten the mood. "Tell me about your mom, then."

"She likes to be in control, just like all the women she tries to set me up with." He sits taller. "My brother sure gave her a shock when he returned from Africa with a fiancée she couldn't approve of."

I laugh, picturing the scene. Jeremy's stories about his mother's failed matchmaking attempts are not exactly endearing. The way he speaks about his brother, though, displays an unmistakable admiration.

I cut a bite of steak, then pause with it on my fork. "Any embarrassing stories I should know about you and your brother?"

"Oh!" He waves a hand. "Too many to count. If we're talking about kitchen-related incidents, he's the cook, not me. There was a time when he tried to bake cookies and used salt instead of sugar. We nearly broke our teeth!"

A chuckle escapes me, and I drop my fork over my meat. "Remind me not to let him near the kitchen at the wedding."

"How about you and Damien?"

So I tell him some of our mischief on the street where we grew up. How refreshing to see Jeremy's carefree side while we exchange funny stories, a side most of his work colleagues don't know about.

When he compliments my cooking, I bob a bow. "Why thank you for your help, kind sir."

Then I scoot back in my seat. "If we're going to practice this fake dating..." Group nights should be less intimidating. "I'll be hosting a Superbowl get-together, and I also hear you have a team-building bowling event in February. Perhaps those are good first times for us to appear as a"—I form air quotes—"couple?"

"Actually, the awards ceremony is not this weekend but the following Saturday. Would you do me the honor of being my date?" He mimics my air quotes.

Right. My friends have been shopping for formal outfits for that ceremony. But... "Only spouses of staff are invited, though."

"You're officially my spouse." The way he says it with a wink ignites unwanted butterflies in my belly. But I know it's nothing.

We make plans for our upcoming "dates" for February, exchanging amused glances. Even though we've just met, an undeniable comfort and ease relaxes me. Sitting here with him, sharing stories, and planning our charade feels fun. Being his fake fiancée, while daunting, also promises to be the perfect recipe for adventure.

CHAPTER 5

Jeremy

Engulfed in a virtual financial-planning session, I navigate through spreadsheets and projections with two accountants and two analysts from our eastern branch. We're deep in discussion, unraveling the financial forecasts and budget variances—a routine yet crucial task that spans our nationwide branches.

"Given the current trends," one accountant chimes in, "I believe an adjustment in our quarterly projections could align us more closely with the annual targets."

The swing of the door has me looking away from the screen, and the session's focused calm shatters as Damien bursts into my office. He slams a photograph onto my desk, its impact demanding immediate attention. I request a fifteen-minute recess before muting my computer. Damien's disheveled appearance, his shirt hanging half untucked, signals a crisis only I can address, and evidently, Jill couldn't have barred his impromptu intrusion, despite her best efforts.

"What is this?" He slaps the desk by the photograph.

It's Zuri and me during Saturday's dinner at their house. While I should be scolding him for his interruption, warmth radiates through me over the instant memories the picture evokes. "What do you think it is?" I roll back my chair. "It's a photo from your party."

He jabs at Zuri's face, smudging it and making me flinch. "This"—he seethes—"with my sister! She's very trusting and..." He huffs, steps back, and rasps a hand over the stubble on his head. "I like to keep my personal life separate from my work life."

I hadn't realized anyone was photographing us, but whoever did captured a moment of genuine connection. We look relaxed and happy as I take the half-eaten chocolate from her hand like a long-term couple rather than people who'd just met.

I choose not to voice these thoughts. Instead, I focus on his apparent intrusion. "I didn't know anyone was taking pictures." Lacing my hands in my lap, I lean back in my chair. I was too "busy" getting to know Zuri to notice who was doing what, let alone someone taking pictures. "If anything, you should be questioning the person who gave you this picture. They took it without Zuri's or my permission."

His anger doesn't abate. He rants about how innocent and trusting his sister is as if to imply I'm some bad boy unworthy of her. It stings, but I keep my composure. I'm not about to discuss my arrangement with Zuri. If only to mention our time in her café two days ago.

My cheeks heat. Was I wrong to enjoy her company? What about how my stomach bubbles up in her presence? I pick up a pen, needing a distraction because Damien might have a good reason to be terrified about the photo.

"You invited me to your party, remember?" It's not my fault his sister and I hit it off. Making my pen spin in my hands, I continue playing it cool while transitioning into my boss mode. "You should be proud of your sister for being a great host. Now if you might excuse me, I was in the middle of a meeting when you interfered."

Damien grits his teeth, fists his hands, and tosses his head back. Whatever he wants to say, he holds his tongue. To be fair, I suggest he make an appointment with Jill if he'd like more time to talk about whatever's eating him up. "At the office, I can only handle work-related matters." Which he already knows.

His chest rises and falls. Then he gives a curt nod, which I take as an apology. He storms out and leaves the photo on my desk. I'm not sure if he meant to leave it, but I smile as I look at it again. It's a snapshot of what Zuri and I could be—a couple who enjoys each other's company. We're not involved romantically. Still, I can't deny the comfort between us, the attraction. I'll stick to the familiarity with her, glad I chose her as my fake wedding date. I had to call and apologize to Clarissa when I declined to meet her for dinner, ending our awkward conversation with an "I'll see you around."

Maybe it's Damien's accusation or the picture itself, but as I look at it, excitement bubbles within me. Okay, it's just fake. Two months until I get through my brother's wedding, and our lives go back to normal—my normal is work. I tried a relationship, putting myself out there, only to get scarred. Plus, Zuri isn't looking for a relationship either, which works out perfectly for both of us.

***

On Sunday afternoon, the golf course becomes our sanctuary away from the office's relentless pace. The breeze whispers through the towering eucalyptus trees, a soothing backdrop as Nico, Wes, and I approach the par three tee box. Best friends and colleagues, we've turned these outings into our weekly ritual, a precious respite unless work demands my attention.

"Ah! Jeremy, my boy." Nico, lean from hours of cycling and always animated, stretches his arms like a bird preparing for flight. His eyes, bright with mischief, scan me. "You have a three-point advantage, but I feel a win coming on. Are you ready to lose today?"

I grasp my 6-iron, the sleek metal cool and familiar in my hands, and give it an effortless twirl. "Every week you say that, Nico."

"And every week he ends up buying dinner." Wes winks. His dark hair shines in the afternoon sun. Unlike Nico's flamboyance, Wes's calmness often masks his sharp wit.

Nico's laugh, hearty and infectious, echoes across the green expanse. "And who ends up footing the bill when we take to the biking trails, huh?"

"You bike to work every day. It's only natural you'd outpace us." I give the distant flag a quick study and tee up my ball. The other two fall silent.

The ball soars through the air, a perfect arc against the blue sky, and lands close to the hole. "Yes!" I pump the club in the air, then step aside so Nico can tee up. "I found a date for my brother's wedding."

"Ah, the mysterious lady stirring whispers in the copy rooms?"

My heart skips a beat while Nico prepares his shot. What? Surely, Damien didn't leave a copy of our photo in one of the copy rooms.

Nico tees up and swings. His ball falls short of the green. He turns with a frown. "Damien's sister, right?"

Wes, usually the observer, nods. "That would make sense. You mentioned she was the only approachable person at that party."

"She's nice." I admit it more to myself than to them. Trusting, as Damien put it.

Wes takes his shot, his perfect form a testament to his disciplined nature.

After following the asphalt cart path to the green, Wes and I wait, putters in hand, for Nico to make his approach shot.

I clear my throat. "She's agreed to be my pretend fiancée. It's a temporary arrangement until Gavin's wedding is over. But..." Talking about Zuri brings an unexpected warmth to my chest.

"A fake fiancée you get along with." Wes's eyes narrow. "That's quite an interesting choice."

"She's different." My fondness seeps into my tone. "Besides being passionate about her café, she's genuine, kind, and wants to give back to the community." My gaze drifts to the horizon, and I'm lost in thoughts of her. "She's perfect for this... arrangement. Best it's someone I get along with, I guess."

I'm the last to putt. As I tap the ball and it rolls into the hole, I can't shake the feeling that, with Zuri, it could be more than just a charade. There was a certain force of nature between us, specifically during our food fight, something that had my fingers linger a tad longer on her soft cheek while I dusted flour from her face. Ideas of what could have be spun in my mind.

Then she stopped by on Friday, surprising me with fruit and vegetables. "Thought you could use some snacks throughout the day, Mr. Workabee." She placed the containers on the coffee table in my office, then talked me into grabbing lunch at Simply Thai across the street. Funny, it hadn't been a struggle to drop my work to have lunch with her. If only I was ready to embrace something real, though.

"If I didn't know any better, I'd say, you have a thing for your yet-to-be-fake fiancée." Nico, always one to speak everything that comes into his mind, points his putter at me.

"I'm not." My words come out too weak. Would I even know what falling in love feels like anymore? It's been a long time since I had that excitement of first falling in love.

The air cools our faces as Wes maneuvers our cart toward the next tee box. He gives me a curious gaze. "Don't you think this arrangement could get complicated?"

"We both have an agreement."

"Not to fall in love?" Wes ticks his head. He's always more practical than Nico and me. Maybe because he's also the most spiritual.

I want to insist I won't let my heart stray again, but the more time I spend with Zuri, the more I want to know her beyond this façade.

Nico parks behind us and approaches, carrying his driver. He's grinning. "Sounds like someone's catching feelings," his Italian accent is more pronounced with his playful mood.

I groan. How'd he know what Wes and I discussed? "It's not like that. It's just... We get along."

"Just be careful." Wes twirls his club with a practiced motion. "Playing pretend can be fun, but what if you fall for her and she doesn't reciprocate?"

They both know what Sonya did to me, and I'm grateful for Wes's concern and reminder. Still, with Wes's words ringing in my ears, I shank my drive. I take a deep breath. I'll be searching the rough for that ball. I shrug. "No one's falling in love."

Nico chuckles. "And if there's falling in love, you can turn the fake into reality." He adjusts his sun visor. "If it doesn't work out, there are plenty more fish in the sea. Just cast your net, eh?"

I laugh despite myself, feeling a temporary lift from my thoughts. "Fish in the sea."

Overhead, screeching seagulls drown my voice. Finding that one person in the vast ocean of possibilities is daunting.

As the afternoon wanes, our conversation shifts to work and the latest office gossip, but my mind remains anchored on Zuri. Each stroke, each putt, reflects the complexity of my feelings for her. Nico's teasing and Wes's counsel resonate, hinting this charade might evolve into something profound.

The sun begins its descent as we conclude our game. Nico, as usual, ends up with the short end of the stick. "Dinner's on me tonight," I declare, having secured a decent second place.

"But you didn't lose," Wes points out, his tone light.

"When I lose our next bike race, Nico will be the one paying." I grin toward Nico, who's wiping perspiration with the back of his hand.

As we leave the course, Wes commends Nico on his viral graphic post for Stone Financial.

Nico growls, "Don't even get me started with the graphic designer."

"She's friends with Zuri." I can't recall her name. "What's her name again?"

"Pain in my chest, if you ask me," Nico retorts, probably only half joking.

"She seemed laid-back when I saw her." I shrug. "At least she gets the job done right."

Nico scoffs. "Trust me, we spend more hours arguing over what goes on the platform or website than getting the job done."

Ever the peacemaker, Wes jostles Nico. "Seems to me, you make a good marketing team."

We approach the clubhouse, the warmth of the setting sun and the camaraderie of my friends buoy my spirits. Thoughts of ring shopping for Zuri and her unique proposal preferences dance in my mind. It could be an uncertain path, but I'm in the safe zone since it's all pretend.

CHAPTER 6

Zuri

An active kitchen always energizes me. It's the one place where cooking brings out the rawest feelings and opens conversation avenues that might otherwise remain unexplored. This resonates with me anew today as I dry a mixing bowl, Damien's voice a backdrop from where he stands at the opposite counter.

Cooking has always been more than a job for me. But I fear losing my passion for it if it becomes too constrained.

"I'm yet to figure out Kress's intentions." Jeremy's last name pulls me back to the present as my brother cradles the red bowl of frosting he's mixing. Damien's wooden spoon slaps the bowl so furiously he might crack it. It's been a week since Lexi printed those photos, but Damien could write a booklet of bad reviews about the picture of Jeremy and me. "All the years I've worked at Stone, Kress has never smiled at me, and suddenly, he's all like a lovesick teen with Zuri."

"Zuri has what you don't have." Across the counter, Olivia's manning the beef stroganoff, her movements rhythmic and assured. Her blonde-highlighted hair, tied up in a ponytail, catches the light when she glances over her shoulder. "Jeremy is one of the office heartthrobs. And guess what else?" She plants a hand on her curvy hip bunching up the tank top she's wearing over gray leggings. "I'll let you beat me in Uno if—"

"Why would a man like him still be single?" Damien demands.

"Because he's been waiting for Zuri all along." Lexi pats her camera, shaking her short brown hair around her face, and jiggles through a silly dance step. "Isn't it great how they hit it off?"

"It's amazing our boss can be friends with one of our own." Olivia leans back against the counter. "Plus, he's a great leader—efficient despite his direct approach to getting things done."

"I can't believe you'd support this." Damien fists his grip on the wooden spoon, still whacking away. I'd better take it from him before he splatters frosting all over. The soft kitchen lighting accentuates his tight frown and the deepness of his emotions. He pulls the spoon from the bowl and shakes it at Olivia. "I thought you were on my side."

His reaction doesn't catch me off guard or deter me. I'm an adult, but he's felt the need to protect me, ever since we officially became orphans, never mind that I was twenty, and he was twenty-two then.

Meanwhile, Lexi moves around the kitchen capturing every moment with her camera, from the soiled spoons to the flour dusting on the counter. She believes each detail adds a personal touch to the recipes I post on my blog.

While she does this for fun, her keen eye misses nothing, finding beauty in the food and the raw, unscripted moments that define it—events that go with it. She captured a detailed moment for Jeremy and me though, so no wonder my brother hasn't stopped talking about this for days.

"I still don't like the idea." Damien continues his complaints, not caring whether anyone is on his side or not.

I sling the kitchen towel over my shoulder and take the dried bowl to the cabinet. Ever since I returned to the West Coast four months ago, I've been unable to ignore Damien's complaints about Jeremy. I'd hoped inviting Jeremy to the party, a plan conceived before I knew him, would bridge the gap between them. Damien had been vocal about the promotion Jeremy overlooked him for. The New Year celebration I organized mid-January presented the perfect opportunity to introduce myself to potential future customers in the Stone Enterprises' building.

"I thought having Jeremy here would ease the conflict between you." I snatch the frosting bowl from his hands, not that he's now doing anything with it other than grip the wooden spoon to diffuse his anger. "If you'd taken the time to talk to him when he was here, you'd realize he's a good person."

Damien's firm jaw clenches. "He was only good because he was too busy swooning over you." His spoon gestures dismissively. "Do you know what he said when I confronted him with your picture?"

"You confronted him with that?" I nearly squeak, my voice far higher than I expected. My eyes widen until they must be about to pop out.

Olivia, stirring the stroganoff, glances over with a disapproving look. "No, he did not." She wags the sauce-soaked wooden spoon toward him, and globs dribble on the tile.

Lexi adjusts her lens, capturing this shift in our dynamics. "Actually"—she sounds chirrupy—"word about Zuri and Jeremy is already milling around some departments at the office."

An uneasy shiver ripples through me. Could it be news about the picture, or were people who came to the house and saw me talking with Jeremy now spreading rumors? If it's the picture, it portrays affection between us, even if there was none.

As long as this doesn't complicate things for Jeremy being the leader. I'd best approach this situation with a tactical sensitivity so I don't add too much ignition to this flambé already burning between my brother and his boss—my soon-to-be-fake fiancée.

Damien rubs his eyes. "The man's a robot."

"Not exactly a robot. He laughs with his friends." Lexi turns to mix the egg noodles, her original task before she snagged her camera to capture the bubbling pasta. "He can be laid-back too, with the right people."

"I heard him laughing with Zuri at the party."

Olivia's mention of Jeremy's laugh sends warm tingles down my spine. I've seen him smile and heard him laugh more times than I care to share.

At moments like these, I'm glad to have my two friends living with us, the perfect buffers during such conversations with my brother. Besides, since they both work at Stone Financial Enterprise with Damien, their insights are the leavening this discussion needs.

Lexi and I moved back to San Francisco when she landed a job at Stone Financial and needed a place to stay. Olivia's lease was up, and her rent had risen. With Damien's permission, I invited both girls to move in with us. While I was blessed to get an internship in a culinary trade school, Damien and my friends have student loans to pay. Plus, he and I don't need a five-bedroom house all to ourselves.

"The party was to help Zuri meet the staff who will be her customers." Olivia wipes the sauce stain from the floor. "It worked. Everyone loved the food, and now, with these rumors, everyone at the office is curious about her and her café."

"The party was a success." Lexi places her camera on the counter. "You can throw more work parties as long as you don't invite *my* boss." She rolls her hazel eyes and crosses her arms, then shudders as if even the thought of her boss brings a tangible tension into the room.

I shake my head as I set the frosting back on the counter. I'm looking forward to meeting all these people, and the idea of hosting more parties now plays in my mind.

"There's no better way to connect than around food." I point to everyone, regardless of whatever issues were unresolved at the last party. I'll make sure Lexi's boss joins us next time. After all,

Jeremy and I bonded over food. From the moment he walked into the door and tested my appetizers, all through sharing chocolates, our conversations never died at all.

The timer dings on my phone, and my sense of smell becomes alert. I open the oven and pull out the pound cake, further releasing the savory scent.

Damien seems to be thinking of something while his gaze drifts toward the window where the neighboring two-story Victorian stands, completely different from ours.

Surrounded by friends in the warmth of the kitchen, I bask in a sense of contentment. This is where connections are forged and where, I hope, understanding can be nurtured.

"This pasta looks ready."

At Lexi's announcement, I hand Damien the strainer. He's always assigned the task of draining the pasta.

"Maybe we should ice the cake first." I place the freshly baked cake on the marble island next to my best-selling cookbook I launched last year. With the stools tucked underneath and out of the way, it makes a convenient workspace. "Olivia, could you check a glaze for a warm cake?"

I included three other options in the book.

"Jeremy invited me to the awards ceremony," I blurt out since I'll need the girls' help shopping. Still, my heart races at the revelation.

"What?" they all exclaim in unison.

Damien slops the pasta into the strainer too fast, and some splashes onto the counter. Olivia's jaw hangs open, her hands pausing from opening the book, and Lexi just blinks, not even bothering to snap our pictures now.

"As his date," I add to get it all out in the open rather than wait for the tension to dissipate.

They fall silent a moment before Lexi reaches for her camera, snaps a picture, and hoots, "I knew it!"

"The event is staff-and-spouses only," Olivia chimes in. "If you're coming as a spouse, then he really likes you."

Damien's reaction, however, is more guarded. "Are you kidding me?" His voice rises. His protective nature is nothing new. He lifts his hands. "Am I the only one who sees how wrong this is?"

"When was the last time you got excited about me having a date?" I counter, meeting his gaze. He grumbles, clearly frustrated, but he'll come around. For now, I won't reveal my arrangement with Jeremy. Instead, I steer the conversation back to our current task. "Let's focus on the cake."

The girls buzz with excitement, while Damien remains thoughtful. He must be unsure of what to do next because he joins us around the island.

Olivia's finger traces down the cookbook's list. "You're missing a key ingredient for our cake." She's snickering, so it mustn't have anything to do with the recipe.

"What would that be?" I play along.

"A dash of fun," she declares, eyeing Damien, then scoops a handful of powdered sugar from the open jar and tosses it at his blue T-shirt. "Lighten up, Mr. Grumpy!"

Damien, now speckled with sweetness, tries to maintain his stern demeanor. Then Olivia smears another handful across his face, and his resolve cracks. The corners of his lips twitch, and he looms over us. "You girls sure you want to do this?"

"Do you?" Olivia counters, mischief playing across her face.

The moment Damien grabs the sugar jar, the room erupts into playful chaos. Armed with the jar, he chases Olivia. With their infectious laughter, a joyful lightness dusts the air as sugary and sweet as the powdery concoctions they're tossing at one another. My mind goes back to my time with Jeremy when I smeared him with flour and had him laughing. Goose bumps scatter my arms at the memory of his tender caress on my cheeks.

I shake my head to snap out of the memory. We're in a fake relationship, and the sooner my brain gets the memo, the better.

"You're insane." Olivia coughs from the sugar as she swats at Damien's chest and his laughter rumbles free.

Lexi's camera captures the moment, the shutter clicking rapidly. "This is perfect for the blog!"

"Good luck cleaning up, you two." I grin, thinking of a similar playful spat they had last week. Only Damien can get away with dumping this much sugar in Olivia's hair.

In the kitchen of our childhood home, I'm feasting on a profound gratitude. When our parents passed, they left the house to Damien and me, and we chose to keep it rather than sell it. This home continues to make memories of love and laughter.

Food truly has a unique way of uniting people, sparking conversations, mending rifts, and fostering joy. Observing my brother and friends, their laughter mingling with sugar-sweetened air, I'm again struck by food's ability to bridge the gaps between us. Not that I expect it to cross the divide between Jeremy and me, of course.

CHAPTER 7

Zuri

In my bedroom, I scrutinize my reflection in the full-length mirror. Adjusting the sleek lines of my dress, Olivia, ever the caretaker, fusses over my hair, her fingers deft and gentle, though it's already impeccable. She clips a white flower pin to the side of my hair. "This is what it's missing."

She's right. The white complements my dark dress.

I nod at my reflection. "Thanks."

Meanwhile, Lexi, with her unbridled enthusiasm, debates the merits of various heels that could go well with my dress and leaves her choices scattered like colorful sprinkles around the room.

"I reckon I'm already set." I tried on my shoes yesterday and made my choice.

My dress, a stunning off-shoulder navy-blue gown, flows to the floor with an elegance I rarely indulge in. It's simple yet sophisticated, and the added elegance makes me feel ready to conquer this evening. I got it on a discount rack with the help of my friends.

But deep inside, I was thinking of looking extra nice for Jeremy. As I smooth a hand down my slim waist, I can't suppress the fluttery excitement of this being a date.

"You look amazing, Zuri." Olivia's eyes sparkle as she steps back to admire her handiwork on my hair.

"You look beautiful too, Liv." I touch the shoulder of her olive-green formal dress, a lovely creation well suited to her. The ruched lines along the waist flaunt her full-figured curves while the high neckline remains modest. Beautiful is an understatement—my friend is stunning as usual. She's styled her hair in loose waves that cascade down her shoulders, adding a touch of glamor to her look. "And, Lexi, I'm glad you walked away with that black dress."

Lexi picks up her camera from my dresser. "I have no one to impress." Her camera clicks away. "Jeremy won't know what hit him when he sees you, though!"

"Exactly." Olivia claps her hands, giddy.

"Stop it, you two." A blush rises to my cheeks. "It's just... we have an arrangement." I feel unease admitting we're just pretending because, when I'm with him, everything between us feels real.

"Pretend or not, you're going to make an impression." Lexi doesn't ask for details when she winks before adjusting her camera lens.

"How did he rope you into this?" Olivia sits on my unlaid bed with its red duvet.

I slide into my wedge high-heels and move to stand by the corkboard I've packed with magazine cutouts of crepes, cupcakes, cheesecakes, soufflés... so many of the recipes I've daydreamed of perfecting. The heels add to my height without compromising my balance or crimping my toes, unlike pointy options might, and with them on, I no longer risk my dress sweeping across the floor. As I touch the maraschino cherry on the shortbread cookie cutout, I recount the story of taking him an apology meal, being asked to be his wedding date, making our dinner at the café, and finally, accepting his invitation to be his date at the awards ceremony.

Then I grip Olivia's shoulder again to make sure she takes this secret seriously. She and Damien tell each other all sorts of secrets.

"We can't tell Damien about the fake-dating part. He's already on edge with me and Jeremy as it is."

She blinks, clearly uneasy about keeping this from my brother. Her lips part, then close. "But don't you think it would ease his mind?"

"Secrets... secrets." Lexi shakes a finger, her brown curls shaking in perfect synchronization.

"I'll tell Damien soon, but—"

I cut myself off, hearing the half tune and humming, commonly my brother's best way to sing songs he doesn't know the lyrics of. Approaching footsteps accompany the tune from down the hall. We all fall silent, heads turning to the door. Damien emerges and walks into my bedroom. Dressed in a black suit seemingly crafted just for him, he exudes polished sophistication.

"Wow, ladies." He lets out a whistle as his bright-eyed gaze sweeps over each one of us. "My roommates clean up nice."

"Your tie." Olivia frowns at him, then leaps up from the bed, ever the caretaker, and adjusts his tie, her movements, both assured and tender, a silent dialogue of their bond.

"This shade of green emphasizes your hair nicely, Donovan." My brother says to Olivia, who tells him he always looks sharp in a suit.

"You cleaned up pretty nice, bro." Truly, the suit brings out a hidden sleek look. My brother is nice-looking when he's not sulking.

"You're going to take everyone's breath away tonight," he comments, a genuine warmth lighting up his face as he tilts his head, surveying me.

"What?" I ask, but he shrugs, leaving me no idea whether he wants to give me any last-minute warning words before I leave.

Last night, I implored him to see Jeremy through a lens not clouded by work-induced bias, but to trust my judgment. It was a plea for understanding, and his current warmth feels like his agreement.

Now, I shuffle my feet back and forth. Our separate departures, despite sharing the same roof and heading to the same place, seem awkward, a logistical quirk Damien dryly notes. "Seems ironic that you're not driving with us. We live in the same house, yet we part ways like strangers."

"You're driving with everyone but me... not awkward at all..."

The doorbell chimes. My hands flutter before my face, but they can't keep up with the flutter in my chest. "Jeremy's here."

Damien blows out an exasperated breath, then rolls his eyes.

"You know how this feels," I remind him, drawing a parallel to his experiences with love, though mine with Jeremy is glazed in pretense.

"Not only has he been in love before but he also has a crush on Jessie in accounting." Olivia pats Damien's back, and he clenches his jaw, clearly affected by this turn of conversation.

"I'll see you guys later." I am poised to lead the way, but Lexi's reminder about my clutch halts me. Olivia's last-minute gesture, a spritz of floral scent, coats me in a layer of confidence.

"Thanks." I blow kisses to my friends and brother before I step out of the room.

I might as well be heading to prom with the school heartthrob. Inhaling deeply, I smooth my dress to steady myself before leading the way downstairs, my companions forming a quiet procession behind me.

When I reach the front door, I hesitate, remembering how stubborn it can be. The last thing I need is to slam the door into Jeremy's face again, especially when we have an event to get to.

I extend my hand toward its handle. My fingers curl around it. With a careful, measured movement, I apply just the right amount of pressure and coax it to yield without the usual protest. The door, responding to the softness of my touch, relents and swings open with quiet compliance.

I'm met with Jeremy's cautious stance. Shared amusement flickers between us, and a chuckle escapes us both—a mutual recognition of the door's unpredictable reputation.

"I thought I'd keep my distance this time."

"I'm glad." My gaze lingers on him a tad longer than it should. He's the epitome of elegance in his charcoal suit, holding a bouquet of peach flowers with baby's breath sprinkled in. And he's looking at me with an admiration that steals my breath away.

"You're... stunning." The raw honesty in his words sends another flutter through my heart.

He then hands me the wavy vase, and a smile lifts my cheek as I accept the flowers. Warmth spreads through me at his thoughtful gesture. "They're gorgeous, Jeremy. Thank you."

I usher him back inside and put the flowers on the island where Damien and my friends have gathered.

"Hey, Kress," Olivia greets and offers him water, but he declines.

"You look sharp, Blackwood." Jeremy tells Damien, and it's comforting when my brother responds cordially.

"You don't look shabby yourself." His tone isn't as hesitant as it was at the party. "If you and Zuri wanna catch a ride with us—"

Jeremy holds up a hand. "We're good thanks."

"Zuri, can I get a quick photo of you and your date before you leave?" Lexi waggles her camera.

"You have a talent for photography." Jeremy chuckles as I return to his side. I'm sure he's complimenting the photo that affected Damien to ambush him at his office. Lexi printed like four copies, hoping I'd keep one, then Jeremy and Damien, while the fourth went into the album we keep around the house.

At her request, we stand by the fireplace. With Jeremy's casual, yet deliberate arm around me, his subtle and intoxicating cologne envelops me.

"Look at you two, all fancy and ready to conquer the world." Lexi winks, her lips twitching before she captures a couple of shots. "How about one where you're looking at each other."

I have no idea what she means.

But Jeremy turns to me, and his strong hands secure my waist. "Like this?" he says, looking at me.

"Zuri, your hands." Lexi indicates I do the same.

Timidly, I slide one hand around Jeremy's waist, and it's shaking as I look into his piercing blue eyes.

"What about—"

"Take the picture already!" Damien's voice booms, cutting off Lexi.

"Relax, Damien." She snaps the shot.

"We gotta get going." Damien smirks.

"Seriously?" Olivia rolls her eyes. "We're never fifteen minutes early anywhere. We're not going to change that tonight. Besides, we have to get our photos next."

Once Jeremy and I finish with the photo, we say goodbye with a promise to see them at the party.

Damien claps Jeremy on the back. "I'll be keeping my eyes on you two." He's probably only half joking.

"It won't be necessary." Jeremy rests his hand on the small of my back, and I get this dizzying longing.

Then, at the need to stand up for myself, I address my brother. "That's if you want me to talk on your behalf to you-know-who," I say, and he frowns, seeming to get the memo of my threat. "Lexi and Liv will show me who she is."

"Don't you dare." He points at me with a somewhat serious glare, and I shrug, my heart expanding.

With Jeremy's hand on my back as we walk out, I lose myself in the moment. Pretend or not, this evening's the perfect recipe for memories. Boy, I'm so in trouble.

CHAPTER 8

Zuri

The grand banquet hall unfolds before us as Jeremy and I step through its towering doors, and the two security guards at the entrance offer warm smiles when he greets them by name. Above, chandeliers twinkle like stars, casting a golden glow over the room. Meanwhile, the murmur of conversations softens the air, punctuated by the delicate chime of glassware as servers dressed in black glide between elegantly attired guests.

In this sea of tuxedos and flowing gowns, I'm grateful I took my friends' advice to pay a tad extra for my dress. With each step, the hem caresses my ankles. Its softness, though, contrasts my firm grip on Jeremy's arm. I seldom attend parties, especially fancy ones. This is a first for me, but I feel confident because that's the definition of my date.

Jeremy, the epitome of grace and confidence, moves us through the crowd with a charm that seems as natural to him as breathing. When we approach a man smiling at him, Jeremy introduces his boss. Just like every man in the room, this one's dressed in a dark suit and crisp white shirt. He's probably five years older than Jeremy, quite young to be the CEO of a reputable financial company.

"My girlfriend, Zuri," Jeremy says as calmly as if he's done this fake thing before.

"You can call me Logan." Logan extends his hand, his grip firm, his eyes kind. "I'm glad you could join us today."

"Jeremy was kind enough to extend the invitation."

"I hope he can bring you to our next game night." Logan then explains the bimonthly dinner he and his wife host for the company executives.

"As long as she's not busy." Jeremy winks at me, and my knees go weak. If he invites me and I have no commitments, yes, please!

Someone joins us, apologizing for the interference, before he requests Logan's presence somewhere else.

With a promise to see each other soon, Logan leaves us, and we move further, though pausing frequently as Jeremy encounters acquaintances. Each introduction brings polite smiles and handshakes. My smile in place, I try to anchor names to faces, a daunting task, but at least, I recognize a few from the party at our house.

As we approach a particular table, a figure cuts through the crowd, his approach swift, his smile wide and inviting. "Jeremy, my goodness!" he exclaims, his gaze shifting to me with a tangible energy. "This must be Zuri Blackwood."

"The one and only." Jeremy rests his hand on my back again. "Why so early today? What happened to coming late and having heads turning?"

"Had to get here to watch you and Zuri walk in." The man winks at Jeremy before glancing at me. Then he leans in to kiss my left cheek and then my right as if we've known each other forever. He steps back. "Nico Marino."

"Nico works with Lexi," Jeremy says.

"I'm her boss or colleague." Nico shrugs, his Italian accent adding an appealing lilt. "Whatever she calls it."

So, this is Lexi's boss.

Nico says how happy he is that Jeremy's lucky enough to have a date who could agree to come with him to the biggest company event of the year.

"Keep your eyes open tonight." Jeremy cuffs his friend's arm. "This might be your night."

Nico lets out a laugh. "This is *not* the place for entanglement."

As more people roll in, the evening grows livelier, and the soft strains of music and the steady rise of conversations create a backdrop to our interactions.

Servers weave around passing trays of hors d'oeuvres and drinks. I decline when one is presented to me. The server doesn't interfere with Nico and Jeremy, aware of their relaxed banter, heads tilted back as they laugh about something.

Jeremy places a hand on my back, a reminder he hasn't forgotten me.

It could be my personal preference, but he stands apart in the room, his allure unmatched. Yet, Nico, with his lean frame, casually styled dark-brown hair, and striking features, commands his share of attention. Stone Financial Enterprises has some nice-looking men, my brother included.

The microphone's sharp crackle breaks through the buzz, and someone announces, "Food's ready."

Jeremy and Nico's conversation stops, and a shiver runs through me when Jeremy leans in close and whispers, "I'm sorry I ignored you." His breath, a ghostly caress, sends goose bumps skittering up my bare skin.

"You weren't ignoring me." My voice holds steady despite the whirlwind inside me. "You've been right here with me the whole time."

He leads us to a table at the front, offering a clear view of the musicians. A woman plays the violin passionately from the corner. Jeremy pulls out my chair.

"Thanks." I slide into it, and he nods.

Glancing over my shoulder, I sight Lexi, Olivia, and Damien a few tables away. Lexi catches my eye and waves, her enthusiasm shining through the crowded room. I wave back, and she raises her thumb at me.

As our table for six fills with newcomers, including Nico, Logan, and his wife, an energetic buzz enlivens the banquet hall. The buffet offers plenty of choices. Steak, chicken, fish, and a variety of enticing sides. The rich scents of gourmet food are enticing. Soon, I savor each bite while lively conversations and laughter weave around me, and the sound of silverware against plates plays a duet with that violinist. The table hums with stories and discussions, especially as Jeremy, Nico, Logan, and a more reserved gentleman find common ground.

Seated next to Jeremy, with Serafina, the CEO's wife, on my other side, I'm caught in conversation with someone new. Despite the hint of her pregnancy, I avoid personal comments, focusing on safer topics.

"I didn't realize Jeremy had a girlfriend until today." Serafina nudges her salad aside. Her bright eyes reflect her keen interest in Jeremy's personal life. "At the bimonthly dinners and game nights, they all talk about personal relationships, but not Jeremy."

At her unmistakable enthusiasm, I wince and halt in the middle of slicing into my steak. I'd better temper her expectations. "Jeremy and I are still figuring things out."

"He seems really into you."

When she nods toward him, I turn his way, his gaze finds mine, and I get it. I think he keeps stealing glances at me. My heart starts to thump, and I look away, then back to Serafina. Keeping my café's financial backing a secret from her is probably a good idea. I doubt he wants his whole company to know about his fake relationship. So I switch the topic to how we met. "It was sort of my brother's party, but I needed to showcase my recipes. I'm reopening the café downstairs under new management in April."

"You're a cook too? My bestie, Vanessa, is a chef. She turned to cooking to honor her late mother and has catered events for Stone Financial." As we return to our meals, the conversation transitions to food—a universally engaging topic that bridges our new acquaintance.

Jeremy rises from his chair beside me, his hand resting on my shoulder, and a strange flutter shivers in my stomach. The proximity, the shared glances—it all feels alarmingly real.

Minutes dissolve into a charged anticipation, the feast has concluded, and the plates are being cleared away. The room, bathed in the chandeliers' glow, hums with expectancy as Jeremy steps up to the microphone. "Good evening, everyone."

He draws every eye toward the front. With such natural charisma, he embodies sophisticated confidence. "Tonight, we celebrate not just the success of our company but also the incredible individuals whose hard work and dedication make everything possible. Each award we present..."

At some point in his speech, I place my hand on my chin. He sure is natural as he speaks to the crowd, some two hundred or so employees are attending with their spouses—for those who have spouses and brought them along.

Cameras capture the event as he calls employees and hands them gifts of appreciation, plaques, or engraved pens for their outstanding contributions and leather-bound planners for forward-thinking and planning excellence.

Then he announces Damien as the Financial Analyst of the Year, and my chest swells as he strides toward the stage, the applause thunderous. "Damien"—Jeremy holds up an engraved plaque with the Stone Financial Enterprises logo over Damien's name and award title—"your analytical skills and innovative strategies have significantly impacted our success. Thank you and congratulations!"

"That's my brother!" I clap, unable to contain my excitement.

"Well deserved!" Nico chimes in at our table. "He's set the bar high for all the analysts."

Logan nods, and Serafina hugs me in congratulations for my brother.

Then Jeremy returns to his seat, his hand finding mine. He laces our fingers together and oh, how I love the feel of his strong warm grip. "You did great up there," I whisper. Even if we're fake, my pride in him is real.

"Thank you." His gaze holds mine, a silent promise that perhaps, just maybe, the façade is crumbling a little.

Nico goes to the stage and hands out awards to people under his team. Then three more company leaders do the same.

I peer over the heads to catch my brother's eye. He's smiling ear to ear, and I wave. He waves back. I'm so proud of him and so grateful his hard work doesn't go unnoticed.

The CEO takes the stage, and applause erupts. Then he calls Jeremy back to the stage. As applause fills the hall, Jeremy clasps his hands in front of him and keeps his head down while the CEO credits him for his innovative leadership and awards him a sleek, glass trophy symbolizing his vision.

Upon Jeremy's return to the table, I stand and embrace him. "Congratulations!"

"Thanks, Zuri." He kisses my cheek, and a camera flashes at us. Then he sits, but his hand still rests on my back. Our shared glances and proximity stir a fluttery sensation that blurs the line between pretense and reality, both thrilling and terrifying me.

The evening unfolds into music, and people move to dance. Everyone at our table leaves to join the packed dance floor.

"Dance with me." Jeremy's breath whispers warmth against my ear, and those fast-becoming familiar waves sluice through my body. He pulls back his chair, stands, and extends his hand to me. With his gaze alight, I can't say no, even if I'm not a confident dancer.

We find a section to the side with enough space for the upbeat song. It doesn't require much skill and draws me in right away. Jeremy is a great dancer. Soon, I've caught up to his rhythm, and we sway in sync. We cover the space around us as he takes my hand, spinning and twirling me to the music.

He grins down at me when the song ends.

I return his smile as he swings my hand. "You have some cool moves."

"Makes it easy when you have the right dance partner."

A slow song starts, and the very air changes. I shiver when his hand curls around my waist and draws me into an orbit of warmth and closeness.

We begin to move, and I glide into the steps. With our fingers interlaced in one hand, I rest my other hand on his chest since I can't reach his shoulder comfortably without stepping on tiptoes. The soft chandelier light bathes us, and the music wraps around us.

"Thank you for coming with me tonight," he murmurs, his breath a whisper against my ear stirring a flutter in my chest.

"Thank you for inviting me." A whisper is all I can manage. Immersed in his proximity, I have to remind myself to breathe. His spicy scent and warmth envelop me, accelerating my heartbeat. "Just so you know, I'm a terrible dancer with slow songs."

"Makes two of us." His smile melts my heart, yet his admission bolsters my confidence. His lips brush my ear. It's just his way of making sure I can hear him through the music, but he has no idea it melts me inside. "You said you took dance lessons. Salsa, was it?"

"You remembered?" My smile breaks through my nervousness. "I never returned to salsa and didn't venture into any other dances after that."

As the song flows, we glide together, our bodies finding a rhythm as natural as breathing. The world recedes, leaving only us in a bubble of intimacy. His warmth and the steady pressure of his hand on my back crafts an alarmingly real connection. The lines of our façade are blurring for me—maybe even for both of us—with each slow step.

Maybe it's all in my head, but there's barely a breath between us. For a fleeting moment as the song nears its end, our lips hover dangerously close, and the rest of the dance floor fades further into oblivion. Like a wave in the ocean, affection swims between us. I have to assume he's leaning forward, because our lips are almost touching, and his breath is sending goose bumps shivering down my spine.

The song ends, the bubble bursts, and Jeremy tears away from me. A flicker of something—maybe confusion—crosses his face as if he is about to make the biggest mistake of his life. He starts walking back, and I follow as if the dance was my idea.

Back at our table, we sit in silence as the couples in the room continue dancing or chatting.

Despite this very real closeness, a gap lingers between us. I reach for a goblet, attempting to quench this more-than-physical thirst, sensing the stir of emotions our dance left unquenched.

"What do you usually do after the dance?" I break the silence.

"People stick around, mingle until they decide to head home." His index finger traces his award statue, and something unreadable adds huskiness to his voice.

How awkward this is with just the two of us at the table! The silence presses in, heavy, charged with the aftermath of our shared moment. I scan the room. Damien's laughing at whatever the woman standing with him is telling him, his head tilted back. Perhaps that's Jessie.

Olivia and Lexi seem engrossed in conversation with the other person at their table. The temptation to escape to familiarity, to dodge the awkwardness, grows.

"Ready for me to take you home?"

Caught off guard, I dip my head and rub at my bare arms. Am I relieved or just saddened?

"Are you usually the first to leave?" I ask, seeking anything to navigate away from the precipice of our earlier connection.

He shrugs, and the gesture speaks volumes yet reveals little. Then Nico returns, his energy infectious, and Jeremy shifts toward him, seeming eager for the distraction.

"Looks like you've been having a good time." The ease with which he transitions into casual conversation with his friend leaves me to wonder about the man's facets.

"Guys, you shouldn't be sitting here." Nico urges us to get back to the dance floor. "We need to keep the night alive."

Jeremy stiffens and barely glances at me. Scratching his jaw, he redirects the conversation to their upcoming golf the next day.

I sit up straighter. This change in him—Does it mean our connection tonight wasn't just my imagination? Did it rattle him? It's not a good time for a relationship while I'm getting my café off the ground, but I tend to forget that whenever I'm with Jeremy.

Deciding to distance myself, I opt for an escape. "I'll hitch a ride with Damien." I stand and snatch my clutch bag from where I tucked it at the back of my chair.

"You're leaving already?" Nico's high forehead crinkles, glistening with evidence of his dancing. "You can't leave your date behind."

If only you knew, it's my date *leaving* me *behind*. But I shake my head instead. "It was nice to meet you, Nico." I have to speak for myself since my date is preoccupied with silence. "Bye, Jeremy."

Somehow, I infuse casualness into my voice, even as disappointment dulls everything in me. "Thank you for tonight." *You're the worst date!* But I hold that in too. "I had a great time." Also true, after all. I just hadn't expected it to end so abruptly.

Jeremy nods. "Of course. I'm glad you enjoyed it." His polite words widen the distance between us with every syllable.

"Wait. What?" Nico scoots closer and moves his half glass of water between us. "Why don't you give your date a ride?"

"It's late." Jeremy still doesn't look at me. "It makes sense for her to ride with her roommates."

Backing Jeremy's rationale despite the ache settling in, I nod to Nico. "Jeremy is right." Nico seems like the life of the party, and his friendliness soothes this rather strange time. Perhaps he'll visit my café. "I hope to see you again soon."

His playful salute is a small comfort as I turn to leave.

The walk to my friends' table blurs as so many emotions blind me to everything else. The laughter and music fade, a backdrop to my internal turmoil. This fake date is concluding before it has a chance to begin.

I'm almost to my friends' table when Damien returns, beaming. His smile vanishes the moment he looks at me. I mustn't be as good at masking my feelings as I thought.

"What happened?"

I squish my face, working my best to act normal. "Any chance I get to meet Jessie tonight?"

"Over here." Olivia ushers me toward the table. "I'll point her out."

Drawn to any distraction, I hurry over.

Damien persists. "Did Kress say anything to make you uncomfortable?"

His face is serious. While my brother used to have a temper, I figured it diffused with maturity. But now he's looking too riled.

"I'm fine, Damien." I speak through gritted teeth not wanting to capture attention. Had he been watching our every step like he promised?

Lexi and Olivia exchange inquisitive glances and I hold up a hand to silence them. "I just want to ride home with you all." Edginess sharpens my tone now, but it's probably not recognizable over the music. "Will that be okay?"

Olivia nods.

"I knew I couldn't trust him," Damien mutters. His gaze, sharp and assessing, shoots toward Jeremy.

And that's when my eyes betray me and my gaze follows his. Jeremy's alone at the table. He turns then as if he knows exactly where to look. His gaze catches mine. I doubt he looks at Damien at all because his confused gaze holds mine in a silent exchange before he looks away.

"I'll be back."

At Damien's declaration, I jerk his shoulder.

"Don't talk to Jeremy right now, please." I have to look at Damien to make sure he understands how seriously I mean it when I say he'd better stay out of this. "I really like him."

The admission is more for myself than for Damien. Maybe I'm the one crossing this line of fake and giving Jeremy cues he's not prepared to take. He was clear. He needed a fake date, period.

"He didn't force you into doing anything, right?"

I burst out laughing and slap Damien on the back. At least, with the music in the background, the nearby tables can't hear us. The girls fall in as the silent observers they become whenever

Damien and I get into a serious argument, but this one is not even an argument, I have no idea what to call it. To keep Damien at peace, I further explain why Jeremy isn't taking me home.

"He offered to drive me, but I told him it'd be silly when you were all here and could take me home."

My brother's tense shoulders ease back into place. He gives me a skeptical look, then glances back at Jeremy's table, but he's not there anymore.

"Congratulations, by the way." I move in to embrace Damien. "I'm so proud of you."

"I'm proud of you too, that you're driving home with us." He draws back and shakes a finger at me before he pulls out chairs for us.

An upbeat song plays, and Damien flicks his fingers, then ushers us to stand. "Let's all go shake it up."

"I'll watch you." I don't dare reignite the feelings of my dance with Jeremy, but I can't ruin the party for everyone either.

"I need to take some pictures." Lexi swipes through her phone, deleting some photos to create more memory. "I should've brought my camera."

I stay with Lexi while Damien and Olivia hit the dance floor.

As we drive home, the others chatter about the dance and his award, but I watch the city lights blur into streaks of color. Like batter blending, this mirrors my jumbled emotions, leaving me wondering what might have been if we'd let things develop. Instead, I'm left reeling from the fleeting moments with Jeremy and nagged by curiosity about what it would be like to be his real girlfriend.

Laying my forehead against the window, I wince at the sting of rejection and question my worth after this abrupt end.

Still, I cling to Monday's meeting for café furniture shopping, my only remaining thread of hope. Until then, I'll keep my distance. He probably needs some space.

CHAPTER 9

Jeremy

Monday dawns with the harsh truth that the world doesn't pause even after a weekend as surreal in my memory as a dream. In the bathroom, I fiddle with my tie, a mechanical gesture that's become second nature. However, I cannot focus on the day's agenda. Zuri invades my consciousness, her image haunting me through two restless nights. Memories of the lilt of her laughter, the velvety touch of her skin, and the shimmer of her eyes linger. Longing shivers through me over my struggle to keep my desires at bay, the battle within not to capture her lips with mine.

The truth hits harder than I dare admit—the thought of plunging back into the depths of intimacy terrifies me to my core, especially after my last venture left me nursing a heart so fragmented I feared it was beyond repair. Yet, with Zuri, the outlook is shifting. Our paths crossed briefly. But now, she's transcending the boundaries of our contrived romantic charade and morphing into something genuine, stirring excitement and dread.

I retreat to my bedroom, and my phone breaks the silence, a reminder flashing from the dresser. It's about the café, the furniture shopping I agreed to do with Zuri. My gut twists. Facing her with my emotions in such disarray feels impossible, and I have nothing tangible to offer her. With reluctance, my fingers type out a message.

Jeremy: Sorry I can't go furniture shopping. I'll connect you with a designer to help you.

I'm busy, and Zuri is well aware of my long working hours anyway.

I press send and silence the voice in my head urging me to reconsider. Then the phone rings, sending a jolt through me. My stomach performs acrobatics as I brace for Zuri's response. However, it soon relaxes. It's just my brother calling.

"Gavin!" I exhale as my tension lifts.

"Don't tell me I interrupted another one of your early morning workout sessions."

"If you count pacing and stressing as a workout, then yes." I drift toward the window overlooking the traffic. Despite my penthouse's proximity to the office, I prefer the solitude of my car for the late-night journeys home.

"Been waiting for the fiancée update—"

"I know." I cut Gavin off, wincing over not keeping him in the loop. Zuri's sudden presence in my life—Would I call it a distraction or a revelation? "It's been hectic." Yes, that's what I'd call it.

"Mom's been hounding me about this mysterious fiancée of yours. What's going on?"

I've never been one to withhold anything from Gavin, yet I've hesitated to bring up Zuri and this web of pretense we've spun.

Exhaling deeply, I massage the tension at the back of my neck. "You know Mom. She's already making ridiculous sleeping arrangements—like Sonya bunking in your room." I grumble at the absurdity of our mother's plans, which place my ex uncomfortably close to my room.

Gavin laughs off Mom's meddling ways, even her ludicrous hopes of him rekindling with his ex-girlfriend, Lucky, over his bride-to-be, Hope.

"And yet, you're letting her orchestrate your wedding."

"Try living in the same town as her." He laughs, but it rings hollow, betraying his resignation to our mother's influence. "But seriously, bro, where are you going to get a fiancée this fast? One willing to travel to Colorado for a week."

"Actually, I've found someone. Zuri." Oh man, listen to how naturally her name flows into our conversation.

"Zuri?"

I chuckle at his astonishment. Then I move about my room to mask the underlying emotions tied to her name. I share how we met, but I carefully select my words. I slide on my watch, needing to keep busy whenever I talk about her. It's my tactic to maintain emotional detachment.

Despite this, when I recount our staged date and the not-so-staged dance, my brother seems to sense the depth of my turmoil. "It doesn't sound like you're pretending, buddy. Are you sure there isn't more to it?"

I falter. Probably a good moment to divert the topic to his wedding plans. "I'm not staying under the same roof with Sonya." I clench the phone and grind my teeth. "Who does Mom think she is to control everyone's life?"

"Chill, bro. I'll talk to Hope. I'm sure she'll host Zuri, and I'll persuade Mom that my best man needs to stay in my house."

"Thanks." A bit of the tightness coiling my muscles loosens, and I flex my grip on the phone, rubbing at the pinched skin where its sleek lines indented my flesh. It's best we avoid any scenarios that might throw Zuri into unwelcome attention or, worse, make her the project of my overenthusiastic mother and Sonya.

As Gavin lists the relatives descending upon the wedding, I'm only half engaged. His earlier observation again gnaws at me, unveiling a truth I'm not prepared to confront.

"Glad you've got yourself that fake fiancée already. Mom's likely to pay you a visit any day."

His words jolt me more effectively than my morning kombucha. "Wait, what do you mean 'pay me a visit'?"

"She's gearing up to interrogate you about this new fiancée of yours. And just so you're aware, she's been briefing Sonya on your impending return."

Seriously? My enthusiasm plummets at the mention of my mother's relentless schemes. By the time I end the call, my thoughts are in a tumult. It's six o'clock—I'm already ten minutes late for work. Today, however, my tardiness isn't without reason.

Conversations with my brother have an uncanny ability to disrupt my schedule, but I look forward to catching up with him. Good thing, he always times his calls before I step into the office.

Mondays unfailingly usher in a deluge of work, but today, the welcome diversion keeps my mind tethered to my responsibilities, especially with the month's end looming on the horizon. The routine is rigorous: reviewing departmental performance metrics, scrutinizing financial statements, and pinpointing inefficiencies poised to derail productivity, among a host of other duties. These tasks, too vast to conquer in a single day, spill over to consume my week with an unrelenting pace designed to ward off distractions. Yet, even this methodical madness cannot prevent my thoughts from drifting to Zuri each night as I check my phone. Despite the long hours crafted to negate the need to bring work home—my attempt at drawing a boundary—the silence of my phone echoes the chasm I've placed between us. It's for the best, of course, though the hollowness now gnawing at me suggests otherwise.

By Sunday, the cycle breaks, and I join Nico and Wes, my confidants in trivial and significant matters on the golf course. Amid our leisurely game, Nico veers the conversation to the subject I've adeptly avoided: Zuri. "So, you're okay with ghosting the charming Zuri, then parading her as your fiancée at the wedding?"

I huff, my evasion settling heavily. "We shared a moment," I confess, acknowledging the depth of our connection for the first time, even as I question my convictions. "A *genuine* moment. And I can't afford that right now."

Wes halts our progress with a gesture of his club. "Those are the complications I warned you about."

A rabbit darts across our path, emblematic of my attempts to escape reality. "I thought I could navigate this fake-dating scenario, but with Zuri, it feels different."

Nico whistles, and a rare seriousness overcomes his usually lighthearted demeanor. "It's a sign, you know. That you're still open to the idea of love."

Resuming our game, I position the golf ball with a focused determination, grip the club, and channel the tumult of my emotions into the swing, striking the ball with excessive force. It arcs through the sky, a physical manifestation of my inner turmoil and reluctant admission. "Perhaps I am falling... just a bit." My acknowledgment lifts an invisible burden, even as the reality of my feelings settle in.

The remainder of the game passes with more jokes and jibes, yet my thoughts incessantly revert to Zuri. Her essence permeates my senses, and her floral vanilla-infused scent lingers in my memory, evoking images of her close to me, her laughter, her touch. Little wonder my focus falters and Nico claims victory over me, a loss that costs me dinner.

During my drive home, the city lights twinkle like distant stars, and my mind circles back to that connection with Zuri. In the brief fortnight she graced my life before I consciously distanced myself, I caught myself looking forward to the workdays with an eagerness I hadn't known, all for the chance glimpses of her during her unexpected visits. The silence that now stretches between us carves a void in my space, a loneliness that hasn't been so evident in years. Perhaps it's time to confront my feelings head-on. Given our arrangement, the fallout of any potential rejection should theoretically be less daunting, cushioned by the pretense of our relationship.

Yet, as I park and reach for my phone, intent on bridging the gap I've created, my thumb stalls above her name. Yes, I'm still wrestling with the resurgence of past fears—a potential heartbreak.

The phone, a silent witness to my internal struggle, remains cradled in my grasp. I'm at a crossroads, teetering between the allure of what could be and the shadows of past pains. Again, caution prevails. I exit the car, the weight of unresolved what-ifs accompanying me, as inescapable as an unbalanced spreadsheet.

***

It's Tuesday. I'm stepping back into the fortress of my office after navigating a high-stakes meeting when the buzz of my desk phone snatches my attention. My mother's name illuminates the screen, and dread nips at me—a prelude to the inevitable storm her calls usher in.

But I answer anyway.

"Jeremy, dear, I'll be in the Bay Area today." She speaks before I can say hello, but it doesn't register until she adds, "We should go out to lunch."

I weigh my options against the immutable force that is my mother's will. "Mom, today's schedule is packed tight with meetings." I barely conceal my plea for a deferment. A mental buffer against her spontaneity is not just preferred—it's essential.

"Absolute nonsense." She dismisses me with the ease of someone accustomed to bending reality to her whim. "I'm already in San Francisco. I'll swing by your office, and we'll dine out. Consider it done."

The battle, as always, ends before it begins. "Sure." A sigh deflates my protest. What else can I do if she flew from Colorado to see me? Already, the call has concluded in our customary, abrupt manner—no declarations of affection.

With the call ended and no indication of when this impromptu visit will occur, urgency propels me. I must address a critical detail before her arrival—my fictitious fiancée.

Scrambling like a day trader during a downturn, I sprint to my sparse desk. Other than a lone pen and sticky note poised next to my computer, the surface is meticulously clear. "Great." I mutter under my breath, my gaze landing on Zuri's photo tucked beside my mouse pad. I'm not clinging to her image, but lately, I've found solace in glancing at it, in reminiscing about the moments we've enjoyed, the future we might've created.

It's a candid capture of us, laughter shared over chocolate, embodying the illusion of a perfect couple. My chest tightens, closing in over the space I've put between us.

I reach for the photo and tap it against my chin. Where could I place this picture to hint at my relationship to Mom? A picture frame would be ideal. I stride out of my office, photo in hand, and spot Jill behind her desk, her gaze on the computer and her lollipop in her mouth.

"Those lollipops aren't good for your teeth," I caution, half-heartedly.

She pulls the candy from her mouth. "I brush three times a day. My teeth can handle it—and your dental plan is good." She smirks. But her gaze shifts to the photo, and her brow rises. "What's that?"

Admitting the oddity of my request, I nod to the family photo on her desk. "Could I borrow your picture frame for a few hours?"

Jill snatches the photo, a grin unfolding. "My, my, my. If this isn't my boss, smitten." Her head tilts. "I'm surprised Zuri hasn't been around since the awards ceremony. You two were the coziest couple on the dance floor."

"I need a frame," I press. "My mother's visiting soon, and I've got to convince her I'm genuinely in love."

"But you are in love, aren't you?" She opens a drawer to reveal a stash of frames. "Lucky for you, I have spares I haven't used yet."

She hands me a sleek, silver frame. "Will this do?"

"It's perfect. Thank you." I stand there, arms awkward at my side.

She inserts the photo before handing it over, one corner sticky where her fingers smudged it. "You can keep the frame, by the way."

"Thanks." I hasten to my office, her warning words bouncing against my back.

"You'd better treat that girl right. She's a keeper, you know."

I don't turn to engage in response. She must've sensed something since Zuri hasn't made any impromptu visits lately. I don't need a reminder of the complexity of our situation.

Back at my desk, I position the framed photo so I can admire it, yet it's visible to anyone entering. This visual cue had better deter Mom's persistent attempts to link me with Sonya. Still, the setup feels like a declaration of a relationship that's both ridiculously nonexistent yet palpably real in my heart.

CHAPTER 10

Jeremy

The instant Mom enters my office, I offer a brief hug—an obligatory gesture—before she takes command of the space, her presence filling the room like she owns every inch. She moves with a deliberate pace, her gaze sweeping over each corner and detail with the critical eye of a seasoned auditor. Today, she's wearing a cream pencil skirt with a matching blazer over a black silk blouse. The pearl necklace and gold earrings speak of her refined taste.

Her attention soon zeroes in on *the* photo. She lifts it with a grace that belies her invasive scrutiny and carries it over to the seating area.

I remain perched on the edge of my desk, a silent observer to her inspection.

Her eyebrows lift. "And who is this?"

"Zuri." I manage, striving for nonchalance. "She's... coming to the wedding with me." It's critical for Mom to understand this. I must dismantle any schemes she's brewed up.

Her gaze sharpens, then narrows, a familiar precursor to a barrage of questions. “Really? Why haven’t I heard about her until we spoke three weeks ago?” Her skepticism is palpable, each word chosen to dissect the truth I’m presenting.

Just as the tension reaches a crescendo, a knock disrupts the charged atmosphere, and Zuri strides in, her entrance as timely as if orchestrated by fate itself. “Jeremy Kress, you are not going to ghost me like that.” Her annoyance renders her even more endearing. The aroma of delectable food wafts from the bags she’s holding, diverting my attention. “Do you have any idea how that made me feel?”

“Zee, perfect timing.” The endearment surfaces as naturally as breathing, even as it catches me off guard. Since she’s oblivious to the additional presence in my office, I flick my gaze toward Mom, then back to Zuri, a silent signal of the company we have.

Zuri halts, her initial momentum tempered by Mom’s analytical scrutiny assessing her from head to toe—invasive, intense, calculating.

“Uh, I should’ve, uh, texted before showing up,” Zuri stammers.

“Actually, I’m glad you’re here.” I push off from my desk to bridge the gap between us. “This is my mother. Mom, meet my fiancée, Zuri.”

I lean in for a light kiss on Zuri’s cheek. Though meant as a mere performance, the act sends warmth through me.

Zuri then moves to the seating area and places the food on the table before she directs her attention to Mom and reaches out her hand. “Nice to meet you, Mrs. Kress.”

"Sara," Mom corrects and accepts Zuri's hand with far more formality than a genuine greeting—a habit of hers that has always irked me.

"You're engaged?" Mom probes, her attention shifting between the photo in her hand and Zuri's bare finger. "For a newly engaged couple, it's quite peculiar that you're not wearing your ring."

"I'm always mindful about keeping my... sparkly, um, ring." Zuri fumbles, brushing her empty ring finger as if to conjure an invisible band. She casts a glance my way, pleading for support. "You know, taking care of the diamond and all that."

"She's a chef, Mom." Stepping in, I position myself beside Zuri, my hand finding a natural place on her lower back. Her casual attire, flowery leggings paired with a red top, opposes Mom's meticulously chosen ensemble.

"I'm not officially a chef," Zuri corrects, her confidence wavering. "I just wanted to cook something special for Jeremy today. After a slight disagreement, he, well, he ghosted me. So, I had to make sure he eats, especially when he's buried in work."

Her explanation warms me to the core, and I glimpse a possible future filled with minor arguments and tantalizing reconciliations. I can't resist pulling her closer, my arm snuggling into the curve of her waist, my lips brushing the crown of her head, my nose inhaling the refreshing mint of her hair.

Mom watches with a critical eye before placing the photo on the table, not where it initially stood. Her gaze then locks onto mine, a challenge in her eyes. "Since your fiancée is here, she might as well join us for lunch."

"No," I need to shield Zuri from any unexpected interrogation.

"I'm quite busy." Zuri steps back in a clear signal of her intentions not to linger. "I appreciate the offer, Mrs. Kress—"

"Sara," Mom insists on the informal address.

"I have a lot on my plate today at the café." Zuri deflects the invitation.

"Was this food prepared in a commercial kitchen?" Mom's inquiry comes from left field, a pointed question that probes more than culinary curiosity.

"Not yet, but I plan to—"

"Do you have a food license?"

"Yes, I do."

I remain silent, allowing Zuri to navigate this conversation. She's more than capable of standing her ground. After all, if our paths are to intertwine more deeply, facing Mom's barrage will be an inevitable part of our arrangement, especially the wedding week. The interrogation continues with questions about Zuri's family, education level, background, and intentions. Zuri wrings her hands and scuffles her flats.

"Mom." I snap my fingers, a protective instinct flaring. "I won't stand here and let you interrogate my fiancée." My voice carries a firmness I rarely use with her, signaling a boundary she's perilously close to crossing.

"You know how many people die from food poisoning?" Mom continues, undeterred. Too bad, she never channeled her relentless scrutiny into her career, choosing instead to organize charity galas and high-society events—arenas where her meticulousness could shine without personal cost.

"I'm aware of the risks of food poisoning, but that won't be an issue for us since you won't be eating her food." My patience thins. The absurdity of the situation isn't lost on me. We're discussing hypothetical health hazards instead of acknowledging the real, human connection forming between Zuri and me.

"I told your assistant to make us reservations at The Almac," Mom announces as if the mention of the upscale restaurant can douse the flames of our confrontation.

With my hand still on Zuri's shoulder, I lean in to kiss her head, her fragrance offering a momentary escape from the tension. Her presence transforms this unexpected family encounter into something I can navigate without losing myself.

Mom's overt disapproval compels me to defend our decision to dine in my office. "Let's not waste Zuri's delicious food." Maybe I can salvage what remains of the day. Mom doesn't have to eat, but after how she acted, no way am I leaving this office.

"I'm not hungry." A dismissive wave accompanies Mom's predictable response. "I'll just have water, if you have any."

Zuri, ever gracious, strides across the room, retrieves two bottles of water from the fridge, and places them on the table before making a swift departure. "It was nice to meet you, Mrs. Kress." She bypasses the formalities of a handshake, offering a wave instead. In her rush, she forgets our façade, leaving without the pretense of a farewell kiss.

Who could blame her for escaping as quickly as she did? Assuming she hasn't called off our deal completely.

I savor the first bite of Zuri's warm steak salad. Inspired by her, I close my eyes and attempt to emulate her practice of pausing before a meal, though I'm unfamiliar with the specifics of her ritual. I'll have to ask her to speak aloud next time, so I can understand and perhaps adopt part of her mindfulness into my routine.

As the enticing aroma soon overtakes the room, Mom ventures a cautious sample of the southwestern rolls Zuri included. Despite her earlier apprehensions, she seems to enjoy the taste and gobbles the entire roll.

"As long as I don't get a stomach bug from this." She dabs a napkin on her red lips.

While I don't expect her to utter a compliment, I can't help saying, "I'm glad you liked the roll, Mom."

She ignores me and shifts the conversation to Sonya—the sole purpose of her visit, I presume.

"I told her you're still single. I can't believe you didn't tell me about this... new girl." She waves her black-painted fingernails, scrunching her face. "She's not even your type."

"I don't think you know my type, Mom." I fork my salad, not liking this conversation.

"You compare her to Sonya? Did you have to go for a woman who looks like your brother's girlfriend?"

Seriously? I've never seen two women who look less alike. "Just because Zuri has the same skin color as Hope's, doesn't make them look alike."

"Still, you and Sonya can work things out."

Tension coils within me. What right does Mom have to imply I'm somehow at fault for moving on after Sonya ended things between us?

"She dumped me, and now I'm the bad guy?" I slam what's left of the salad back onto the table. "I'm more than capable of making my own decisions."

"Sonya learned a lot, which could be good for giving her a second chance." Mom continues despite my obvious frustration, and an unwelcome nostalgia for what was misting her eyes.

As the conversation steers dangerously close to the boundaries I've been trying to set, I set down my fork and hold up a hand. "Can we, for once, not discuss my love life?"

She offers a smile that lacks genuine warmth. "Sweetheart, your happiness is everything to me."

"Is it?" I challenge. Her actions and words often feel misaligned with the notion of my happiness being her priority. "If that were true, you'd understand I'm capable of managing my own love life." With that, I'm marking my autonomy, reminding her my path to happiness is mine to navigate, regardless of her intentions.

Long after Mom's departure, the office grows quiet as I work overtime. Today, I need the extra hours after the unintended disruptions. Amid the solitude, I glance at the furniture catalog Zuri left in one of the food bags, a reminder of our missed appointment. Did she want my input on her café's interior? If so, her gesture touches me. Unlike Sonya, who preferred to present her decisions as done deals, Zuri's approach is refreshingly collaborative.

I push back from the computer, unable to refocus on the digital reports flickering on my screen. Thoughts of Zuri nudge me toward action. After my mother's behavior, I should reach out with an apology. I open my text app.

Jeremy: Sorry about how my mom behaved today.

Zuri: Sorry I couldn't stay. Your mom is intense.

Jeremy: Don't worry. You'll have time to brace yourself for her at the wedding.

Zuri: Are you sure you still want me as your date?

Jeremy: Absolutely. You're the perfect date. And I've checked out the catalog you left.

Zuri: I wanted your opinion, regardless of the designer you suggested.

I want to share my opinion with her. Well, mostly, I just want to see her.

Jeremy: Can I take you out to dinner tonight, so we can go over the furniture options?

Zuri: I'm cooking here, but if you're willing to discuss furniture, I can plan for a late dinner. How late are you working?

It's already six. My place is a short distance from the office, so I'll have ample time to freshen up.

Jeremy: Pick you up at seven?

Zuri: Seven, it is.

Excitement jitters through me, an adrenaline and anticipation I haven't felt in ages. The pretext may be the furniture, but it's Zuri that has me rushing off. Everything about this feels right, a sharp contrast to the day's earlier tension.

CHAPTER 11

Jeremy

Porch lights illuminate the street to Zuri's house. I trace the paths I navigated on my last visit. Yet, tonight, I'm driven by the need to mend the gap I created between us. A crisp breeze slips through my half-open window, offering a brief respite that's as refreshing as it is fleeting, failing to ease my apprehension. As Zuri's house edges into sight, my grip on the steering wheel tightens, the leather beneath my fingers a tangible anchor in the stormy thoughts.

In her driveway, I park behind a blue Buick. I blow out a breath. Has Zuri confided in her brother and friends about our unconventional relationship? My abrupt disappearance couldn't have cast me in a favorable light, considering the sharp look Damien shot my way at the awards party. Yet, since he hasn't confronted me, Zuri must've kept our situation discreet.

I tap my fingers against the steering wheel, hesitating to step out of the car. Just how should I announce my arrival? I could walk to the door, but I'd rather not run into Damien. Opting for simplicity, I reach for my phone in the console and fire a concise message.

Jeremy: I'm here.

My fingers tap faster as I await her reply, each tap amplifying my anxiety. When my phone finally vibrates, the air whooshes from my lungs.

Zuri: Okay. Coming out.

Anticipation, coupled with the chance to explain myself in person, dispels my tension. Focused on our reunion, I exit the vehicle as she steps through her front door. I rush to the passenger side and open the door for her.

Her black dress sways at her knees, and the porch light warms her features with an ethereal glow. The red handbag slung over her shoulder adds a splash of color to her ensemble.

"Hello." Keeping her chin tucked down, she fiddles with her handbag straps as she approaches.

With her near now, I get a close look at her dress. It clings to her, accentuating her well-proportioned figure. Keeping one hand tight on the door handle and the other to my side, I resist the urge to lean in and kiss her cheek. "You look stunning." I'm not just saying it—it's the truth.

"Thank you." Her fragrance envelops me as she walks past to settle into the seat. I close the door and move around to get to my seat.

The drive commences. In a jumble of nerves, I blow out a breath. "I–I wanted to apologize." The words emerge, barely steady. "For ghosting you. It wasn't fair."

A pause stretches between us. The streetlamps flash intermittent light into the car, illuminating her sitting there, arms crossed, gaze evaluating. "Why would you ghost me for an entire week?"

Nine days, but who's counting? At a stop sign, I draw in a slow breath. "I've been doing some thinking." The car idles. Easily enough, I can drive forward now, but just how can I steer this conversation where it needs to go? I pass through the intersection, and as we continue along, I confess my confusion regarding the blurry lines between our pretense and genuine moments. "I don't know about you, but I got caught up in emotions during the dance."

"I sensed that too." She shakes a finger at me. "Too bad, it only happened to you."

Her playful response has me reaching out. I smack her leg. "Liar."

"Some people can't handle the truth, you know."

Ouch. That hits a nerve. I couldn't handle the effect she had on me—still has on me—which is mostly why I'm here with her rather than at my penthouse ordering takeout.

She tucks her chin down again, and her lips wobble while she picks at a seam on her handbag. "I thought you found me unworthy of you."

Whoa! I wince as the revelation strikes deep. My thoughtless actions—my running from this preoccupation I have with her—caused those insecurities.

"That's not true." In fact, nothing could be further from the truth. Her feelings of unworthiness mirror my fears. "And I felt bad all week for ignoring you."

Here we are, trying to maintain a delicate balance, yet if I continue my avoidance, I could jeopardize not only the façade of our engagement but also this underlying connection we're struggling to define.

Soon, we arrive at a cozy Mediterranean-themed restaurant offering dim lighting, creamy stucco walls, exposed ceiling beams, and well-loved wooden tables and hardwood floors. Lush plants add the only color to its earthy tones while pottery and old wine bottles line the shelves. Soft music plays in the background, the soothing ambience a reprieve from our turbulent conversation. I vetted this place on my phone earlier, seeking a less crowded place with good food, somewhere less formal so it didn't appear too obvious as a date. Now, spices and fresh bread tempt me with mouthwatering scents.

Plus, the restaurant's tranquil atmosphere eliminates the need for reservations. A young woman welcomes us and escorts us to a vacant table tucked away in a corner. Before departing, she hands us the menus. "The server will be with you shortly to take your order."

Flickering candlelight bathes the space in a warm glow, accentuating Zuri's features and casting an intimate veil over our table. She slides into the padded bench along the back wall and sets her purse amid the cushions, leaving the wooden chair facing her for me.

"I've been thinking." She clasps her hands on the table, her eyes bright. "I don't want you to pay me for the café."

"Why's that?" I stiffen. Not that I can blame her for backing out of our arrangement.

"Well..." Her hand covers mine on the table, and its warmth seeps deeper than the skin, clouding my judgment with a pleasant haze. "Maybe just help me buy the appliances. The rest, you can help me with your business management skills, to see if I can start with whatever I have. Or you can loan me the rest, and I'll repay you."

"How about I invest in the café instead?" I have the money, and I'm always passionate about helping fund local community businesses. But I don't need to broadcast that. "You can repay me in two years when the business yields profit. Plus, you have a charity to support, and I want to help you fulfill that dream."

"Thank you." She takes her hand back, and I miss her touch. "But what if it doesn't succeed?"

"As long as I'm your business advisor, your business isn't going to fail." I'll use all my local connections to broadcast her business, though I also don't want to overwhelm her when she's just starting out. "It'll succeed, and you'll be in the profit margin sooner than you expect."

She braces an elbow on the table and plops her chin in her hand. "Now, can you please explain why you're so afraid of relationships?"

I shake a finger at her. "If I remember, you said you're not into dating either."

She deflects that with a lighthearted shrug. "But I didn't act so closed off when we had a moment during the dance."

"I've been let down before." Her sweetness disarms me, compelling a confession I hadn't planned on sharing. "I guess I'm afraid of jumping into something and getting hurt again. But avoiding you wasn't the answer."

The admission hangs between us.

Her eyes reflect a shared pain. "I'm sorry about that." A shadow fleets crosses her bright-eyed expression. Maybe she, too, understands the sting of a breakup. "It's hard to let someone in when you're scared of getting hurt."

The server returns to take our drink orders, and we both request water, having not yet delved into the menu. When prompted for our meal choices, Zuri turns to me for a recommendation, so I ask the server for their signature dish since neither Zuri nor I have any food allergies.

Once the server departs, Zuri refocuses on me, her curiosity piqued about my ex. "I'd better start getting to know all the people I'll meet at the wedding."

"Sonya is just like my mom."

"Controlling?" Zuri probes, catching me off guard and eliciting a laugh.

"I hadn't seen it that way when we were together, but looking back four years after we split, it's clear now."

"How did you two meet?"

"Our families are close." My gaze fixes on the candle between us, its light flickering uncertainty. "My mom always envisioned us together. We were engaged for one year and had plans for a wedding...."

The story emerges, revealing a chapter of my life I rarely unpack.

"Why would she elope when she was engaged to you?" Zuri's voice rises over the music.

Is there perhaps a hint of protectiveness within her shock? Thinking so prompts me to delve into the painful recount of betrayal.

"One day, she's detailing her dream wedding that she spent an entire year planning with her mom, then the next day, six months before the supposed wedding day, she elopes."

And my mother was the bearer of such unexpected news.

"That's brutal." Zuri's hands cup her face, her palpable empathy heartwarming. This gesture, simple yet profound, tightens something within me, leaving me grateful yet aching over her genuine concern for my past hurts.

But it's time to redirect the conversation. I shift the topic to another chapter of my life. "Before Sonya, there was someone else during high school. My mom wasn't her biggest fan, but that didn't stop me. I was really into her... even considered marrying her right after college graduation, partly to spite my mom. But college happened, distance came between us, and she moved on. She was married by the time I finished college."

The waiter approaches, the arrival of our water, marking a pause in our dialogue. Around us, ambient restaurant sounds fill the space, the gentle clink of silverware against porcelain and the murmur of distant conversations adding layers to the evening's atmosphere.

Once alone again, our conversation takes a more reflective note. We delve into our insecurities, the lessons etched into us by past loves, and the protective barriers we've erected around our hearts. This revealing exchange draws us closer through personal vulnerabilities.

As food is served at a nearby table, the aroma of roasted vegetables and seasoned meats breezes toward us, a perfect complement to our deepening conversation. Engrossed in this unusual conversation, I share more information than I've ever shared with anyone. I even delve into my family and my mother's overbearing nature, which has somewhat jaded my view on relationships.

"Ooh." She reacts with exaggerated concern. "Does that mean I'm getting the worst version of you?" Her playful shiver prompts my laughter.

"Actually, you're seeing the best version of me that's been absent for quite some time," I tease, but there's truth in those words.

"I'm glad." Her finger traces the rim of her glass. "How did you start working for Stone Financial?"

She seems interested in understanding me beyond the superficial details required for the wedding façade.

"After I graduated, I started as an analyst at a midsized financial firm, eventually getting promoted to a senior analyst position. Then, at one of our family gatherings, Eric, the founder of Stone Enterprises, mentioned he was looking for someone to lead their marketing efforts. I jumped at the opportunity and began my way up to COO."

Zuri sinks back in her chair, her curls bouncing around her delicate face. "How did Logan become CEO if Eric is the owner?"

"Eric stepped down to spend time with his family. He left the company in his brother Logan's hands."

"So, you're friends with both the owner and Logan?"

I nod. "Our families have been friends for years, and my brother is close with Logan. It's one of those things where my brother's friends became my friends as well."

But the spotlight's been on me for too long. "You and Damien grew up here in San Francisco?"

"We sure did." She beams. "We have so many memories here. I'll have to show you around all the places we used to find trouble."

"You, getting into mischief?" I mock a gasp and arch a brow, this side of her intriguing me.

She laughs, and the sound's quickly becoming a favorite. It stirs something deep inside, desire. It's been so long since I felt anything other than hurt, so these awakening emotions are—What? Overwhelming? Unwelcome? Addicting?

"You have no idea." She shakes a finger at me, those curls quaking with her laughter. "From sneaking into late-night shows at the Fillmore to dodging security at Ocean Beach for midnight swims, San Francisco was our playground, and we knew every nook and cranny worth exploring."

How well I can imagine their spirited youth spent in the heart of the city, adding layers to the woman sitting across from me.

My curiosity shifts. I brace my wrists on the table's dinged edge, leaning in. "How did your parents die?"

Her features darken, and my chest tightens. "Mom died in a car crash. Dad had a heart attack when we got the news. He never recovered from it and passed away a month later."

I reach across the table and cover her hand with mine. "I'm sorry about your loss."

"Thank you." She dips her head, and her curly bangs hide all but her tightly pressed lips. A deep breath raises her chest before her smile returns. "But we're here to talk about furniture."

Right, so we are. Um... "I left the catalog in the car."

"I have one." Our hands separate as she reaches for her handbag from the bench. She produces a magazine, moves the candle aside, and places the catalog between us. As she opens to the first page, we both scoot forward, and wisps of her hair brush against my forehead. The simple tickle awakens every part of my skin, and I try to focus on the chairs she's showing me.

"You-you"—her whisper cracks—"you said, you took a look. What stood out to you?"

I flip through the pages, pausing at each of the three sets that grabbed my attention.

"These are too catchy for a lunch café," she says of the final set and turns back to the set I showed her in the middle. "We'll go with this walnut set."

Wow. She chose one of the options I pointed out. My chest puffs out. "You trust my judgment that much?"

She then leans back, and I do the same. My chair legs squeak against the hardwood floor, and I exhale slowly, already missing the proximity we shared.

"That was my second choice, and since it's on your list, it's the winner."

Odd that she's seeking my opinion and not consulting her friends. "I'm sure your friends have a keen eye for design."

"Your contribution, especially with the financial aspect, makes you a significant part of this café. Your opinion matters a lot."

Taken aback, I pledge. "Then I'll be more than happy to assist with the business planning, ensuring the café starts off on the right foot."

"Wow, thanks for the vote of confidence."

At her lighthearted sarcasm, my smile broadens.

The server delivers our Mediterranean feast, and Zuri does that thing she does before every meal. "I just observed that you close your eyes. I assume you're praying?"

She smiles, clasping her hands together. "Prayer is part of my daily life, not just at meals." She shares about her faith and how it deepened following her parents' passing. "We grew up attending church, but for a time Damien and I drifted from what our parents taught us."

She then waves in a shooing motion. "Oh, you got me started. Sorry. I'm rambling."

"No, actually, I like hearing the things you're passionate about." Each time she speaks, I find myself drawn into her world.

"As for praying before meals, it's my way of recognizing my reliance on God," she explains, looking at our spread. "It's a chance to express my thanks for His blessings, including the food we eat."

Her perspective resonates. "I've never thought about where my food comes from before eating it," I admit, then feel a sudden boldness. "Would you mind saying the prayer out loud?"

"Sure." She pushes the plate aside and extends her hands toward me. As we join hands and she begins to pray, her words flow with a moving sincerity, making me eager to embrace this moment and her faith.

After we take turns washing our hands, the meal unfolds with more escapades from our past adventures, including her spontaneous road trips and my misadventures in the corporate world. Each story and shared laugh weaves a stronger connection and hints at the deeper understanding and companionship forming between us. For the first time in what feels like forever, I'm experiencing a genuine connection, something that transcends the pretenses of our arrangement and offers the potential of something meaningful.

"Jeremy Kress, you're becoming a good friend," Zuri remarks, causing me to pause and put down my fork. Her fork suspended in midair, she searches my eyes, earnestness and reticence in her gaze. "I don't know if..." She stops and bites her lower lip, clearly holding back thoughts she's unready to share.

I understand. My feelings for her run deeper than our façade, yet I'm cautious, terrified of the uncertain and potential rejection.

"I like you too, Zuri," I blurt out, then regret my lack of restraint. "I mean, as a good friend." What a bumbled attempt to mask my true feelings! Yet my affection for her extends beyond what I anticipated. This unnerves me, even as a part of me remains eager to explore the possibility of "us." Curious about her past relationships, I venture. "What happened with your previous boyfriend?"

She lays down her silverware, and her shoulders slump despite her laughter. "He was Damien's best friend."

"And Damien throttled him, I guess?"

"I ended up straining their friendship." Her shoulders curve in further, though her chin remains high. "He cheated on me, and Damien found out before I did. It escalated into a fistfight."

Right. He's a deeply protective brother, and here I am, treading into a "pretend" relationship. I give myself a silent warning over what comes with being close to Zuri. "I can tell Damien's not someone to mess with. Especially when it comes to his sister."

"Ever since then"—she shrugs, a sigh slipping loose—"he thinks he needs to protect me from all men."

"I'm glad he's looking out for you." And I am appreciative of her brother's vigilance. After all, without his protectiveness, Zuri would probably be dating someone else by now, and our current camaraderie might not have been possible.

On our drive back to Zuri's house, our conversation meanders through the wedding details. Then a quick nod sends her curls bouncing, and she shifts her whole body to face me. "Since you have a nickname for me, I'll be calling you Jer."

I chuckle. "Jeremy's already the short form of Jeremiah, but sure, Jer works." How natural it feels, having her here beside me. Zuri's the first woman I've driven in this car since I bought it two years ago. For staff events, we always opt for the company car with a driver.

I flex my grip on the steering wheel, the vehicle feeling somehow different after that realization. But I'd best focus on the discussion, so I share the bizarre sleeping arrangements my mom has made for the wedding with my ex uncomfortably close to my room. "She's yet to be convinced about us."

"We'll just have to make her believe." Zuri pats my arm, her confidence on full display. "It shouldn't be too hard."

It should be too easy since I'm starting to have feelings for her. Or could that complicate things? Either way, her statement reminds me of another necessary task—choosing a ring for her. I'd planned to let her pick one out, but knowing now how she values surprises, I'll select one myself and add authenticity to our... arrangement.

When I park in her driveway and turn to her, the glow from the driveway lights illuminates her, almost a beacon. The urge to discuss taking our arrangement into the realm of reality gnaws at me, yet the fear of rejection stifles my words.

"Thank you for tonight," is all I say.

"I had a good time too, Jer," she whispers back. Her intense gaze locks with mine, and a current of unspoken possibilities zaps the air. We stare at each other, my heartbeat races, and her breathing escalates.

"I'll get going." She grips her purse on her lap.

Before I can sabotage this arrangement, I look away and swing my door open. I rush to the passenger side to open her door, and she steps out, her scent lingering— peppermint and something floral, uniquely Zuri that leaves me dizzy. Unable to restrain myself, I catch her hand and draw her close. I lower my lips, my mind screaming not to go for hers. Unsure why I chose today of all days to listen to my conscience, I instead let my cheek brush against hers, pressing a soft kiss to her skin. "Good night," I whisper to avoid crossing lines our fake engagement hasn't prepared us for.

"Good night," her warm breath against my neck ignites a shiver down my spine. With a final wave, she heads to her door.

I'm left alone, my thoughts swirling with this... *affection*. My heart is still racing, and a whirlwind of what-ifs drives away all rational thought. Who knows what our next engagement will bring?

CHAPTER 12

Zuri

With this afternoon's temperature a surprising midsixties, not cloudy and not sunny, I stand on the first tee box near a red ball stuck in the ground. I'm told that's where ladies tee off. Driver in hand, I'm ready to launch my first-ever game of golf. Jeremy and his friends, Nico and Wes, watch me. The tight knot in my stomach is about to cut off my breath. I punch a tee into the soft ground and set my ball on top.

Jeremy and I arrived well before the others so he could show me how to play. With thirty minutes of instruction, he hopes I can swing into their friendly competition. What was he thinking?

"You've got this, Zee."

Jeremy came up with that nickname on a whim, and he uses it so naturally. His encouragement boosts my confidence. I take a deep breath, close my eyes, and recapture each step of the drive as Jeremy instructed me. Opening my eyes, I set my stance and swing. The ball arcs through the air, a decent drive that earns me claps and Nico's chuckle.

"Not bad for a beginner."

"I guess I have a good teacher." I grin at Jeremy, and his affectionate smile makes my knees weak.

"Good teacher or not, we all know who's buying dinner." His Italian accent light with his jesting, Nico takes his place with the driver.

I like how he says everything like it is. While Jeremy and Wes have done nothing but praise me, Nico has been clear I can't win as a newbie. I'm not hoping to win. I'm just enjoying being here, seeing Jeremy relax with his friends. They're casual today, all dressed in polos and chinos. Wes's sun visor shades his eyes while Jeremy's tucked his own sunglasses atop his head. Their banter and teasing eggs the game on.

Four holes later, I'm again taking my stance when Nico calls out, "Keep your eyes on the ball!"

"Here." Wes walks up, his dark hair shiny around his visor, his soft tone a stark contrast to Nico's vibrant energy. He stops just close enough to demonstrate without invading my space. "Try shifting your weight through your swing. It might help with your control."

"She's doing great." Jeremy's protective tone warms me. "You're all taking this too seriously."

Mindful of Wes's advice, I attempt to adjust my stance. I swing. The ball takes flight and, predictably, veers off its intended path. A collective groan rises, followed by laughter.

"Looks like we're going on a treasure hunt again." Jeremy shakes a finger at me.

I don't mind treasure hunts, but I *am* delaying the game. Later, as Wes leads the charge into the rough in search of the rogue ball, I can imagine forming a connection with Jeremy's friends. Already, there's a bond over our shared laughs and frustration whenever I veer the ball off course.

As we drive our cart to the next hole, Jeremy's shoulder nudges mine. "How are you liking golf so far?"

"It's fun, actually. Easier than I thought." No one ever accused me of being athletic, and I'd gladly exchange these clubs for a beater and a set of serving spoons. So this isn't an activity I'd choose. But the fact that he invited me when he came to church with me earlier makes me feel special. He must enjoy my company as much as I enjoy his, and I'm happy to tap into his world. The afternoon sun warms my skin, and the breeze ruffles my hair. "So this is how you spend your Sunday afternoons?"

"Wes and Nico can't seem to play without me. I'm left with no choice."

Nico cranes his neck and shouts from ahead. "Remember, Zuri, the loser buys dinner!" While his competitive streak is evident, his sense of fun underpins the game.

I'll definitely be footing the dinner bill, my fleeting streak of beginner's luck having deserted me on too many holes. When we wrap up our game, they ask me to choose a restaurant, but today isn't about me. It's about tapping into Jeremy's world, including his favorite hangouts. So I hold up both hands. "Please take me wherever you guys prefer to dine."

"It's time to introduce you to Romano's." Nico winks. "I never win, so I rarely qualify to choose where we eat."

Romano's turns out to be an Italian restaurant, and fresh vegetables heap an entire table on the side. The man behind the glass-covered pastries greets us, his accent thick. He smiles when he calls Nico and addresses him in what I assume to be Italian.

A dark-haired middle-aged woman greets us and leads us to our seats. From the music, the workers, and the enticing scents of garlic, pesto, pizza, and freshly baked bread, I feel like I've stepped into a theater of Italy in San Francisco.

As we settle into the eatery's rustic charm, a server not in uniform brings us water and allows us time to peruse the menu.

This restaurant must be family-owned if no one is wearing a uniform. But oh, snap! My eyes all but go wide as I study the menu. For a simple restaurant, the prices are steep.

As if Jeremy can read me, he leans in, and his warm breath whispers against my ear. "I've got this covered."

"But I lost," I protest, caught between gratitude and keeping the rules of the game.

"And you played well." His hand touches my arm.

"For the love of dinner, just accept," Nico says, scanning the flat menu. Apparently, he's not one to miss anything. "What kind of man do you think Jeremy would be to let his girl buy dinner for all of us?"

His girl. Excitement thrills me. Is this what he calls me when he's with his friends? For the last two weeks, we've hung out at least ten times, including the day I invited him to watch the Superbowl with us. So, yes, we've seen each other almost daily, mostly to discuss different financial strategies and business planning for my café. Still, there's always such casual banter, and it ends with a quick bite together. We've tried to steer away from romance, but every so often, we get caught in heated glances. And many times, we've almost kissed when he drops me off at home. He already paid for the fridge and furniture. The fridge was delivered on Friday, and the furniture will be delivered in two weeks. Time has flown, and we're already at the end of February.

The server returns to take our orders.

I settle for pizza, and Jeremy does too. Wes orders soup and salad, and Nico orders spaghetti. Before they bring the food, Wes reads the pamphlet and facts about Italy, then quizzes us.

"I'll be cheating if I answer." Nico rocks back in his chair, and clasps his hands behind his head, leaving Jeremy and me to respond.

We then talk about the day's game, and they share stories of their golfing adventures. I listen, laughing along, feeling more and more a part of this circle of friends. The delicious food brings a perfect end to an enjoyable day.

But one of the moments I cherish most is the simmering anticipation that builds as Jeremy drives me home. Unspoken words always zap between us in those final minutes in the driveway. Our gazes meet, flitting between each other's eyes and lips, ensnared in a mutual struggle of what-ifs and maybes.

Tonight, the routine's even more charged. As I clutch my purse in my lap, my resolve wanes under his steady gaze. His scent, a comforting blend of sandalwood and a hint of rosemary, dominates the car. The porch and garage lights filter through the windows, casting us in a delicate dance of shadow and light. My gaze, almost of its own accord, drifts to his lips, sparking a flurry of thoughts about a kiss yet shared.

His chest rises and falls, his polo clinging to his broad shoulders. Then he breaks the silence with a sigh. "Well, I'm glad you hung out with me today."

So the evening has come to an end.

"Yeah." I swallow my disappointment as my fingers brush against the door handle, ready to exit the world we've created. In a burst of urgency, Jeremy leaves the car and rounds to my side. I've already stepped out, and we nearly crash into one another.

His hand finds its way to my waist, and he pulls me into an unexpected embrace. My heart races—or is that the echo of his? I grip my purse as if it's the only anchor in a storm and fold my other arm across myself, creating a barrier. After the dance in January where passion flared only to be doused by his withdrawal, I dare not let my guard down again.

"Hey." He breathes out, his voice a rumble that vibrates through the space between us. His chin dips to meet my gaze, his breath feathers against my lips, and shivers slither down my spine. I brace for more. My eyes close in anticipation, and my body tenses, then relaxes as his lips graze my cheek instead. The gentle, almost-kiss isn't what I'd hoped for, yet it leaves a trail of warmth in its wake.

"Good night, Zee." He steps back, the distance between us widening once more. His gaze lingers on me, a silent conversation in its depths.

"Good night, Jer." My voice barely rises above a whisper as our momentary closeness leaves bittersweetness on my tongue. What would it take for him to break the barriers he's set, to turn our pretense into something real?

The fleeting contact on my cheek only intensifies my longing. Now, with every step I take away from him, the tantalizing possibility of a real kiss teases me. What would it feel like? Reaching the door, I steal a glance backward, half-expecting him to be waiting as he usually does until I'm safely inside. But today, he drives off.

Maybe he'll be ghosting me again.

My hands tremble as I fumble with the key, struggling to fit it into the lock. I could knock, but I need to regain my composure before encountering my house companions. Nothing about today felt like pretense. It had nothing to do with getting our stories straight for Jeremy's mom. His presence at church today, alongside Damien and my friends, and then his spontaneous invitation to join him and his friends for golf—all this was remarkably real. It shouldn't be a challenge to convince his mom or anyone else that we're a couple in love. If this isn't a sign of us opening up to each other's worlds, then what is it?

***

As February blends into March, my interactions with Jeremy unfold into an exhilarating whirlwind that defies our pretended romance. It's as if we're navigating the brink of something real. Each shared experience draws me deeper into his world. I'm thrilled when he expresses interest in joining me for my next weekly volunteer commitment at Crina Medical. Aware of the necessity for a background check, I ensure he completes the forms two days in advance, securing his approval by the time we're scheduled to volunteer.

On Thursday afternoon, Jeremy and I find ourselves in the rehabilitation center's cafeteria area, standing with two patients. The air is fragrant with simmering foods, and the sound of clattering pots emanates from the kitchen through the open doorway.

I observe Donna as she pours a cup of flour into the mixing bowl, her hands trembling. Across from us, at the round card table, Jeremy assists Greg with the same task. Yet, Jeremy's attention seems more focused on catching any stray flour, diligently cleaning up after Greg's minor spills.

"What next?" Donna's inquiry draws my attention back to her. She's now playfully running gloved fingers through the flour. Each week, I meet different patients, as only a few are brought out at a time, and their participation varies based on their condition and interest in cooking.

A warmth spreads through my chest as Donna delights in the simple task. I reach for the baking soda and a measuring spoon and place them beside the plastic bowl of chocolate chips. "Now, we add baking soda."

"Okay." Excitement tinges Donna's voice as she shakes the remaining flour from her hands into the bowl, her face glowing beneath the fluorescent lights.

"What's your favorite thing to bake?" I pass her the spoon.

She shrugs, a slight smile on her lips. "Anything, really. It's nice to do something... to not be cooped up."

As she scoops the baking soda from the container, half of it spills from the spoon. I'll need to sneak more into the recipe to ensure our cookies turn out well. Normally, a simple batch of chocolate chip cookies takes me five minutes to mix, but here, it could take double that time, depending on the patient's condition. This is precisely why we stick to straightforward recipes.

Soft chatter and gentle movement surround me. Each volunteer, including Jeremy and me, has donned blue aprons embossed with the Crina Medical logo. Given the need for close supervision, volunteers are paired one-on-one with patients when possible, ensuring both safety and the therapeutic benefits of the cooking process. We keep it simple: no knives and uncomplicated tasks.

While some volunteers prepare dinner, others, like us, focus on desserts—mostly baking, which is deemed highly therapeutic. We concentrate on pouring, mixing, and sometimes decorating.

More workers and volunteers weave in and out of the kitchen, carrying trays of food or setting up tables beyond our room. Deep laughter from our table snaps me back to the present. Jeremy is laughing heartily, thrown back by whatever Greg, the middle-aged man across from us, is saying. Greg, caught up in the fun, tosses a handful of flour into the air, punctuating his joke.

"And then I told him, 'You can't trust atoms—they make up everything!'" Greg chuckles, the flour dusting down like snow.

While Donna meticulously measures her ingredients, I can't help but smile at the sight of Jeremy, so engaged and lighthearted. When his gaze meets mine, my heart skips a beat, fluttering with a warm tingling sensation. The kitchen's warmth, the laughter surrounding us—it all melds into the perfect backdrop for this moment.

Greg's question about the next ingredient pulls Jeremy's attention away, but not before our eyes share a silent conversation. Observing Jeremy, so out of his usual element of spreadsheets and reports *and* so genuinely relaxed, I realize he's the missing ingredient that my life had been lacking.

In the end, Donna and I move to help Jeremy and Greg finish mixing their dry ingredients. While Donna and Greg add the eggs and melted butter, Jeremy and I get the cookie pans out. The four of us work together, scooping spoonfuls of cookie dough onto the baking trays. I move each tray back to the cart between our tables.

A chef comes by to collect the cookies and transfers them to his cart to wheel into the kitchen for baking. "Dinner is ready whenever you are," he says.

"I'm starving." Greg tosses his gloves into the trash can. Donna follows suit, and they both head over to the dining area.

Jeremy and I stay behind to clean up the workspace.

"Can you believe I pulled off the recipe without reading it?" Jeremy comes up beside me, his warm breath against my cheek sending tingles throughout my body.

"Without Donna and my help, you and Greg wouldn't have managed it." My cheeks ache from smiling. Standing next to him, I'm reminded of our height difference.

"That's why I always need to be on your team in the kitchen." He brushes a kiss on my cheek before lifting the white plastic bowl of flour. "Where do we put all this?"

Right. We have to clean.

I work with Jeremy to dispose of the leftover flour. It's not much, but it's always easier and more sanitary to have things poured from the bag, rather than having patients dig into the bags themselves.

As we clean, he asks about the process of dinner. "We sit with them during dinner and engage with them." I wipe down the sticky flour on one end of the table while he takes the other end. "Patients who don't want to interact usually don't come to these events."

"I never knew how much cooking could mean to someone," Jeremy admits as he collapses and folds the table.

"And the interaction that comes with it." I follow him as he carries the table to the back room where others are storing theirs.

"I'm not sure what interaction I'm going to offer," he says. "But as long as you sit at the same table, I should be okay."

He drops his gloves in the bin by the back room, and I do the same. "You did just fine with Greg," I squish my face in mock-seriousness. He imitates me, chuckling as he takes my hand.

As we walk toward the hum and activity of the dining area, hand in hand, my heart is overflowing. Every step with Jeremy deepens my affection, my feelings fermenting and rising like bread dough warmed by the spring sun.

CHAPTER 13

Zuri

Besides him accompanying me to the monthly cookout at the mental hospital, we went to another company event—bowling—as a couple, and I teamed up with Jeremy. The air buzzed with the clamor of tumbling pins and spirited victory shouts, a backdrop to our connection. Even Damien, who has been slow to warm up to Jeremy, shows signs of thawing, especially after receiving recognition at work. His gradual, if reluctant, acceptance feels like a victory in itself.

Our adventures span from rain-soaked hikes through lush forests, breathing in the rich aroma of wet earth and foliage, to hours spent collaborating on the café's renovation, business strategy, and necessary insurance coverage. Insurance is something I'd underestimated, but so crucial. In addition to collecting data, he created a slideshow that outlined a vision for the new-and-improved café. I still don't grasp all the business lingo, but I can leave the business planning for him. He's smart, experienced, and confident—which boosts my confidence that my business won't be a flop.

Jeremy has woven himself into my daily life. The meals we share, whether planned or spontaneous, remain each day's peak moments. I've learned so much about his personality—the things that make him laugh, the quirks that make him Jeremy, and the aspirations that make him driven. With each revelation, my heart grows fonder.

Yet, as our connection deepens, so does the complexity of my emotions. One question haunts me: Is this merely an act, or have I fallen for him? The answer seems clear, especially now as I stand in my café, supposedly working, but instead imagining what he's doing at the moment. He's all I can think of.

I should be supervising the final touches, but being in the building is just an excuse to have delivered lunch to Jeremy earlier. The painters are busy at work, covering the walls in the sage green that should be the perfect soothing color to add a calm freshness to the space.

The man on the ladder strokes the brush alongside the ceiling, the color transforming the room. But the corner looks slightly off. Maybe he just needs to add another coat.

I walk over to the person mixing paint, his back curved over on the tarp covering the floor. When I approach, he stops stirring. "Can we make that corner brighter?" I point to a spot near the window. The rain outside has changed from pouring hard to falling softly. "I want the sunlight to show off the colors."

He shakes his head. "Ma'am, I can go get another color if you like. But then we have to paint the whole wall again so it matches. If it looks dark to you right now, remember it has to dry."

Right. How silly of me. Then I ask if he needs something to drink, but he tells me he still has the water I gave him two hours ago.

Time is flying as we get closer to the café's big opening day at the end of April. Every day, I feel more excited and nervous. More than a dream coming true, this is showing a part of me to the world.

My time with Jeremy these last two months has been like a storybook romance. To our friends and even my brother and Jeremy's assistant, we seem like a couple. Jill lights up when I come to see Jeremy and always says, "Go right on, sugar," even if he's in a meeting online.

I find reasons to visit, sometimes just to see him, and he always makes time for me. He never seems bothered, just calls for a fifteen-minute recess and steps away to focus on me.

And I enjoy these moments more than I thought I would. His office has become a special place where our pretend relationship feels more real. Every time he smiles at me, my heart thrums, and I forget we're a fake couple.

Jeremy might feel the same way too.

With these thoughts in my head, I retreat to my makeshift office in the kitchen where my computer awaits on the counter. I have to add pictures to the recipes to upload on my blog.

The rain's rhythmic slap against the windowpane weaves a serene soundscape as my fingertips dance across the keyboard. The air, still tinged with fresh paint, makes me want to bake something to replace the artificial smell with a warm, comforting aroma. Maybe I'll bake some cookies to thank the painters for their hard work.

I stop typing the recipe to upload the photos Lexi took a few days ago. The clock on my computer says it's three. The new fridge buzzes in the background. The freezer was salvageable, so I didn't have to buy a new one. All the appliances remind me of my temporary relationship with Jeremy—a deal we made.

I've taken two weeks off to focus on getting the café ready. Besides editing blog photos and volunteering at the rehab center, I've attended a networking meeting with other café and restaurant owners to hear their insights and explore potential partnerships. I've also been finalizing permits, insurance, and other legal requirements for the café. Additionally, I've met with potential suppliers at the farmer's market and conducted research to get a feel for café trends in the area.

My blog followers, especially those in San Francisco, are excited about the opening, so the café should do well once it starts. I'll be able to pay back Jeremy for any money borrowed from him.

Falling for him complicates things, which is why I insisted on a loan rather than accepting his money. We haven't agreed yet on whether he'll let me pay back or not.

Lost in thought, my name barely penetrates until I hear it again, clearer this time—the one that only one person calls me. "Zee."

Jeremy's in the doorway, his smile soft, tender. He's rolling up his sleeves, a gesture that offers a glimpse of his strong forearms, a view I've come to appreciate more than I'd like to admit.

"I didn't realize you take breaks from work." My heart light, a flutter in my chest, I rise to my feet.

"Just wanted to see if you have any snacks tucked away." A spark lights his eyes.

Approaching, he opens his arms the way he's done so much lately. It's become familiar and comforting in the days since our golf game. Stepping into his embrace feels like coming home. His arms encircle me in a sheltering warmth, and I allow myself to relish the closeness.

"I wanted to show you something," he murmurs against my hair.

"Yeah?" I draw back, my arms still loose around his waist.

"Got a minute?" He tucks my curls back from my cheeks, holding my gaze.

With a wink, I indulge in our charade. "I always have time for my fiancé." The title still tastes sweet, though it's coated in sorrow whenever I think of how soon this will be over.

He takes my hand, laces our fingers, then lifts our hands, and kisses the back of mine. It sends shivers down my spine.

"Where to?" I inquire as we head toward the elevator.

"It's a surprise."

The elevator ascends in silence. The numbers rise higher, and soon we pass the fifty-eighth floor. "I've never been past your floor."

"We're going up another, to the boss's office."

The elevator doors part.

Emma, familiar from company gatherings, greets us before Jeremy leads me on. We navigate through corridors to a door marked Rooftop Access. He pushes it open, and the city unfolds before us, its buildings glisten like jewels under the rain.

We step onto the rooftop, the rain envelops us, and its caress adds shimmery magic to the moment. Jeremy faces me, both hands holding mine and his gaze intense beneath the cloudy sky.

"You know it's raining." I taste the raindrops trickling onto my lips. Jeremy's eyes, alight with an unspoken fervor, hold my gaze, and my pulse accelerates.

"This might all seem fake, unrealistic." He squeezes my hand, the rain softening his words to a whisper. "But you are real to me, and every moment I spend with you highlights my day. So, let's imagine, just for now, that this moment is real."

His statement hangs between us as his words sink in. Just what is he trying to say?

He reaches into a pocket and retrieves a small velvet box—revealing a ring that gleams even under the storm's shadow. My breath halts.

"Zuri." A quiver in his voice underplays my name. "These last two months spent with you have been some of the happiest moments in my life. What began as pretense has turned into something very real for me. I find myself thinking about you at random moments, looking at my door anticipating your arrival at any given time of day. I care about you, more than I ever expected."

The rain's patter fades into the background. Unshed tears blur my vision as the world shrinks until it's only us, two hearts in the midst of a rain.

"Would you consider us? Take this leap with me?" He holds up the ring, sincerity brimming his blue eyes. "Will you marry me?"

I study his face, and while I need a ring for his brother's wedding, he's looking at me like I'm everything to him. Even if his proposal is a charade, it stirs something genuine within me, and my tears stream to join the rain. Jeremy and I could be something real, and maybe this is our turning point.

"You should say something," he prompts. Is that fear in his eyes, the same fear lacing his tone?

"Yes!" I say, my heart beating, and somehow, I have no hesitation whatsoever. "Yes, Jeremy." Laughter and tears choke my voice. "Yes, I'll marry you."

He lets out a long breath, clearly relieved from whatever fears as he slips the ring onto my finger, its presence anchors the pretend moment in reality. My pulse hiccups when he lowers his face toward mine, and determined for something to happen this time, I step on tiptoes and grip his shirt collar.

Our lips touch, and my knees mush like jelly. Jeremy Kress is kissing me! A slight abrasion from his beard rubs against my skin, but who says I intend to complain? He's kissing me without hesitation or any indication he's playing a game. He's kissing me as if this engagement means something to him, as if he's fallen in love with me and he's been thinking about this day and this proposal. When his fingers move through my wet hair, shivers course down my neck and through my spine, igniting every nerve with a startling intensity. I kiss him fervently, with such longing that the world beyond us fades. This kiss, unlike the timid experiments of my past, feels like the real thing. My first three kisses? They all pale in comparison.

Raindrops fall on our lips, and that's when I realize we're catching a breath. Embarrassed by how eager I acted, I try to hide by ducking my head.

"Not bad," he says, his breathlessness mirroring my ragged breathing. He then tips my head to face him. His gaze searches mine for confirmation of this shared dream. I nod, too overwhelmed for words. This surprise engagement is a wish fulfilled beyond my wildest dreams.

He smiles, a shy, uncertain smile that sends my heart soaring. Then he leans close, and his arm offers support as my legs threaten to give way. "Lexi would love a photo of this."

Before I can protest the lack of a camera, he produces his phone. Our cheeks brush as he captures the moment—two figures, joyously drenched in rain, but both happy and sincere.

When we return indoors and step into the elevator, my mind is in a whirl. The proposal, that kiss—it transcends the realm of pretense, plunging me into a sea of raw emotion. My heart races, excitement coursing through me so strong I scarcely notice our arrival on his floor until Jill's greeting snaps me back to reality.

"Hello, sugar." She beams, her smile infectious as she eyes our drenched clothes. "Why are you all soaked?"

With a surge of joy I can't contain, I flash my newly adorned hand. "I'm engaged."

How surreal those words are!

"Yes, we are." Jeremy chimes in, his tone brimming with genuine enthusiasm, devoid of any previous hesitations.

Jill squeals, steps away from her desk, and closes the distance between us. As she examines the ring, the diamonds catch the office light in a dazzling display, and she nods her approval. "Jeremy Kress, I might have sold you short."

"And why's that?" he asks.

"You've made a wise choice." She gives me a knowing look. "Congratulations are in order."

"Thank you." He pats my shoulder. His gaze dips, slow and heated as it skims my dress. "Jill, could you retrieve the duffel bag from the conference room closet? It contains spare company shirts, and my fiancée needs to change out of her wet clothes."

The way he articulates "my fiancée" resonates, frosting our current façade with a sweet layer of undeniable reality.

CHAPTER 14

Zuri

"You're engaged?" Damien erupts like a pressure cooker with blocked valves. Disbelief sends him into a coughing fit as the cereal he's been munching catches in his throat.

It's only hours after that moment in the rain. Now, I'm huddled with my friends and brother around the kitchen island making dinner. Chicken and vegetables roast in the air fryer. The kitchen lights catch the diamonds on my ring, scattering tiny stars across the marble surface.

Olivia, eyes still wide, twirls my finger, inspecting it at every angle, her voice bubbling over. "Look at it, gleam!" Her eyes sparkle almost as much as the diamonds. "It's gorgeous!"

Lexi leans closer, her grin infectious. "This calls for a celebration." She claps. "We have to throw an engagement party for you two!"

"No way!" Damien's objection slices through the warm cheer. "You two hardly know each other, and you're already engaged?"

"We're not rushing into anything." I hold up my palm in an attempt to soothe his concerns. "We need at least a year to plan the wedding." If only he knew the full story.

"The man can have any woman he wants, why you?"

Ouch. Low blow, bro. I try not to sound offended. "Because I'm that one woman for him?"

But he must've sensed my deflation. "You're too good for him, and I'm—"

"He's too good for me." If things work out, Jeremy outshines me. "He's resourceful and skilled. His insights have been helpful in my business planning, and he's smart and decisive, quick to seize command."

"You mean bossy." Damien rolls his neck from side to side, tension radiating from him.

"He's good at what he does, and you know it." Olivia waves a dismissive hand in Damien's direction.

"Kress is practical. I like that," Lexi adds. "He focuses on doing what's necessary rather than dancing around things."

I smile. That's all true.

"What Damien won't tell you"—hands on her hips, Olivia eyes me, then Damien—"is he's admitted Kress is selfless when it comes to mentoring and supporting any team member's growth and skill."

Damien gives Olivia *the* look. But at least he's seen some good in Jeremy. "This is not about work."

Olivia dismisses him, her pre-dinner snack, cereal, abandoned. She loops an arm around my waist, and her ponytail tickles my neck as she leans in. "How did he propose?"

Lexi, ever the documentarian, waves her camera, apparently already thinking about the visuals. "Put your hand back on the marble. We need to get a shot of that ring for your blog followers."

Whoa. No way. I shake my head. "I'm *not* posting any engagement photos on my blog." The girls know, so they must hear the unspoken word *fake* engagement.

"Don't spare any details." Olivia hugs me tighter, eyes wide. "How did he propose?"

Damien retreats into a brooding silence, face buried in his hands, so I spare him the full intensity. "It was like something out of a movie, on the rooftop...." My voice rises as I recount the proposal, omitting the electrifying kiss now indelibly imprinted in my memory.

"Wow!" Olivia jostles me, then spins us around the kitchen. "That's *the* most romantic proposal ever!"

My friends' reaction stands in stark contrast to Damien's silent skepticism, far more obvious than the lines between truth and fiction, which now seem as delicate as the sparkle on my engagement ring.

With Damien's brooding as my cue, I signal the girls, mouthing for them to give us a moment. They retreat, leaving us in unspoken tension. I edge closer and lay a hand on his slumped shoulder. "Damien?"

His eyes, shadowed with concern, meet mine, brotherly worry tautening his features.

"You can't keep getting upset over every guy I date." I jab him in the rib cage.

"He's my boss, Zuri."

"And he's entitled to happiness too, isn't he?"

Damien's frustration manifests in a huff, the bowl of cereal pushed aside. "I never pictured him with my sister." He runs a hand over his short hair, still chuffing. "I never should've invited him to that party."

"Come on. You believe in divine matchmaking, don't you?" After all, where's his unshakeable faith?

Or is it wrong of me to pull that on him when this is all pretend?

Maybe I *am* getting too lost in this pretense. But right now, I fear my brother losing it on Jeremy before we even finish the deal.

His shoulders droop further. "Everything's moving too fast. You two haven't even had a real argument."

"Oh, but we have." I'm thinking of our spat during our first outing at the awards ceremony. "He's really nice to me."

I slide onto the stool beside his. Then I let my words whip up a recipe of Jeremy not only as a partner but also as a man of substance before I top off the concoction with our plans to visit his family in Colorado for his brother's wedding.

Damien grips the back of his neck. "Oh man. Meeting the parents already." His posture relaxes. "I guess you're an adult who's capable of deciding your destiny."

"I made it on my own in Florida." Back when I left San Francisco after I ended things with his best friend.

"Lexi did keep an eye on you there."

"Hey." I stand straight and whack his shoulder. "I'm so insulted you think I need someone to take care of me."

"I'll try to get used to this... Jeremy." He quirks a brow, and his sarcasm signals a truce.

"And I'll support you too when I invite Jessie over." My threat at playing matchmaker draws a mock glare.

"Don't you dare." He ruffles my hair. "Do you know how embarrassing it'd be for my little sister to play matchmaker?"

I laugh. "It's just as embarrassing when you go off fighting my battles with my supposed boyfriends. You ambushing Jeremy with our picture was mortifying." But even as I cross my arms in a pout, warmth radiates through me because, surprisingly, Jeremy still has the photo on his meticulously clean desk. Hope sugarcoats me whenever I see our picture there.

The girls surge back into the room, gushing out their excitement for the engagement party.

"Hold on." I raise a finger, needing to make this as casual as possible. "There's one condition." Their chatter ceases, their gazes on me. "We host the party here, and part of the fun will be testing out some menu items." A culinary trial run, of sorts.

Olivia's eyebrows crease together. "You're planning to cook for your engagement party?"

My decision is non-negotiable. "That's the deal, and you're all pitching in by bringing your friends." My gaze slides to Damien. "That includes inviting Jessie."

He responds with a dismissive headshake.

I press on, outlining the dual purpose of the gathering. A chance for Damien to interrogate Jeremy with any lingering questions, a thought that brings a reluctant agreement from my brother.

The real challenge now looms ahead—convincing Jeremy to green-light this celebration of our "pretend" engagement. Maybe that won't be hard—after all, the whole fake-engagement thing was his idea. Plus, this presents an opportunity to have him invite his circle, including Lexi's boss. She needs to build that volatile relationship in a setting far removed from work pressures.

***

It's a lively Saturday morning a week later as Jeremy and I navigate the farmer's market. Fresh-picked produce, aromatic herbs, and grilled delicacies scent the air, vendors hawk their goods, and shoppers exchange money for their finds—all creating an energizing vibe.

His arm brushes mine as we meander along. "So, your mom wasn't into cooking, and you picked up the reins on your own?"

"Since Mom was a busy interior decorator, she preferred to heat precooked meals. I got sick of those and started watching cooking shows, and Mom joined me, watching and brainstorming dinner ideas. But she always said they were too complicated, and she didn't have time. Still, that sparked a passion in me, to explore and experiment with new recipes. And we really connected when she had fun reheating my meals."

"Hence, your belief that food unites people."

A cart filled with squash nearly intercepts our path. I tug at Jeremy's hand, steering him clear, before we halt at Trish's booth, my go-to for fresh veggies.

"Ah, my favorite customer!" She beams. Beneath the green floral wrap twisted around her head, her gaze skims Jeremy.

"This is Jeremy." My chest expands, never mind that our engagement is a façade. "My fiancé."

"Nice. When's the big day?" She shades her eyes against the midmorning sun behind us, her dark-brown skin glistening.

"We're still settling on a date," Jeremy replies. "But we're aiming for something that feels right for both of us."

Trish nods and hands me a bag since I always forget to bring my reusable one. I reach for a bunch of lettuce but replace it with a superior bunch.

Jeremy, ever meticulous, examines the kale. "You always manage to find the best greens."

I chuckle, my fingers probing the kale's lush dark leaves, the crisp texture cool in my hands. "The darker, the richer." As the stand becomes more crowded, I edge closer to Jeremy and signal it's time to move on, then hand Trish money for our vegetables. "Looks like we've got everything here."

"Nice to meet you, Jeremy!" She waves, and Jeremy waves back, calling out his own "nice to meet you too."

Next, we stop at a stall flowing with fresh fruit. Jeremy's hand pauses over a peach, cradling it with tenderness. "Are you thinking of including a fruit salad on the menu?"

"A fruit salad was on my mind, but now you've got me thinking." I take the peach. Its fragrance evokes memories of sun-drenched days beneath Grandma's backyard peach tree. "Perhaps a peach cobbler with ice cream could be a hit."

"Hard to go wrong with ice cream." He selects more peaches with deliberate care and tucks them in the bag.

As we meander through the market, I nudge his arm with mine, still surprised he insisted on coming to the market with me instead of burying himself in work. "Don't you have a million things to do at the office?"

He shifts the tote to his other hand, giving me a sideways glance. "I wanted to be here with you, especially since you're taking on the cooking for our engagement party." His sincerity envelopes me like a warm hug. Then he drapes his arm over my shoulders, and the hug becomes real as he teases me about our unreal situation. "Just promise me you won't be cooking at our wedding." He winks. "I mean that's if my mother takes it too far and we end up getting a fake marriage during our one-week visit to Pleasant View."

A thrill zips through me. "Now that would be something else."

I've stopped pretending about our relationship ever since that kiss. Although Jeremy hasn't initiated another kiss or ventured into any recipes for emotion since his proposal, our connection has only deepened. We find comfort in each other's presence, a semblance of a couple in the way we interact—holding hands, sharing glances, minus the kisses, save for the occasional peck on the cheek.

But the idea of marrying Jeremy, even in jest, fills me with an undeniable excitement.

At a fresh-herb stand, basil and mint scent the air. Jeremy lifts a sprig of rosemary, for a closer scent. He holds it toward me, his eyes alight. "Here, smell this."

The rosemary's earthy, pine-like aroma envelops me as I breathe it in. "I love that smell."

"It reminds me of your hair," he whispers in my ear, and shivers tingle down my spine as his breath brushes my skin. My conditioner has mint and rosemary, but I'd never imagined he'd noticed or would remember what my hair smells like.

Gathering the herbs into a disposable container, our hands converge on the next selection. The brief touch sends a pleasant jolt through me, and the electric connection lingers when he asks. "What herb is this?"

His deep-blue gaze ensnares me, my mind adrift in their depths until he lifts the herb for inspection and pulls me back to reality—well, our *fake* reality. "Ba–sil," I manage, but my voice betrays the flutter in my chest.

We meander on, each stand a burst of color as vivid and real as my growing emotions. "Which of these spices adds heat to a dish?" he inquires, pausing before a stand arrayed with exotic spices, the air rich with cinnamon, cumin, and curry powder.

"Cayenne pepper." I point to the fiery-red powder nestled among the assortment. "Though Tabasco or jalapeno peppers will do the trick."

When he uncaps the cayenne pepper, his face as curious as a child, I stifle a snicker. "I love how involved you are in this."

"It's all a part of the fiancé package."

We continue through the market, getting ripe tomatoes, succulent berries, and fresh bread alongside the essentials for the gourmet dishes I've planned for tomorrow's dinner. When we're making our way out of the market, he steers me toward a flower stand.

"I'll take a bouquet, please." He smiles at the vendor, an elderly man. While Jeremy reaches for his wallet, my gaze is drawn to his selection—a bouquet of wildflowers, their hues vibrant and untamed, nestled within a hand-painted ceramic vase.

He hands me the vase, and I touch the soft petals. The simple elegance strikes a chord within me. "They're perfect." I breathe out, struggling to contain the joy in my voice. "Thank you."

The man looks at us, head tilted to the side, and a twinkle in his eye. "You two make a lovely couple."

Jeremy's hand finds a gentle rest on my back, affirming his presence. "That we do."

As our eyes meet in a shared recognition, my cheeks warm under his gaze and the vendor's kind words, and my response is little more than a whisper. "I couldn't agree more."

We leave the market behind. The sun climbs higher, emitting more warmth, and I savor this... this sense of completeness to the life we're weaving together, fake or not.

"This bag is heavy." He moves the bag to his other hand before I offer to share the load. But he just winks at me. "I'm hoping, by carrying this, I won't have to be part of the cooking."

"I thought you liked food wars in the kitchen?"

"I literally still have flour from the last food fight when you dumped it in my hair."

"No, you don't." I roll my eyes as the sunlight catches the sleekness of his hair. I divert my focus to the vase I've tucked against my side. But that doesn't stop me from looking back, from admiring him in his blue pants and striped button-down. This is his casual attire as compared to the suits he wears throughout the week, and the casual look suits him.

On the drive back, we rehash his market experience, then discuss tomorrow afternoon's party.

"Nico and Wes are willing to forego golfing to come for your food." He winks. He must've raved about my cooking to his friends. "I might've hinted to Nico you'd be whipping up something Italian."

"As long as he doesn't hold me up to any standard."

Jeremy drops me off at my house, and I can't bring myself to unlatch the door, the moment bittersweet, the end to a perfect morning. Then not only does he open the door for me to step out of the car but he also carries the tote to the front door. What a gentleman!

"If it's okay, I'll not bother coming in." He sets the bag on the porch. "Have a great afternoon, Zee."

I hug the vase closer, and the petals tickle my cheek as I duck my head. "You're sure you don't want to stay for lunch?"

"I have to head to work."

"You're such a workaholic." I tap his shoulder, highlighting the contrast between his professional commitments and the personal time he's chosen to spend with me today.

"That's not all true—at least not lately." His gaze latches to mine, and his voice dips. "A workaholic wouldn't leave work to help his fiancée shop for food."

As our gazes linger, my mind grapples with his statement. Lately, he's not a workaholic, and he makes the effort away from work to spend time with me. Unbidden, my gaze drops to his lips and the memory of our rooftop kiss rushes back. That moment of real intimacy now feels like a distant dream.

He leans in and presses a kiss on my cheek. "See you tomorrow."

I nod and watch him walk back to the car, then drive away, the warmth of his peck still tingling on my cheek. Today was more than a trip to the farmer's market. It was another food connection that grows stronger with each passing day. With every meal we share and every ingredient we select, we step closer to a recipe for something increasingly real.

CHAPTER 15

Zuri

The café buzzes with excitement between the new tables and chairs. Guests, instead of sitting, drift from one laden table to another, selecting seconds, their conversations a lively hum in this space now opened up by the demolished wall. It's all one expansive room, yet half-furnished, the final touches are reserved for the grand opening still three weeks out.

On such short notice, the turnout this Sunday evening is modest. The few friends from Stone Financial we rallied up form pockets of casual banter—standing in relaxed clusters or navigating the food spread. I'd planned to have the party at the house, but Jeremy suggested that, if we're cooking menu items for my café, we might as well give the appliances a test run.

Laughter mingles with the clinking cutlery and the occasional chime of glass, and fulfillment warms me. I *am* a chef if people are enjoying my food.

With a frosting container in my hand, I assess the pans and food trays on the card tables along the wall. Creamy risotto, southwest rolls, stuffed sandwiches, and more dishes tease me with their sizzling aromas.

Nico and Wes, Jill and Naina, mingle with some office employees. Damien and Olivia stand with two others in their circle while Lexi moves around snapping photos.

I smile as Jeremy, my perfect—even if fake—fiancé, ambles toward me, plate in hand. The most relaxed I've ever seen him, he's dressed in jeans, his casual short-sleeved button-down untucked. A grin splits his face, and my heart melts.

"The basil sandwiches hit the mark, Zee." He offers me his plate with a half sandwich. "Eat something."

Gratitude swells within me, a tiny, fragile bubble. "Thank you." He knows I haven't eaten, proof he's been by my side throughout the afternoon. I've been too wound up making sure everything was perfect and I had enough food on the tables.

I accept his plate and offer him the small frosting bowl I forgot to put out earlier. "I made this for your cookies."

His jaw drops, and his exaggerated gesture somehow doesn't feel out of place. "Thank you."

Something warm unfurls in my chest at the exchange.

"Have you tried the southwestern sa–salad yet?" That catch in my voice betrays my apprehension as my gaze flits to the table where the salad's still untouched. I wanted it on the menu, but if it's not appealing to anyone now, no one will order it either.

"You made the mistake of making me the spring rolls and jalapeno poppers first." Jeremy offers a lifeline, his presence a comforting constant. He hadn't been able to come to church with me, probably so he could arrive to help me set up.

"Here's my critique now." We turn to see Nico moving toward us, plate in hand with his half-eaten pasta and grapes. He forks the rigatoni noodles. "You're a decent chef."

"The best." Jeremy plucks a grape from Nico's plate.

Nico's eyes gleam. "You got a pen and paper? You're gonna need to take some notes if pasta's going to be on the menu."

"We'll remember," Jeremy says.

I don't miss the "we," meaning partnership. I like that. I didn't realize I was in need of romance until he took residence in my heart.

"If we forget, I know where to find you," he adds, and I assure Nico I have a good memory too.

Nico's brows rise, and as he clears his throat, I ready myself for his blunt assessment and brace for whatever facts he has to share. "This pasta needs more salt. It's too bland for my Italian taste buds."

"If you listen to Marino..." Lexi remarks from across the counter where she snaps a photo of the lights. That, too, is a new addition.

"Don't listen to her," Nico jests, pointing in Lexi's direction, his critique now a battle waged on multiple fronts. "You wanted us testing the food for honest opinions, right?"

I nod, stifling a laugh as Lexi grumbles about her annoyance with her boss.

Jeremy's apologetic glance is a balm, a silent promise of support as I devour my sandwich, a small defiance against the critics that loom large.

Critics, I realize, are a necessary evil, the crucible through which my culinary creations must pass.

Jeremy winks and mouths his apology, no doubt for his friend's bluntness, but while I fear critiques, I'd rather know what to change now before I serve it to customers.

"To truly consider this Italian..." Nico seems to overplay his accent now. "It needs a real tomato or a cream sauce, not just a brush of butter and herbs, then"—he brings his fingers to his lips and kisses them—"bellissimo."

"Not everything is meant to overwhelm your taste buds, Marino," Lexi's retort slices through Nico's culinary critique with her characteristic sass. She shifts and redirects her camera toward us, immortalizing the moment.

"I bet you're a terrible cook." Nico arches a brow at her. "Bad cooks can't handle criticism."

"Like you can cook," she snaps back. "It's your lack of sugar-coating that needs work."

I understand why Lexi often claims she can't stand her boss. She detests being micromanaged, and Nico is unapologetically outspoken about everything.

"As usual, everything tastes so good." Olivia walks toward us.

"Thanks, Liv," I say as Jeremy takes the empty plate from me.

Damien discards an empty foil pan into the trash, apparently savoring the last bites of his meal.

"Zuri." Wes approaches, dabbing his lips with a napkin, his voice carrying an expressiveness unusual for his reserved demeanor. "Those chicken quesadillas were to die for."

My chest warms. "You're welcome to take some home for leftovers."

"I would love that." He nods. "Ever thought about introducing a vegetarian option? It could widen your appeal."

Jeremy chimes in, endorsing Wes's suggestion, and I find myself nodding.

"How about incorporating a simple Indian dish?" Naina steps closer. "Paneer tikka masala, perhaps? It's vegetarian, and I can provide you with a recipe."

I nod again, although I'm not too confident in making exotic dishes, let alone making them for customers.

Guadalupe throws in her idea of adding taquitos to the mix, while Chi leans toward a more global flavor with orange chicken. Jill, not to be outdone, suggests fried chicken for those seeking comfort food.

"As her fiancé and business advisor," Jeremy speaks up, and I like how he says her fiancé. He can probably sense my burgeoning panic at the overwhelming suggestions. His tone is firm yet open to future possibilities. "We'll take all these suggestions under advisement after the first year's performance."

"As usual, Sis, the southwest rolls were my favorite." Damien circles back to us. "Jeremy, what's your favorite of the dishes Zuri makes?"

"I like everything Zee makes." Jeremy winks at me, his arm finding its place around my waist, hinting at preferences known only to us. His favorite meals won't be featured on the menu. The spring rolls are still up for debate since he thought starting with six or seven items on the menu was a better proposition than drowning myself with so many items and risking having supplies go to waste.

"My, my." Jill claps. "I'm so glad my boss has a cook for a fiancée." She wags her brow.

As he kisses the top of my head, a twinge pinches my chest. We're lying to some of our favorite people.

Jeremy's friends know about our fake engagement based on what Jeremy said, but none of them act like it. I'm not sure Jill knows, but I hate that I didn't tell Damien, especially when he slaps Jeremy's shoulder. "I underestimated you, man. My sister sees something in you, and that's what truly counts."

"Thanks." Jeremy's hand moves from my back to grip my shoulder. "I'm the fortunate one here," he murmurs, his affection not giving any indication this is just for show.

Naina's eyes brighten, her olive complexion glowing under the soft light as she asks to see my ring.

I extend my hand, and the diamonds catch and scatter beams in a dazzling display. Jill, along with a few others, draws closer, captivated by the ring's brilliance—a tangible representation of our charade. Their compliments cascade around us, and Naina's accent adds a unique melody to the admiration as she sings out. "It's sooo beautiful."

"You've outdone yourself, Zee." Jeremy's breath against my ear sends tingles of awareness through me, dissipating my doubts. "You're officially a chef."

"How did we forget jamming up the tunes today?" Damien asks, his broad chest rising and falling beneath his untucked button-down. He then redirects his gaze to Olivia. "You wanna get the playlist going, Donovan? I'm gonna prep the game."

"I'll take your phone." She holds out a hand, and he passes over his phone.

He then announces a surprise. "We're gonna split up into"—he eyes the group as if doing a mental calculation—"four teams."

Then he gives me a genuine smile that squeezes my heart. I should tell him soon about Jeremy and me. But it's almost too late. He's gonna be so mad. Ugh.

"Should we get out the cake first?" Lexi jitters toward the fridge, but Jeremy and several others prefer to let the food digest first.

We pull four tables close together and sit around for the card game of spades. Traditional spades is played with four players in teams of two, but for sixteen of us, we set up four separate games, each with its own set of four players. As the game unfolds, laughter tints the air. Jeremy is on my team, and we're up against Lexi and Nico. They ended up together when everyone besides Jeremy and me had to draw random partners. Since they can't agree on anything, Jeremy and I easily win.

An hour later, Olivia slices the cake, and Jeremy and I serve. Lexi stops me to photograph the sliced cake on the plate I'm carrying.

"Did you *have* to invite my boss?" She speaks under her breath as Nico's laugh bursts from where he's carrying the conversation.

"He's Jer's bestie."

"Jer?" She pauses her picture taking and cocks her head. "I'm not even going to assume you two are still pretending."

My cheeks heat up. I have no definite answer because, while I like Jeremy and we act like a couple, he hasn't declared anything official. "As far as I know, we're still—"

"Keep telling yourself that." She snaps a picture.

Then I redirect the chat to Nico. "You should give your boss the benefit of the doubt."

She rolls her eyes. "At least, the party is almost over."

That argument might have me in the middle—a battle I'm keen to avoid since Nico is sort of my friend too.

As we eat cake and others get second servings, Damien tilts his head back, laughter booming as he shares a moment with Nico and Jeremy. It's the food, undoubtedly, that weaves us closer together.

Shortly later, people mill around the tables as we pack leftovers for everyone to take home.

"We need to make this a habit." His tone light, Damien seals a disposable container and hands it to Jill. He nods at Jeremy, his expression sincere. "But next time, you two are up against my team."

"I can guarantee Zuri and I can outplay you." Jeremy hands Wes his share of leftovers.

Wes raises his container in salute. "As long as Zuri's in charge of the food, count me in any day."

"You just saved me from another night of takeout," Nico chimes in, his grin wide. "Count me in for hangouts like this."

"Here's to Zuri's café." Naina lifts her water glass. A collective cheer rings out, food containers and glasses clinking in testament to our unity and friendship old and new.

"And many more nights like this." Damien's sincerity tugs at my heart. Now, I'm faced with another dilemma. I could unravel the lie or nurture my faint hope Jeremy and I might truly fall in love and eliminate the need to correct any wrongs.

CHAPTER 16

Jeremy

Sunday night wraps us in warmth inside my brother Gavin's house while we dine with him and his fiancée, Hope. Zuri and I arrived in Pleasant View two hours ago, which gave them ample time to get acquainted. The dinner table is still flowing with half-devoured exotic dishes Hope made for us. Now, our stomachs satisfied, we sit surrounded by the lingering aromas. The pendant lights cast a warm glow over us and illuminates the open space stretching into the living room.

Hope is recounting her experiences since she arrived in the States six months ago. "Gavin's made it easy for me." Her voice carries a blend of African and British inflections, her skin, a shade deeper than Zuri's, glows under the light, and her deep affection for Gavin warms her dark eyes. "The biggest challenge has been adjusting to the winter."

"Yet, you're always eager to hit the slopes every weekend." Gavin nudges her shoulder, and she's so delicate I almost warn my brother to be careful. But she's proved her spunk, and besides, I've seen his tender care for her. Even now, his voice is soft, and his eyes, blue like mine, shine with affection.

"That's because I want to be confident on skis before the snow season ends." She spreads out her hands, including us. "Maybe we can all go skiing before Jeremy and Zuri head back to California."

"Definitely." I give Zuri's shoulder a reassuring tap, my hand resting behind her chair. In her yellow top with dark leggings, she appears casual for a relaxed night, but uncertainty now glosses her eyes.

"I'm rarely around snow, let alone ski." She bites her full lower lip. "Unless watching the Winter Olympics counts?"

"Don't worry. I'll teach you." The idea of being on the slopes with her excites me.

"Gavin taught me in January." Hope recounts her experience. "I'm not great at it yet, but it's fun. You'll love it."

"Yes, you will." I wink, then sense my brother assessing me.

When I look at him, he has that knowing smile as he asks, "You never told me how your engagement party went."

I mentioned the party during our phone call the night before we gathered with our friends.

"Zee should give you the details." I nod toward Hope, who's now leaning forward, eager for how we handled a fake-engagement party.

"Why me?" Zuri asks.

"You're more into the details than I am." She was the mastermind behind the party. My role was mere support, following her lead.

"My friends already know Jeremy and I are a pretend couple." Zuri's hands animate her story while Gavin rubs Hope's back as they listen. "I couldn't say no when they wanted to throw us a party."

"We ended up hosting the party ourselves." I chime in, my arm resting behind Zuri. "And we didn't just host. We cooked and served everyone."

"It was buffet style." Zuri turns my way with the gentle smile that always stirs something deep inside me. "Okay, we did put in some effort to prepare the meals."

"She wouldn't let me hire a caterer." My protest is half-hearted, a playful jab at her independence, even though she was wise to win over people to spread the word.

"That was a perfect chance to test out my recipes." Zuri then addresses Gavin and Hope. "Turns out, your brother can really cook."

"Really?" Gavin raises his eyebrows in mock surprise and I offer a modest shrug.

"I have no choice when Zuri summons me to her café for dinner," I say. "That's if she doesn't end up smothering my hair with flour."

"Food wars." She elbows my ribs.

"I have to warn you about her 'food wars' in case you ever find yourselves in the kitchen together." My fingers trace over her shoulder. Her exposed neck tempts my touch, but seizing any excuse for contact feels right. Her skin is soft, and her figure so enticing.

"I'm looking forward to witnessing these kitchen battles." Hope glances between Gavin and me, her amused look suggesting an unspoken understanding.

There's no need to convince anyone of the authenticity of our relationship. The easy back and forth of our conversation, not to mention our laughter and shared looks, speak volumes more than any pretense ever could.

"Can I see your ring again?" Hope scoots forward.

Zuri, without hesitation, extends her hand across the table, allowing the diamonds to catch the light. As Hope examines the ring, rotating Zuri's finger to get a better look, pride surges through me. Perhaps she would be okay with turning our relationship into something for real.

"Quite the ring for a fake engagement," my brother quips.

I shoot him a look that says "back off," but choose a lighter retort. "Well, why not go all in?"

"It's funny that your friends are in on the act." Hope releases Zuri's hand. "Yet they threw you an engagement party."

Gavin gestures between us. "Maybe your friends are hoping you'll turn this façade into reality."

Zuri slinks back, seeming to retreat into herself as she wraps her arms around her body. "My brother doesn't know."

Despite sharing a home with him and her friends, she's yet to break the news to him, a decision she seems confident in, though not entirely comfortable with.

"Why haven't you told him?" Hope's eyes fill with concern reflecting Zuri's inner conflict.

"He's protective of me. Since Jeremy and I are, well, pretending..." Zuri's voice drops as she glances at me, and I drape my hand over her back for comfort perhaps or just because it's become natural for me to keep my hands on her. "I've been waiting for the right moment. But the longer I wait, the harder it's become, especially now that he's gotten used to Jer."

Hearing her use Jer endearingly tightens something in my chest.

"I feel like"—her whisper dips even lower—"like I'm betraying my faith by lying to those I love."

I keep silent. Hope and Gavin are spiritual and can best comfort Zuri.

"I can relate to thinking God is not on your side." Hope clasps Zuri's hand. "I feel like that a lot of times. Gavin has helped me understand the nature of God."

"We help each other," he adds, then delves into their journey of faith since they met in Uganda.

Gavin's story with Hope—finding each other after his past heartbreak—makes me appreciate their bond. He's found peace and happiness with her, a stark contrast to his past turmoil.

Zuri then sits up straighter, her clasp on Hope's hand seeming tighter. "So, do you think we can convince Sara about us?" Her eyes, alive with a playful spark, flash my way, and she nudges me.

"Given my brief encounter with her at Jer's office, I think I need all the pointers I can get before I meet her tomorrow."

She's laughing, but I can hear a genuine concern beneath her light tone.

"You don't need to convince her in any way." Dismissing the notion of any required pretense, Gavin drapes his hand on Hope's shoulder.

"I agree with Gavin." Hope nestles comfortably against his side.

Their unanimous front, paired with Zuri's mischievous smile, sparks a warmth within me, a silent acknowledgment of the bond we've formed. Yet, beneath this friendship lies a looming dread—the end of our pretend relationship is near, a mere six days away. We've yet to discuss how we'll navigate our final day, despite the deep dive into this charade.

While it terrifies me to risk another relationship, Zuri is different, and I'm hoping I still have enough time to work up the nerve to confess how I feel. No doubt, she likes me. After all, when I kissed her on the rooftop, she kissed me like she'd been thinking about kissing me.

It's not just the kiss, though. We've had plenty of sweet moments. But, more importantly, we like each other and enjoy spending time together.

The evening progresses, and Hope and Zuri connect with an ease that comforts me. Not that I ever doubted Hope's ability to connect, given her easygoing personality.

As we begin clearing the table, Hope shares more wisdom with Zuri about facing my mom. "No matter how convincing you two are as a couple"—she scoops food into a glass container—"Sara always has a scheme."

Gavin takes the container from Hope and puts it in the stainless steel fridge. "No one will ever be perfect for Mom's boys unless she's chosen them as our spouses."

Good thing Zuri is staying with Hope instead of at my parents' house. I shudder thinking of Mom's original sleep arrangements. I turn on the water and snatch the dirty plate from Zuri. "Is Mom still planning to have Sonya stay at the house?"

"Lucky and her parents are also staying the night at our house, starting Thursday."

Lucky? Seriously? Mom's still in touch with Gavin's ex? "Two days before the wedding?"

"The families have been friends for years, so that figures." Gavin reaches for another food container, keeping his foot on the fridge to wedge it open. He calmly accepts Mom's plans, even when they include uncomfortable arrangements, unlike me with my unvoiced reservations.

"She's not happy you're staying with me by the way," he says. "Either that or the fact that Uncle Luke gets to stay in your room instead."

"It will be a good thing for Mom to bond with her brother, don't you think?" I stack the drippy plate into the dishwasher.

He shrugs. "They haven't seen each other in a long time. She's probably more anxious about how they're going to cope under the same roof."

Speaking of family members, Gavin and I discuss the relatives anticipated at his house for the evening.

Meanwhile, Hope and Zuri are chattering about wedding preparations. I hear something about Hope's plans for her bridesmaids that week.

"Gavin and I were planning to show some photos of our time in Uganda."

"I want to see your adventures from Uganda!" Zuri clutches both of Hope's hands, giddy, her curls bouncing. Man, she's so adorable.

"Once the food's put away, we can flip through a slideshow. Hope's got it all ready for the ceremony." Pride deepens Gavin's voice. "It will be showcased during the ceremony."

Soon, we settle onto the sofa. We watch vibrant images of their time at a hospital with the children, as well as them both standing in front of a breathtaking waterfall, and then their traditional ceremony that, with its informal nature, radiates authenticity and warmth. They look so happy, and a thought occurs to me about my upcoming best-man speech.

As I adjust my position, my leg brushes against Zuri's. She doesn't seem to notice with her attention fixed on the TV, but I'm contemplating moving again so I can repeat the sensation. *Focus, buddy!* I clear my throat. "These pictures are perfect. They'll help me add depth to my speech."

Gavin, lounging with ease, extends his arm along the sofa back behind Hope. "You know me better than anyone—no need for a formal speech." He winks. "Unless you want to mention all those times I had to clean up your messes."

"Seriously?" Yes, he's teasing, and while I want to out him for his old habits of leaving his shoes in the middle of the house and letting the nanny clean up after him, I give him a free ticket so I don't scare Hope.

"If my time with Jer is anything to go by"—Zuri jumps in with a playful defense—"I'd say he's the meticulous one. It seems like he's the one always cleaning up."

My chest swells, more from her eagerness to defend me, than from her words themselves. I wrap an arm around her, drawing her closer, trying not to notice how well she fits or how good she feels. "You know me so well." My voice cracks, the warmth in it unmistakable.

Gavin throws us a curious glance and smirks. "How long have you two been acquainted?"

"Long enough to actually like each other." Hope taps his chest.

"But I'm more eager to hear how you two met." Zuri's eyes sparkle under the dim lights, her proximity thrilling me. "Please, do tell."

"It wasn't your typical meet-cute story." Gavin grins as he faces Hope, his voice warm. "Hope had—and clearly still has—such an incredible spirit."

"And Gavin is very bold." Hope's eyes light up. "It all started when he defended me from my mean boss. He was the first person to stand up for me."

As they tell their love story, Zuri oohs and aahs, her hand resting on her chest as she takes in all the details. She asks questions, clearly not wanting to miss a step in their love story. Yes, this beauty's a romantic.

We laugh and reminisce about their time in Uganda. The night stretches on until almost midnight when we drive the girls back to Hope's place, a cozy ranch house—one of the investment properties Gavin will sell or rent after the wedding.

I hover by the door with Zuri standing not far from me as Gavin and Hope share a tender good-night kiss in the living room. My gaze drifts to the African wall hangings and a woven basket on the coffee table. It's best I look anywhere but at Zuri as my mind whirls with the possibility of kissing her again.

"It's a great place," she says, and I manage a glance at her, her hands clasping her luggage.

"You have my number," I mention, completely off topic. My mind isn't in the game. *Stay cool, buddy. You can do this.* I stick to the phone sentence I was trying to say. "Call me if you—"

"Get nightmares?" Zuri says playfully as she bites her lower lip, and I struggle to look at her without thinking of how those lips taste. "With the mountains and all, a mountain lion or bear could be chasing me down."

I laugh, though it's strained. My glance inadvertently seeks out Gavin as discomfort over their intimacy tightens my gut and heats my skin. It's not just their affection that unsettles me—it's the growing realization of my desire for Zuri. The longing is becoming increasingly hard to ignore. I take a step backward, and I hit the closed door. But at least, the slight distance keeps me from reaching for Zuri and kissing her senseless right in front of my brother and his fiancée.

"Breakfast." My mouth feels dry, and my gaze catches. "We'll eat together. Gavin and I." What's with me? I'm struggling to piece my thoughts into coherent sentences. "We'll pick you up."

Restless, I rub the back of my neck, an attempt to distract my hands. Memories of our kiss flicker through my mind, haunting yet precious. The ease with which I could kiss her again battles with my resolve not to toy with her. That kiss was real, filled with our raw emotions.

But before I dare kiss her again, it's crucial that Zuri grasps the depth of my feelings. So how do I reveal my true feelings and risk investing in us?

CHAPTER 17

Jeremy

Gavin's house is nestled close to Pleasant View Trail, so we hit it early. As we jog, I breathe in the freshness as opposed to San Francisco's urban rush. Remnants of snow linger on the distant mountains, inviting me to ski soon. But here, the scent of pine and damp earth signals spring in full swing.

Gavin, keeping pace beside me, talks about his honeymoon plans. "Hope wanted to go to Niagara Falls, and I'm looking forward to it." His steady voice sends humid puffs into the cool morning air. Despite our vigorous pace, the calmness about him surprises me, given the upheaval he experienced nearly two years ago when he was left standing at the altar.

"So, how are you feeling about the wedding?" I speak not only as the best man but also as his brother concerned for his well-being.

Gavin pauses, then stretches, and a muscle pops in his shoulder.

"I was nervous a month ago. I overlooked so many red flags with Lucky, but Hope hasn't given me any reason to doubt her love for me."

A critter darts across the trail too fast for me to discern if it was a squirrel or a gopher.

"These last two weeks, I've had peace about it. Hope and I are starting our marriage with God being our foundation. That's a big deal. She suggested we approach the ceremony differently to ease my nerves."

He continues, reflecting on the challenges of their families' acceptance and their journey together. "Hope's been incredible throughout, even with her family's hesitance. Her dad couldn't make the trip due to health reasons, and Mom... Well, she's coming around."

I hardly believe him, but I won't voice my doubts.

He resumes a slow jog, and I fall in step.

Colorado's serene beauty surrounds us, our shoes pummeling wet leaves from last fall. The aspens stand tall and leafless, but in two months, they'll be flourishing and blending in with the evergreens.

The trail curves, and we slow to navigate the bend. The morning sun peeks through the canopy, dappling the ground with patches of light.

"What about you?" Gavin veers into my personal territory. "You seemed at ease with Zuri last night."

"She's... easy to be around." I speak between breaths. "We respect each other, and she values my opinions." The memory of her trusting me to choose the café furniture warms me anew, even as my feet pound the winding trail. "We laugh at each other's jokes."

"But is there more? Beyond the arrangement?" Gavin digs deeper, his question slicing through the morning's tranquility.

"It's complicated." Because of my back and forth. But it shouldn't be. Zuri is nothing like Sonya. "There might be something more."

"I'd say don't wait too long." He jogs past me when the trail's muddy edges make us run single-file. "Getting right back at it helps you not get too comfortable in your single life. Emotions have a way of sneaking up on you when you least expect it."

I'm well past "getting right back at it" —Sonya left me four years ago. Yet, there's Gavin, not only way ahead of me on the trail but also blazing a trail in this thing called love. His advice, born from experience, resonates deeply. I've seen him navigate his share of emotional turmoil. Now, his journey to finding happiness with Hope is a testimony to the unexpected paths the heart can take.

If only he knew my emotional turmoil since Zuri came into my life! I've enjoyed having her in my life more than I'd expected. As we navigate the trail's curves, Gavin's advice not to wait too long echoes in my mind. I don't want to go back to my life without Zuri in it.

We continue our run, the conversation shifting to lighter topics, the early morning exertion a backdrop to our brotherly bond. Birds chirp overhead while our footsteps rhythmically pound the earth beneath us. Both create a meditative soundtrack to the quiet morning.

Near the end of our trail, the physical exertion rejuvenates me, as does the clarity of mind that comes after a workout. Then Gavin slows, signaling the end of our run, and we come to a stop, our breaths heavy, the cool air a contrast to the warmth emanating from my body. We stretch in silence, a necessary conclusion to each run, yet my mind is far from silent. It's still grappling with my burgeoning feelings.

"We'd better not let our ladies wait too long for their breakfast." Gavin grins.

"They're probably still asleep." That is if Zuri slept well in an unfamiliar place. "I was thinking of taking Zee to the arcade today if you and Hope want to join us."

I then nod to the first people we've encountered on the trail.

"Hope and I planned to spend the day with you, so yeah, let's show Zuri our old stomping grounds."

I chuckle, grateful to have this time with my brother and his help in making Zuri's stay as enjoyable as possible. I can't guarantee what awaits us during our dinners in my childhood home though. That's why I flew in a day earlier than Mom expects so we could settle in before I thrust Zuri into Mom's orbit.

***

Daylight blends into darkness as we pull into the driveway of my childhood home nestled in the mountains. After a day spent showing Zuri our quaint town and revisiting our favorite spots, we feel rejuvenated, and ready for the family gathering.

"You grew up here?" Zuri whispers, nudging my arm.

I sort of understand why she's gawking. "That's right... my neck of the woods." A spacious three-story home with a full basement for just four people is way too much space.

"Wow. It's... lovely."

"Thanks."

We walk up the path and a florist's van is parked among the many cars scattered beyond the driveway on the pavement that expands into the front yard. I hadn't realized relatives were arriving four full days before the wedding.

"Seems some family members arrived earlier than expected." Gavin leads the way with Hope by his side. Zuri and I follow, absorbing the sights—the expansive yard and stately mansion backed by sprawling land. Unseen around back, there's a pool, hot tub, and spaces filled with memories, including Gavin's almost-wedding disaster two summers ago.

As he pushes the door open, noise and laughter spill out, welcoming us back into the fold. Aunt Patty, clad in her signature brown suit, strides toward us, her brown eyes widening. More gray streaks through her auburn hair than I remember. She beams and opens her arms wide for an embrace. "Oh my! Look at you boys."

Her warmth envelops us as we step into the hallway, the air fragrant with the fresh flowers from the vast bouquet on the cabinet.

"Aunt Patty." Gavin wraps her in a hug before I take my turn while complimenting her timeless appearance. I love her simple soap scent, so different from Mom's preference for luxurious perfumes.

"You both have beautiful ladies at your side." She steps back, taking in Hope and Zuri, and her familiar kindness warms my heart. I introduce Zuri as my fiancée, and Aunt Patty's embrace is as welcoming as her smile. Gavin presents Hope, his bride-to-be, and Aunt Patty cups Hope's cheeks, her welcome starkly different from Mom's often-reserved greetings.

Then she wags a finger between Gavin and me. "I'm not happy that you boys haven't visited me in so long." She turns to Hope and Zuri, grasping each of their hands, and urges them to coax us into visiting her in Oklahoma. "There's more than enough room, y'all know. And we ladies can have fun while the boys enjoy the property and get on their fishing adventures." Laughing, she lets go of them. "Boys, did your mom tell you your uncle built another house for his 'collection'?"

The click of heels echoes through the hallway, prompting us all to turn. Mom, the epitome of grace and poise, approaches and now commands the space. "Are you guys coming in?"

Aunt Patty rubs my back. "I figured if I didn't keep the boys here, you may never give us the chance to catch up."

"Don't tell me you're still convincing them to come to your farm." Mom waves her black-painted nails toward her sister, Aunt Patty.

"I like her farm." I lean in to peck Mom on the cheek.

"We're planning a visit next summer." Gavin embraces Mom.

Aunt Patty leaves and promises to be back from her car in a few minutes.

"Hope." Mom nods toward Gavin's fiancée, her smile not quite reaching her eyes—a frostiness veiled in politeness.

"Nice to see you again, Sara." Hope gives a little wave, her half smile underscoring the unresolved distances between them. I admire her resilience in agreeing to let my mother orchestrate the prewedding events, despite Gavin protesting that she didn't need to honor Mom's wishes.

But now, the spotlight's on me, and in this moment, Zuri and I must maintain our act. I draw her closer and kiss the top of her curly hair. "Zee, remember my mom, Sara. Mom, Zuri."

"Your fiancée?" Mom's eyebrows arch as she takes in Zuri. "I assumed you two would've ended things before the wedding."

Zuri's soft hand squeezes mine, and I square my shoulders, meeting Mom's skepticism with a seriousness I hope masks the hot fury blazing within. "What gave you that idea?"

Unfazed, Mom scans Zuri's left hand. "I see you're wearing your ring today. After your little fight, ghosting or whatever it was, I figured—"

"It's called a couple's fight, Mom." I grit my teeth. "I'm sure you and Dad get those sometimes?"

Clearly not, because Dad just puts up with whatever Mom directs.

She dismisses the tension, her focus shifting to the evening ahead. "It's going to be a marvelous night." With a flick of those black nails, she ushers us to follow her. "Morgan has dinner ready."

Right. Her ability to glide over family discord is a practiced art.

When we emerge into the main room, several of our family and friends are standing around, others are seated, and most are holding glasses containing amber or red liquid. Their chatter rises, combining with Mom's harping on the florist to move the flowers away from the space designed for the wedding cake.

"All right, everyone." Her voice pierces through the vast room. "The boys are here."

"Welcome!"

"Woo-hoo!" voices resound from the crowd.

My father stands from where he's sitting with four gentlemen, all dressed in formal suits. His smile meets his eyes, and I grieve for him. He's always willing to put up with Mom's antics.

Then my brother whispers, "Ho boy. There's Sonya."

Heels click on the smooth floor, and a familiar figure emerges from the library. She's dressed in a snug cocktail dress, certainly for show, revealing more than it should. My emotions go into a freefall. My hand slides from Zuri's back to her side in a futile attempt to shield my heart.

Catching my mother's eye, I see a flicker of understanding or perhaps a challenge.

"It's been so long since you've seen family friends. What better occasion for a reunion than a wedding?"

With that, she's dismissed my discomfort, having orchestrated this moment for her own reasons. How can she not see Sonya was a bad investment that squandered years of my life and left me emotionally bankrupt?

CHAPTER 18

Zuri

"Stay true to yourself." Hope's advice rings in the back of my mind as a woman, the kind I see on a magazine cover, strides toward us, all long legs and exposed skin. Her calculated focus zeroes in on Jeremy, and my heart clenches.

I scarcely belong here in this elegant setting with its posh occupants. This feels more suited to a high-end TV drama than reality. But then, maybe that's what I need to remind myself. None of this *is* my reality and this man beside me is nothing more than my fake fiancé.

The ease with which Jeremy's hand slips away from mine doesn't just sting—it releases an avalanche of doubts. Uncertainty crashes over me, challenging my every rehearsed response.

It'd help if I knew if he was shocked or surprised. Or both? But our connection wavers, and all I sense is the communication between him and this woman as he gawks. I catch snippets of Gavin and Hope's conversation with a man they greet warmly as

"Dad," yet my focus remains tethered to Jeremy and the blonde with perfectly painted red lips.

"Jeremy dear, aren't you going to introduce Sonya to your friend?" Sara's voice puts an end to the silent exchange. "What's her name again?"

Her feigned forgetfulness crafts a dismissal I cannot ignore. Her gaze flits between Sonya and me, then settles on Jeremy, clearly pleased with this reunion she's orchestrated.

But this is why Jeremy brought me here. This is my role. Regardless of the undercurrents of discomfort, I reclaim his hand and my role. As Jeremy seems to shrink under the pressure of the situation, I suck in my tummy and stand taller. Despite my slightly elevated shoes, I still have to crane to peer up at Sonya. And somehow, I introduce myself with a veneer of confidence. "I'm Zuri. Jeremy's fiancée."

I mask a smile, and while it's courtesy to shake hands, I suspect Sonya, like Sara, dislikes shaking strangers' hands. That works out for me. I have no intention of being embarrassed should I get dismissed. I simply wave.

"Sonya," she sings-songs her own introduction and shifts her gaze to Jeremy. Her stilettos put her almost to the same height as Jeremy. Her cocktail dress hits midthigh, far too revealing and fancy for a casual family dinner. My bohemian pants fastened over a long-sleeve top feel underdressed, save for Hope, Jeremy, and Gavin who seem equally casual.

"Sara didn't tell me you were engaged."

Jeremy finally returns my grip on our hands. He clears his throat and apparently remembers I'm here. "Mom's been too busy to remember everything."

"Jeremy and Sonya have known each other since they were kids," Sara cuts in, then highlights the shared history between their families.

"Jeremy told me everything, actually." I find strength in my role. After all, we've been preparing for this for over two months. "You're back in your town after some time away, right?" I let my brow rise as I address Sonya. What I'm saying is that she's recently divorced.

I think she gets the memo. She finally gives me her full attention. Her face hardens as she peers down at me, and her confidence almost wavers under my gaze. Despite the victory, something pinches my chest over causing her discomfort. I'm not like that, one to give such cheap shots.

A middle-aged man steps right between Sonya and us, diffusing the tension, and pats Jeremy's shoulder. "Son."

"Dad." Jeremy engulfs the man in an embrace,then steps back and places his hand on my back, gently nudging me forward. "This is Zuri."

To my surprise, the man puts out his hand to shake mine. As he asks if I was born in Colorado, I try not to think much about why Jeremy didn't add fiancée to his introduction.

"I'm a San Francisco native, but I've always wanted to visit Colorado." As the conversation shifts, my shoulders relax, and I allow myself the first deep breath since entering the house, relieved to steer away from my earlier discomfort.

"I'm hoping to take her skiing tomorrow." Jeremy shifts his hand to my waist.

"Let's make our way to the table for dinner. Come along, everyone." Sara claps, slicing through our conversation with an air that brooks no argument.

I survey the expanse around us—a seamless transition from the main living area to what must be the dining room. This section of the house, too, boasts a lofty ceiling and floor-to-ceiling windows that bathe the space in the dying light. Each nook, be it beside a grand piano or atop a side table, plays host to fresh flowers, their subtle fragrance—a blend of roses and something sweet—mingles with the rich aromas wafting from the kitchen. Mom would have loved to have decorated such a place. And I must admit Sara's done a beautiful job.

A whole procession surrounds us, their voices and chatter making the room lively. As we approach, I notice servers who were previously a blur in my peripheral vision, now navigating the room with loaded trays.

Jeremy and I stop at one of the two linen-draped tables beneath the chandelier. Before each cushioned chair is a plate, and floral cloth napkins wrap around the shiny silverware.

Sara, with a practiced grace, directs one of the couples toward a table near the fireplace. "Find your name," her command emphasizes the evening's formality.

"It's just a casual dinner, Mom," Jeremy mutters under his breath.

Her heels click against the floor as she turns, her gaze piercing to where Jeremy and I stand, his hand frozen midmotion over a chair he'd been about to claim. "Jeremy, you're next to Sonya tonight." She indicates across the table where Sonya is already ensconced. Then she offers us a nonchalant glance before accepting a wineglass half filled with red liquid from the server. "Your fiancée can sit over there with Gavin and Hope."

She directs a semblance of an apologetic smile my way. "I didn't realize you'd be joining us."

I bite the inside of my tongue to swallow the sting of her words as I nod. Hope warned me about Sara. So did Jeremy. And I even witnessed it in that brief moment in San Francisco. She has a knack for commanding a room and leaving others feeling slightly off-balance. But it doesn't take a genius to know that the seats by the bride and groom are the most coveted. Her placing me there as if it's the only open space for an afterthought guest is ridiculous.

"Zee is sitting here with me." Jeremy's firm tone leaves no room for protest as he pulls out a chair for me.

Wow, there's the confident COO I know.

He then takes the seat beside me, dismissing his mother's directive. With a defiant flick, he rearranges the name cards and tucks them beneath the decorative centerpiece as if to erase any evidence of the original seating plan.

"You can't just mess up my seating arrangement."

Sara's complaint is a distant murmur as Jeremy focuses on me, his actions a silent rebellion. "Would you like something to drink besides water?" he asks. And, with that gentle defiance in his gaze, I can picture eighteen-year-old Jeremy defying his mom when he dated the ranchers' daughter.

"Water's fine."

He touches my hand. "I promise I'll get you some kombucha tomorrow, though I'm sure yours tastes better."

His compliment and consideration warm me more than they should.

With Jeremy's rearrangement, Sara relocates two people to the next table and moves Sonya to the chair across from us, then positions herself beside her. The table, designed to accommodate a dozen, feels more confining than I expected. Even when compared to the more expansive table by the fireplace where lively chatter rings out between Hope, Gavin, Patty, and Gavin's dad. All the relaxed people are at that table.

Too bad, Jeremy didn't drag us over there.

Dinner is finally served, steak and lamb, accompanied by an array of sides.

Cutlery chimes against porcelain, offsetting the steady hum of conversation, and I remain tense and out of place, despite Jeremy's presence.

With Sara's intensity cutting through the room, I don't blame him for his silence. Goodness, even I don't want to talk—far too mentally exhausted by her manipulative games.

Yet, undeterred, Sara presses on with her agenda. It's clear now why she chose to position herself next to Sonya, overlooking her husband's presence at the other table. "Sonya, sweetheart." Her voice rises above the chatter as she swirls the red wine in her glass. "Why don't you tell Jeremy about your new position?"

Sonya sits straight, dabbing at her lips with a napkin before flitting her gaze to Jeremy who's focused on slicing his steak with savage force. "I'm now the curator at Opulence." She nods and elaborates on her role, engaging in the sort of art acquisitions that would appeal to the most discerning of collectors.

"Good for you," Jeremy mutters, a harsh sarcasm seeping free. He reaches for his water and takes a sip. "A private art gallery suits you well."

Sonya, seeming oblivious to his disinterest, chatters on about the elite art gallery. "The challenges keep me engaged."

I bite into my steak, letting myself savor the meal. There's just the right amount of salt and garlic, and hmm, it's tender.

Sara's every question orchestrates the conversation between Jeremy and Sonya, and with how fast he's eating his steak, he must be uncomfortable. I slip my hand under the table and place it on his free hand, squeezing it. He looks at me, and the wordless thank you in his eyes reveals an endearing vulnerability.

Sara, watching my every move, shifts her focus to me. "If I remember correctly, Jeremy's fiancée is an aspiring chef, isn't she?" she probes, her untouched meal forgotten. "Something along those lines?"

"She's not just aspiring." His defense catches me off guard, and the protective edge to his words warms me from the inside out. "She's an exceptional chef."

"Because you're not a picky eater." Caught in a moment of self-doubt, I downplay his praise. "Anyone can whip up spicy food and appetizers."

"My Jeremy doesn't eat spicy food."

"Only in this house I don't," he says. "You don't ever want Morgan to cook anything you don't add to the menu."

Jeremy had said his mom liked micromanaging, but I didn't realize she controlled whatever the chef cooked.

"Zuri's food would make you want to try spicy food." He gives me a sideways glance, smiling. Wow, that's the first time he's smiled since his mom came onto the scene—that alone becomes the highlight of this night.

"Hmm." Sara pinches her wineglass stem, then touches Sonya's arm. "Remember that time you and Jeremy took a cooking lesson from Morgan?" Apparently, she's sticking to her agenda—her obvious intent to rekindle the flame between Jeremy and Sonya.

"It was Jeremy's idea." Sonya glances at Jeremy flirtatiously. "I'm not sure why he thought we could pull off making pizza from scratch." She inspects her fingers as if searching for something. "I still have the scar from the oven burn."

"That was your first year together, right?" Sara lifts her wineglass toward Jeremy. "I knew then you two belonged together."

"Well, that was then." He draws out a sigh. "Now, we're all looking forward to making new memories, aren't we?"

As the final course brings in a more relaxed dessert session, the atmosphere changes. Laughter mingles with the clicking of silverware on dessert plates and the scent of chocolate and coffee. Gavin and Hope have taken the seats across from us, and Sonya has relocated to the table's far end next to another sophisticated woman probably her age. The lack of formal introductions at the beginning of the night leaves many faces still unnamed.

Patty strolls to our table, dessert plate in hand. "What do you two lovebirds plan for this week leading to your wedding?"

"Speaking of plans..." Sara, seated next to Gavin's left, swirls her chocolate-covered fork. "We're all going to the ski cabin tomorrow. We'll ski for the next two days."

"What?"

Gavin and Jeremy's simultaneous protest cuts through the nearby chatter. "Jeremy and I were planning to take Hope and Zuri—"

"That's perfect," Sara cuts off Gavin. "The cabin can accommodate twenty-five. It'll allow us plenty of family bonding during the wedding week. With Jeremy staying at your house, Gavin, I figured we'd plan a different location for all of us to reunite."

Jeremy gapes at me, then raises a hand. "That sounds great, Mom, but did you consider everyone's plans? Zuri and I had discussed exploring the town."

"Oh, pshaw." Sara brushes aside his concerns with a dismissive wave. "There'll be plenty of time for town exploration later. This is about the family reconnecting."

His eyes narrow. "By reconnecting, you mean...?"

"Most of our friends here." She flutters her hand around. "It's been a while since we all spent time together at the cabin."

"What better time to connect with everyone than at a wedding?" Hope touches her groom-to-be, probably to convince him Sara's plan is all right.

By the time we leave for Hope's house, I'm so ready for a break from Sara. I underestimated her. Now I'm wondering how I'd fit into Jeremy's family should Sara ever become my mother-in-law. The question weighs on me when I sit with Hope at her dining table, sipping chamomile tea at ten o'clock.

"I always need a cup of tea after being in Sara's presence." Hope cradles her delicate cup, the steam from it curling into the air as she tests a sip. Her need for tea is understandable after the emotions Sara stirs up.

"How did she manage to convince you to let her take charge of your wedding?"

Hope shrugs, her silhouette blurry with the dim lighting barely reaching us from the seating area. "Sara is controlling, but she loves her children." She nods to an African art piece on the wall. "I grew up with my father and stepmother. I still doubt they ever loved me."

She then shares her upbringing, challenges, and struggles, and facing Sara's overbearing involvement in her children's lives pales in comparison. "Even though Sara tried to reunite Gavin with his ex and is *still* hoping she'll convince Gavin to leave me for her idea of a perfect woman, I'd never come between them. I love Gavin, and it's important that he doesn't have a broken relationship with his mom because of me. Sometimes, it puts a strain between Gavin and Sara, especially when he ignores his mother's calls out of frustration."

She settles her cup back on the table. "I had to realize this isn't just my wedding. It's her oldest son's wedding, and she wants to be part of planning it. I couldn't take that away from her. At least we're getting married at a different venue, not his childhood home."

I shiver, probably from the thought of dealing with Sara on such a personal level. "You're far more patient than I could ever be."

"Don't worry about Sonya." Hope grasps my sleeve, then rubs my arm. "Despite her renewed feelings for Jeremy, he only has eyes for you."

My thoughts drift to his behavior—to how he seemed unnerved upon seeing Sonya. I bite my lip as our time in the car on the ride here lingers in my mind. "He became so quiet. I'm not even sure if he regrets bringing me along."

If he wanted to convince his ex that he's happily moved on, he probably wishes he picked someone sleeker and more sophisticated. I've never considered myself self-conscious, but tonight, I felt everything I lack in height and beauty compared to Sonya and Sara.

"Trust me, Sara's presence can shake anyone's confidence."

That I can believe. But am I strong enough to endure it? Is he?

Later, curled up in bed, I reach for my phone. There's a group text from my friends. They want an update on my trip.

Flopping on my stomach, I shift to the edge of the bed and thrust my phone closer to the bedside light as I respond.

Zuri: Jeremy's mom is out-of-this-world intense. I'll need all the prayers.

I put the phone on the nightstand, but before I slide it out of my hand, it beeps.

Lexi: Show them the fire, the real you.

Olivia: Why would she be intense when you and Jeremy are literally not even pretending to be in love?

I chuckle. Then type.

Zuri: Maybe that's what scares his mom. She wants Jeremy with the other woman.

Olivia: Lucky for you, you're not the other woman for Jeremy.

Lexi: When are you going to see the family next?

Zuri: Headed skiing tomorrow. Two nights in a cabin with Jeremy's mom and an ex.

Lexi: Don't forget to take some pictures of the snow.

Olivia: Don't let anyone intimidate you. You're beautiful, confident, and you are you.

I smile. It's so typical of Olivia with her sweet and tender caring nature.

Zuri: Thanks, girls. I'll call you when I get there tomorrow. On the bright side, Jeremy's brother and fiancée are so sweet, and they'll be there too.

Lexi: That's all you need on your side.

Olivia: Stand strong.

Their words comfort me, a reminder of the strength and support I have, regardless of the challenges Sara or the upcoming ski trip might present. With my heart lighter, I text my promise to call them tomorrow. Surely, the events and view will be worth facing his family dynamics.

CHAPTER 19

Zuri

With the ski poles in my gloved hands, my heart pounds against my ribs as I walk sideways on a beginner slope. A giant mountain stretches before me, snow gleaming under the afternoon sun. Despite the layers of warmth I've cocooned myself in—snow pants, heated gloves, a thick coat, an insulated neck warmer, and a snug helmet—yet the cold still finds its way across my skin.

I don't need to glance over my shoulder and past several heads and vibrant coats to sense Jeremy's presence. He's there, waiting and looking at me as long as Sonya hasn't made it back down the steep slope to talk his ear off.

"Now move the right ski and the right pole," my instructor, Lena, says from the side, her voice soothing my mounting anxiety. "And the left ski to the left pole and slowly move uphill."

I move sideways, using the technique I've worked on during our time on the small hill. I'm so not athletic, and only Popsicles should be frozen while holding onto sticks. But while I'd rather be steaming myself over a hot oven, I'm not going to let this mountain best me.

As soon as we'd arrived at the cabin, I was eager to check out the skiers before my first try on the slope. But Jeremy suggested the best way to learn was by being on the slope rather than observe. So I took Hope and Gavin's suggestion for an instructor. This way creates less friction between Jeremy and me should I get frustrated during the strenuous lesson.

"Remember to bend your knees as you climb further." Lena's words float over the distant laughter and the ski lift's unending hum.

I bend forward, finding my balance in the snow, and follow her instructions.

Then with a deep breath that does little to steady my heart, I push off. My descent is anything but graceful. The series of clumsy stumbles culminates in an undignified sprawl in the snow.

"You got this, Zee!" Jeremy shouts from below as I stand, and his encouragement motivates my brief, embarrassed laugh.

Then Lena reminds me to adjust the angle of the skis to the slope. Using her skis, she instructs from beside me, shifting side by side with practiced ease.

"Now climb further using the duck technique we practiced at the beginning. If you start sliding, fold your knees toward the snow."

Every tumble's more demoralizing than the last. A child glides by, making me feel like a failure. And then, as if summoned by my growing frustration, Sonya sails past in a pink ski coat and pants. "Zuri, still in the same spot?" she taunts, her athletic figure disappearing down the slope. She's a pro skier, so she's only on the intermediate hill to stay close to Jeremy.

Every bit of me deflates.

"I'm not cut out for this." The fight drains from me as I brush the cold wetness clinging to my face, hot tears threatening. Clumsy, soft, and awkward, I'm as out of place as a marshmallow in a salad.

"You're doing great." Lena motions toward the ski lift. "Everyone starts somewhere. Let's try a longer stretch this time."

Her proposal seems absurd given my current track record, but she dismisses my doubts with a simple laugh. "You'll find your rhythm."

Another lift slides by as I repeat the same exercises, but I gain more confidence with each attempt. When Lena, at last, tells me I'm ready for the lift, a thrill courses through me.

Although anxious, I let the strange, uncovered ride scoop me up. Then I lower the metal bar to secure myself in place, Lena's assurance of the lift operators at the beginning and top of the slope comforts me.

Once we slide off the lift, we stand higher this time. The resort below sparkles, a constellation of life and light against the fading daylight, and our ski cabin is a distant shadow in the tree silhouettes beyond the lodge. I take in the steep slope. My chest constricts, and blood slams my ears.

"Focus on the feeling, not the fear," Lena whispers, clearly having dealt with nervous students like me a lot.

Empowered, I steel myself for the descent. The sooner I conquer this hill, the less opportunity Sonya will have to weave her way closer to Jeremy. With this newfound resolve, I push off once more to prove to myself that, short and awkward and all, I am capable of doing anything I set my mind to.

"Only use the skis to control your speed forward." Lena's words float behind me, carried by the breeze as adrenaline, confidence, and excitement empower me with every graceful arc and controlled slide. This is fun. I want to do this all day tomorrow.

"Great job, Zee!" Jeremy's unmistakable pride propels me forward. Through the crisp mountain air, his figure crystallizes—Sonya at his side fades into insignificance when his smile, bright and unreserved, captures my focus.

As I reach him, something inside me swells. "I'm getting the hang of this!" I exclaim, toss aside the poles, and fall into his open arms.

"You crushed it." He holds me at arm's length, and those blue eyes gaze at mine. "I'm so proud of you!" His warm words envelop me, and in a heartbeat, his lips find mine. He's finally kissing me again! While the first kiss was loaded with emotion and hesitancy, this one is slow, deliberate, and maybe double emotion. It anchors me to the moment.

A groan of annoyance has me pulling back. Right, Sonya's here. I see her turning away. Her departure slices through the enchantment.

"Ready to call it a day?" Jeremy's casualness belies the moment we've just shared. Was his affection a performance to provoke

Sonya? No, surely not. The sincerity of his kiss proves otherwise. "Care to have some hot chocolate?"

There's a promise in his question.

"That sounds perfect." My arms find their place around his waist as I seek the warmth of his presence. His dark ski coat and mine create a slight barrier between us, but I savor the warmth of his gaze ensnaring me—making the world stand still. Time to probe the boundaries of his act. "I reckon Sonya bought into our little act."

"We do make a convincing duo." He seals the statement with a kiss atop my head.

Then Lena slides down to us. A cloud of vapor puffs from her mouth. "Zuri, your progress is astounding."

"I'm still struggling with confidence on the slope." I shift to stand beside Jeremy.

"If you still want, we can meet again tomorrow."

"She's skiing with me tomorrow." Jeremy's strong arm secures me against him, and a protective certainty wraps around me like a warm blanket.

Today, I've learned more than to navigate the slopes—I've also embraced the beauty in striving and in falling and rising again. So surely, I'm ready for the more challenging slopes of our relationship.

CHAPTER 20

Jeremy

The three-story ski cabin has always been a hub of friends and family memories, and the chatter now with a group of eighteen brings it to life again. Whether Mom had hidden motives this time or not, most of us enjoy skiing. Our family's love for the outdoors and the sport had Dad buying this small ski resort that provides no public housing accommodations, just a lodge that sells merch, rents ski gear, and offers hot food and drinks.

We're still sitting around the table after the dinner and dishes are cleared. Even Sonya and her folks and three of Mom's friends with their daughters remain. Pity their sons couldn't join—seems they've got better things to do than hang around being micromanaged by their moms. In this miniature society, the men, much like my dad, bring in the dough, but the women command the home.

I've claimed a place at the end of the long table with my dad, brother, and Aunt Patty. She's making us laugh as she talks about my cousin, Trent's latest adventures with the tractor shows he hosts on the farm. "He'll be here on Thursday *if* he can find someone to watch his unruly dog."

"I haven't seen him in ages." I muse aloud. Our last squabble—something trivial about Mom—flits through my mind. Trent always had a rebellious streak, opting for starting a band after high school. That didn't pan out, but teaching music in their small Oklahoma town makes him happy.

"What do you mean Trent is coming?" Mom's voice pulls me back as she peers past the trio separating her from her sister. Mom's always alert, taking in everyone's conversation if she's not too busy directing the conversation.

"He knows how you like a definite answer, and he wasn't sure." Aunt Patty lifts her Diet Pepsi, her preference over the wineglasses most women her age have in front of them. "But he wants to be here for his cousin's wedding."

"Not when he didn't respond to the invitation." Mom speaks over the people next to her. "Where's he going to stay?"

"There's still three vacant rooms he can stay in." When Dad soothes things over, Mom's glare has his shoulders drooping. Clearing his throat, he turns his gaze back to Aunt Patty. "Sara knows what's best, of course."

I grit my teeth over how my father always has to play along with Mom's plans. For this, I'm grateful Sonya ended things with me. I wouldn't want to be in Dad's position where my opinions don't count in my own home.

"He can stay at my house." Gavin raises his hand, clearly eager to put an end to this dilemma.

My gaze drifts past the two people separating me from Zuri. She and Hope are deep in conversation. Hope leans her head back and laughs at whatever Zuri is telling her, her laugh exuberant, her emotions seeming so much larger than she is, and my chest expands seeing Zuri relaxed. Her articulate hands speak along with her, her curls shake around her full cheeks, and her eyes shine. What's she talking about? Is it her mishaps on the slopes?

I'd opted out of skiing today so Zuri could have her first lessons on the slope with less terrain. She preferred to go with a trainer, afraid to disappoint me in case she didn't grasp skiing. I'm still impressed by how fast she embraced the slopes. My only frustration earlier was Sonya constantly appearing at my side and reminiscing about our past.

As people start leaving the table, I look forward to hanging out with Zuri for whatever time we can get before bed, but she and Hope move off to help the workers tidy up the kitchen. Some people scatter off to the main room. Others linger by the fireplace seating area with the mountain view. Sonya and Gavin's ex, Lucky, remain by the kitchen table, their laughter loud as they chat with the other women their age. Gavin and I join our girls in the kitchen, rinsing plates, loading the dishwasher, and sweeping with the workers.

"I'm sorry. Did I miss a spot with the mop?" The woman's heavy Hispanic accent obscures her words, but the concern knitting her brow as she scans the crumbs I'm sweeping from the already mopped floor—makes her meaning clear.

I stop to smile at her. "You've done a fantastic job."

Zuri, unable to hold back her amusement, playfully tosses a kitchen towel my way. "Leave it to Mr. Detail, and we'll be here all night."

"I just love cleaning," I assure the woman. Truth is, seeing any remnants on what's supposed to be a clean surface bothers me.

After cleanup, Dad asks us to join him for a round of pool in the game room. So, while Gavin and Hope play shuffleboard, I play pool with Dad, and Zuri watches, cheering for my dad when she realizes he's losing.

"Traitor!" I whisper in her ear as I chalk my stick.

She covers her mouth, but she can't stifle her chuckle. It blends with the hum as a dozen of us engage in various table games.

"At least someone's on my side." Dad nods at Zuri, his gray-streaked hair fluttering with the movement.

I win and reassemble the balls in the triangle.

"I think I have a chance of beating Gavin," Dad says.

"I'll beat Jeremy for you." Zuri rests her hand on my back, and her eyes sparkle beneath the recessed lights. "As long as we play Ping-Pong."

With Gavin stepping in to challenge my dad at pool, Zuri and I pivot to the Ping-Pong table. Her confidence with the paddle and her precise shots catch me unexpectedly.

"Forehand smash!" she exclaims over the murmur and the thwack of balls hitting each other on the tables. Her paddle slices through the air, and the ball zips past me. I scramble to counter, but she's in her element.

"Spin shot," she calls out next, her wrist flicking in a way that makes the ball dance unpredictably on my side of the table. Each term she uses, each move she makes, is a revelation.

"I'm going to assume you play this every week?" I lob the ball back into play, impressed yet strategizing my next move.

"Not exactly." Her paddle circumvents the ball effortlessly, and her mouth quirks. "But Damien taught me how—and don't you dare ask him for lessons so you can beat me."

"Hmm. He's joining us golfing one weekend later this month, perhaps we'll opt for Ping-Pong instead. I have a game room with a Ping-Pong table at the penthouse, and you can join us if you let me win today."

But she doesn't let me win. Despite my defeat, pride swells my chest as I draw her close for a hug, congratulating her on her victory. This moment between us is meant to be genuine, but sensing someone's gaze, I turn. Sure enough, Mom and friends in the lounges by the bumper pool are gawking and perhaps talking. For their benefit, I lean down and plant a kiss atop Zuri's hair. Her scent makes me dizzy with longing, the kind I hadn't thought I still had until she came into my life.

Pretend or not, Zuri and I belong together. That's becoming more clear with each passing day.

"Ready for shuffleboard?" I nod toward the previous players vacating the table.

"Never played it before." She clasps my hand and swings ours between us. "But if I learned to ski, I can handle a table game."

"I don't underestimate you, for sure." I weave us through the crowd, her warm hand in mine a steady anchor. My gaze drifts, landing on Sonya, who's watching from the window where she stands with Lucky.

I shiver. She's not down here to play any of these games. She has other plans that shouldn't involve me, but they do. She's somehow a part of my life, both a friend of the family and responsible for my dented heart. Now, she's dragging me along in this twisted game I have no control over, but maybe I should be grateful. If it weren't for her breaking my heart, I wouldn't be here with Zuri now.

Shuffleboard turns out to be a great diversion as I explain the rules and techniques to Zuri.

She's a quick learner, willing to try everything. We tease each other, laughing as we play. I take it easy on her, ensuring the game remains fun rather than competitive—though I still end up winning.

She congratulates me, stifling a yawn, clearly exhausted. The high altitude, especially being in the snow, has a way of taking a toll on anyone. Then she tips her chin to where Dad and Gavin are wrapping up another game. "I'm sure your brother would like to take you up on the pool table too."

Dad high-fives Gavin. My brother grins.

"Seems your dad lost again."

"A friendly competition is exactly what the groom needs." Adrenaline ignites a fire within me. "I'm ready to take him down."

While Gavin and I are deep in our pool game, Hope and Zuri engage in a fast-paced match of air hockey, their laughter and banter floating over to us. Meanwhile, our conversation drifts to the upcoming bachelor party. I must ensure I make the groom happy. "You still want to play table games on the eve of your wedding?"

"Boating would be legit, but the lakes are still icy here." Gavin studies his shot, his focus on the game. "Number thirteen ball, right rear corner pocket."

"I could fly you and the guys to San Diego or San Francisco for a beach day if you want." Those alternatives might appeal to him.

Gavin chuckles, executes his shot, and sinks the striped orange ball. "Tempting."

An all-too-familiar laugh overshadows our game. The atmosphere shifts, and Sonya's perfume invades our space, unwelcome and too familiar. She steps closer to me, with Lucky maintaining a cautious distance behind her. "I see you still haven't lost your touch with this game."

Memories of past winters spent at the cabin with our families rush back, but I'm not in the mood to stroll down memory lane. Keeping my response light, I maintain my focus on the table. "I still have some skill left."

Gavin takes another shot, sending the cue ball spinning toward its target. The number 10 ball ricochets off the far wall, nudges the number 15, and rolls into the middle pocket in front of me. Nice shot. And now, number 15 is in the clear. If he keeps this up, he'll clean the board, and I won't get another turn. Still, I assess my future shots in case he misses. I'm in the lead, after all, with only two solid balls left to sink.

Sonya's challenge breaks through my concentration. "After you and Gavin finish this round, how about you and I go head-to-head?"

Gavin eyes the layout of the remaining balls. Then his gaze flicks between Sonya and me. He smirks, a subtle show of support for my waning lead in our friendly game. "I doubt you'd win, Sonya."

"You never know." She raises her chin, making her stance clear.

In a pickle, I scramble for a polite way to decline without creating a scene. "You and Lucky can play after us."

"I'll just watch." Lucky's voice floats over the rim of her wineglass.

So I need another excuse to avoid the match. Hope and Zuri rejoin us. Perhaps I can use it as my out. "Zuri might want to play again."

Sonya's gaze flits between us. "Surely, Zuri can spare you for a few minutes." Sonya's always relentless, just like my mom.

"I'm going to call it a night." Zuri closes the gap between us. She steps on tiptoes and brushes her lips against mine.

I wrap my arms around her, cuddling her soft body, and escalate our simple peck into a gentle kiss. This public display, intended or not to signal to Sonya, becomes a moment of genuine connection between us.

"You're sure you don't want to stay?" I murmur against her lips, my heart racing. I'm caught in the warmth of her proximity, but her nod confirms her decision.

"I'll tag along." Hope approaches Gavin with an affectionate embrace. "You should stay and play Jeremy again. That skiing took a toll on me."

As the game with Sonya unfolds, Gavin's a silent pillar of support. He engages minimally with Lucky, his focus on the game and the dynamics playing out. My strategy against Sonya is simple—and effective.

A quick win hastens her departure from the game table and allows Gavin and me to resume our competition. But I soon regret not calling it a night after playing Sonya because she lingers, her presence an irritating reminder of past entanglements I'd rather forget.

Yet dodging her isn't an option when she leans in, her voice silkily suggesting, "Would you like to take advantage of the Jacuzzi after?"

Seriously? I grunt. "Headed to bed."

"How about skiing tomorrow, for old times' sake?"

My plans are set. "I'm skiing with Zuri."

I swallow a laugh when Lucky positions herself close to Gavin, barely masking her true intentions. "Ready for the big day?"

"No reason not to be." He keeps his gaze on the pool table.

Right. It's not like he thinks Hope will be a no-show like Lucky was. Somehow, I keep the comment to myself.

Gavin is as competitive as I am, but we're both on the same page as we struggle to concentrate on the game with Sonya and Lucky circling like predators. We just need to finish and call it a night. While the duo keeps laughing at their own jokes, I win one round, and Gavin wins one. We settle for a rematch tomorrow and retreat to the sanctuary of our shared room and its two single beds.

"I should've left as soon as Zuri left." I slide under the covers.

"Lucky for you, Hope knew you'd need backup and asked me to stay."

I chuckle and clasp my hands behind my head as I stare at the dark ceiling. Our conversation drifts from the day's plans to our current predicaments. "I'm gonna hit the trail early if you and Hope want to come."

"Hope's not a morning person anymore," Gavin says. "It's good you're going early. Otherwise, Sonya seems bent on clinging to you."

"Doesn't seem Lucky is ready to let you go either."

"That's up to her. I haven't given her any reason to keep chasing me. The sooner she stops taking Mom's advice, the sooner she could get herself out there." Gavin's bed creaks as he turns over. "Good thing you have Zuri to save you from Sonya's drama now."

I smile into the darkness. "Zuri did great in her ski class." The memory of our kiss lingers. I can almost still smell her sweet mint breath. "I thought when I kissed her in front of Sonya I made things clear I've moved on."

"You kissed Zuri today?"

"Uh-huh!" My lips tingle at the admission. "And I kissed her on the rooftop—in the rain, no less—the day I slipped the ring on her finger, and I just..." Adrenaline surges through my body. Man, that kiss took me by surprise. "I didn't just slide the ring on her finger and walk away. There were words before that. They just flew out of my mouth and didn't seem forced or anything."

My chest tightens from the way Zuri makes me feel. During our silence, I can hear the occasional shuffle of footsteps passing through the hallway.

"When you kissed Zuri today, was it just for show or because you wanted to?"

"It's both." How can I explain? "Showing off motivated me to do something I wanted to do."

"You and Zuri..." Gavin clears his throat. "Bro, I can see you two ending up together. You're yourself around her."

I nod, the weight of my next words pressing on my chest, needing release. "How do I break free from this pretend arrangement and transition to the real deal?"

"It's simple. Communication." He exhales, long and deep, a contented sound I envy. "My relationship with Hope is stronger because we both trust that God is at the center of it, the foundation. Whenever we pray together, it helps us look at things from God's perspective." He talks about the essence of relationships and God's ability to connect each one to the right person. "All that takes prayer."

I tell him about Zuri's faith in God. "She's told me bits and pieces about prayer. I don't know if she'd want me if I don't believe in her faith."

"Those are all things you two can work out before you take another serious step."

"That's *if* we take another step." Why would she even want me after meeting Mom?

My heart deflates at the possibility of Zuri not wanting me, so I talk about the impending bachelor party instead. "I've booked the Inn on Main for the party. Hope can bring her bridesmaids there if she wants to after they finish with whatever the girls are doing. The Stone siblings who'll be in town for the wedding also plan to join us for the bachelor party."

"Looking forward to catching up with the Stone boys I haven't seen in a while." Nostalgia leaves husky tones in his voice.

"Logan wasn't sure he'd be back from Italy by Friday," I mention, recalling my boss's plans during his globe-trotting commitments.

In the quiet of our room, amidst the distant laughter from other rooms, I'm glad to have this moment here with my brother once again, planning another bachelor party for him, a real one this time with a bride joining him at the altar afterward. I'm mostly glad he's not letting his past pain define his current newfound happiness. If he can move on, so can I.

CHAPTER 21

Jeremy

The morning's chill nips at us as Zuri and I disembark from the ski lift, our boots shuffling into the untouched snow. April is not usually busy with its hit-and-miss snow, and this early, barely anyone's out yet. The mountain's northern side is less populated but still as beautiful. I'll be taking Zuri there this afternoon if she wants to hit the more challenging trails.

The rising sun casts a luminous alpenglow over the familiar peaks, transforming the slope into a shimmering expanse.

"I guess waking up early means I can fall without an audience." The navy wool scarf covering her mouth and neck muffles her lighthearted comment. "Lexi and Olivia won't believe I was up skiing at six a.m."

"I'm so proud of you." Especially considering I hadn't given her much notice when I texted her late at night, and she responded this morning willing to ski this early.

"I take it you and Sonya caught up with your past last night?" Her voice holds an edge.

Jealous? Perhaps she's as into me as I'm hoping. My chest swells. While I'd like to update her about last night's events in her absence, I'd rather leave Sonya and the exhaustion that comes with her out of this moment.

"You're here with me, not Sonya," I say. Does that fully convey the depth of my focus and affection for her?

"You go first." She moves her ski pole to the left, shifting her ski along with it.

"You don't think you need me close by?" I seek her face hidden behind her goggles and scarf, but I have to imagine her smile.

"We're going to move slower if you wait for me."

As asked, I take the lead, glancing back to ensure she's close. She's hesitant at first, slow, but she seems to remember the basics. Angling her skis, leaning into turns, which is what it takes to get through the slope.

As we glide down, her initial hesitation melts away, replaced by a burgeoning thrill as she kicks up the speed and her joyful laugh echoes around us. Her bravery and zeal draw me all the more, and when we make it down, we agree to take the lift again for another run. But first, we seek comfort in the warm cabin and hot chocolate. Adrenaline surges through me at Zuri's excitement to hit the slopes again. A few people have shown up, but not enough to crowd the resort. So we queue for the lift, ready for another exhilarating descent. Then a familiar figure hurries up.

"Mind if I join you?" Sonya leaves no room for denial. Dressed in a white hat and jacket, as pristine as the snow itself, her presence casts a chill over me—her intentions likely not as pure. Her impeccably disastrous timing seems as if my brief spell of happiness conjured her presence. She climbs into the lift with a dramatic entrance and seems like she's stumbling, so I catch her to help her back in.

"Thanks, Jeremy." The morning breeze carries her words as the lift starts its ascent.

"Hi, Sonya," Zuri greets.

"Oh, Zuri." Sonya turns her head back, acting as if she just noticed Zuri's presence. She waves dismissively, then eyes me with Zuri seated next to me. "It was fun catching up with Jeremy last night."

With tension brewing, I don't say anything. Neither does Zuri.

We jump off the lift. Before we can embrace the slope, Sonya stumbles into my chest as if she's had a tumble. I have to stagger to get my balance as I extract her off me.

I sense Zuri's assessing gaze. But I'm not confident enough to look at her, especially when Sonya stands on my other side raving about how talented I am at pool.

Great!

"I was hoping maybe tonight Zuri can let you off the hook again, so we can utilize the Jacuzzi."

My hands tighten in my gloves. Enough is enough. It's time to end whatever game she thinks she's playing.

I look at her through my goggles. "Sonya, we need to talk."

"Of course," she sings out, apparently having no clue of my brewing anger. "That's what I want too."

"I'll meet you two down there." Zuri launches herself down the slope with a grace that belies her learner status. Anger seems to fuel her skill, leaving me between frustration and admiration.

I'll catch up with Sonya's drama later.

"Wait, Zee!" My voice barely catches the wind as I shift to set for her, but Sonya's grip halts my momentum. At the sudden pullback, my skis skid, and my balance wavers again. I lean toward the snow, planting my poles and skis to steady myself.

"What do you want from me?" The question escapes in a burst of anger, my patience worn thin. I pry my arm free from her grasp. I lower my thermal scarf from my face so nothing can muffle my words or obscure their meaning. "*You* jilted me. *I* moved on."

"I thought we could talk." She lowers her ski mask to her neck. "Try again."

Her words are read from the script of Mom's playbook.

"Did my mom put you up to this?" I shift my skis to create a safe distance between us, irked by visions of her throwing herself at me and kissing me the way Lucky kissed Gavin to upset Hope. Being friends, Sonya and Lucky share the same tactics.

"You eloped with another guy without as much as a breakup. Now, you think you can waltz back into my life?" My rising voice must betray my frustration. "Do you see me as some kind of back-up plan?"

Her jaw drops. She mustn't have anticipated any resistance.

"Did you think I'd be here waiting for you to decide?"

She fumbles with her gloved fingers. Her insistence on reclaiming my attention now seems even more misplaced.

"I'm sorry for everything." Her apology is somewhat hollow, but it's relieving to get an overdue apology in any form.

"Don't be. You have your life, and I've moved on too." I shouldn't have barked at her in the first place, but seriously!

She nods, a silent acknowledgment passing between us. Then she presses her lips together. "Zuri is lucky."

"I'm the lucky one." *If* I can figure out a way to work on my speech to tell Zuri I've fallen deeply in love with her. But I did that with Sonya, and look where it got me. Back to square one.

Yet Zuri is different from Sonya. I know that deep down. Maybe I'll tell her after she opens her café, when she's not distracted from starting a business.

"As long as we can always remain friends?" Sonya's voice pulls me back.

"What choice do I have?" I wave toward the cabin, hinting at the unchangeable family dynamics where past relationships linger like unwelcome guests. "Our families are friends."

"Race you down?" She quirks a brow, her tone light, and pulls her ski mask over her mouth and nose.

"That I can do." My competitive spirit ignited, I reposition my scarf, determined to claim this victory as my own. With my skis and poles firmly in the snow, I descend the slope, a flurry of motion, and ski past her, crossing the finish line first, though she's right behind me.

"How do you always win? You hardly ski in California," she asks as we make our way to the wooden shelter where a few people are sliding on their snow gear.

"Just because Mom doesn't fill you in on everything about me, doesn't mean I don't find time to hit the slopes." Honestly, I pretty much save skiing for whenever I come home.

"You were always the adventurous one between us." She laughs, reminiscing about a time when my impromptu ski escapades left everyone worried and amazed.

This time, her laughter is more relaxed than forced. I'm glad we talked things out instead of me ignoring her.

Zuri is standing on the lodge's porch. Her bright blue coat, one of the spare ones we keep in the cabin for guests, complements her skin tone and fits her perfectly, emphasizing her well-balanced figure. Man, she looks so fun to hold.

She's taking pictures, or so I think until she glances my way. Then I sense the storm of emotions assailing her face—sadness, disappointment, perhaps even betrayal. Ouch, that strikes a chord within me.

Does she feel sidelined or threatened by Sonya? If so, I must mend the oncoming rift between us.

"Meet you back at the cabin for breakfast." Sonya's words fade into the background as I make my way to Zuri.

But Zuri turns, pretending to take a picture and acting as if she can't see me.

"Hey, Zee." I set down my skis and shove my gloved hands into my pockets, hunching against the uneasy weight hanging between us.

She finally faces me when I stand beside her. Her half-hearted attempt at a smile lacks the usual sparkle in her vibrant eyes. "Ready to head back?"

I nod. How'd I get into this mess of an ex and a fake engagement turning far more real than I anticipated?

Zuri's skis were rentals, which leaves me carrying my set as we navigate through the early skiers bustling into the shop. We make our way to Gavin's Forester in the lot.

Opening the door for her, I sense her quiet resignation as she slides into the passenger seat. After loading the skis and settling behind the wheel, I kick up the heat, and the blasting air drowns our silence. Then I back out of the nearly empty lot, easily navigating around the dozen or so other vehicles.

"Why did you bring me here if you still want to be with your ex?"

Whoa. Thrown off by the accusation, I draw in a slow breath. "Where's that coming from?"

"Where do you think? I thought I was supposed to be your buffer. Instead, you used me to attract her attention. Now, you two are laughing like you reconciled. She can't seem to keep her hands off you, and you're right there to catch her as soon as she falls."

My grip tightens on the steering wheel as if I can steer the conversation away from this impending collision. Mom and Sonya's manipulations are exhausting enough without Zuri losing it on me. "Look, Zee, I'm already stressed with everything. I don't even see why you're mad."

"I'm your fake fiancée. I get it." She twists the ring on her finger, and it stirs an unexpected reaction.

"I like it when you act jealous." The words escape me before I can gauge their impact. "No more fake-fiancée act." At least I'm not the only one falling.

She sits silent, her hands folded and her gaze on the winding road. Then I come to the stop sign before turning on the loop to our cabin, and she huffs. "You may forgive me if the months of hanging around you and kissing you made me get carried away. Some of us have feelings."

"I do too," I say. I want to elaborate, but our drive ends too soon when I pull the car in front of the ski cabin. Once I park, she swings open her door and exits with a haste that leaves me trailing, and my attempts to call her back are lost with her retreating footsteps.

I almost catch up at the entrance as the front door closes behind us. But Hope and Gavin, seated at the island with steaming cups, greet us. The warm interior is a stark contrast to the chill settling in my heart.

The kitchen teems with life, pans clanging and food sizzling. The sausage, eggs, and bacon aromas mix with the coffee scenting in the air. Despite the feast, my appetite for reconciliation is what needs to be fulfilled. Zuri's cold shoulder as she asks Hope and Gavin to be excused forecasts a stormy day ahead. How are we to navigate the next three days as a "couple"?

As the day unravels, Zuri ensconces herself in her newfound companionship with Hope, Dad, and Aunt Patty, ignoring me. When she sits far from me during lunch and dinner, my heart clenches. Perhaps she needs a break—it aligns all too well with our departure from the cabin that evening.

Yet, this perceived need for distance doesn't deter me from gravitating toward her in the back seat. There's ample space, yet I scoot to the middle seat to close the gap between us, to bask in her presence and the subtle fragrance that is uniquely hers.

This proximity, while soothing, is equally agonizing when she drifts off to sleep, her head finding rest on my shoulder. Her warmth seeping in through my flannel is a bittersweet torment I willingly endure.

The spell breaks as we pull up to Hope's house. Zuri awakens, her movements quick and disoriented. She pats down her rumpled hair, a soft murmur of apology escaping over her unintentional closeness.

"I wasn't complaining," I say as she tears out of the car and rushes for the sidewalk. No, I can't let her leave like this. I need to bridge whatever gap has formed between us, to reassure her no apology is necessary for such a tender, fleeting connection. But she's gone. I slide into the front passenger seat before we back out of the driveway.

"Whatever you did to Zuri must be really bad." Gavin guides the car on the narrow road to his house.

"Playing pool with Sonya last night wasn't my best idea." I grip the back of my neck.

"You got your answer." Gavin must be revisiting our conversation from last night. "That's your cue she's into you. A fake fiancée wouldn't be bothered when you hang out with your ex."

I don't have to say anything because that makes sense.

For the first time, I'm looking forward to tomorrow's dinner at Mom's house. Zuri will talk to me the moment Mom's cold welcome sets her uneasy. It's a lousy thought, but what choice do I have?

But the next day, we don't have to pick up Hope and Zuri to drive with them to Mom's house. Hope's friends and bridesmaids drive them and join us that evening. I only get a fleeting hello from Zuri. With Mom disregarding her manipulative seating chart tonight, Zuri sits with Hope and her new friends at the long table by the fireplace. Her avoidance stings more than I care to admit, a silent rebuke for yesterday's missteps.

At least, I'm seated next to Gavin, and Aunt Patty's on the other side of Gavin with Dad and Mom across from us. With nine of us at a table for twelve, a few empty chairs remain between us and where Lucky and Sonya have seated themselves at the end of the table. After returning from the cabin, some people needed a break and went back to their homes, intending to return to the wedding at the event center rather than stay the night.

Now, servers carry loaded trays of food and place platefuls before us. My mother stands and summons everyone's attention. The murmurs turn to silence.

"Gavin is going to, um, pray for us." Despite the day's adventures, her hair is perfectly in place. "You're the reason we're gathered here tonight."

A silence descends upon both tables as he prays. A few collective amens resound afterward, so I'm glad to add mine now that I know why people pray before eating.

The towering decorated cake on the other side of the kitchen makes this wedding more realistic.

"For some reason, all your grandparents decided to get here tomorrow," Mom grumbles, moving her fork through her steaming pasta. Dinner was simple tonight, salmon and pasta with baby broccoli. "That means we'll have the rehearsal dinner before your bachelor party."

"As long as we're done by seven." I rest my fork on the salmon, and my gaze flicks to the other table. Zuri's head tilts back as she laughs with the other women, her eyes sparkling with unrestrained joy.

I recognize two of the women, wives of our friends. The guys stayed home to put their kids in bed and let their wives come here tonight.

If only Zuri was laughing at something I said. Her gaze finds mine as if she's aware of me looking at her. She nods before looking away.

Laughter at our table pulls me back. Maybe it's the lighthearted meal or whatever it is, but Mom appears relaxed as she recounts some of Gavin's childhood memories. Childhood adventures that have Dad and Aunt Patty laughing.

"Not that long ago, Gavin turned the backyard into a mud-wrestling ring." Mom's blue eyes twinkle as she shakes her head.

"And Jeremy, always the faithful sidekick, jumped right in without a second thought." Dad lifts his drink in a toast. " I recall your mother looking at you both covered head to toe in mud—she was too overwhelmed to get upset."

"Don't tell me you laughed about it?" Aunt Patty, in her brown coat, wags her Diet Pepsi.

"Crazy as it sounds, I laughed." Mom beams as if the memory is like yesterday, yet I was nine and Gavin eleven.

"But you still scolded us for ruining your flower garden," Gavin says.

As the remnants of the summer rush into my mind, I wag my fork at Mom. "You made us work with the gardener to replant those flowers if my mind serves me right."

"Since then, I make sure the gardeners plant the lilies in perfect rows." She's smiling at me.

I must smile too. I'd been very particular with the gardener on how I wanted the rows planted straight. The man had to inquire of Mom if he could do as I asked, instead of the zigzag pattern previously used.

Mom has some flexibility when she chooses. Like then, or how at the cabin and tonight she ignored the seating chart. My parents are wonderful, and I have no doubt they love us. I don't like how Mom disrespects Dad at times and he lets her get away with it. But they're still together, so I guess their arrangement works out just fine.

We continue talking and laughing, and our chatter and laughter mingles with the clinking of silverware against porcelain.

Then the doorbell shatters through, and everyone falls silent.

Mom calls for one of the servers to answer the door. Soon, a loud bark resounds as something black barrels straight for the kitchen, charging with the fervor of a storm. Mom squeals. "Don't tell me that's a dog."

We all pivot as the dog launches itself at the cake and topples it from the stand.

I leap, and so does Gavin. "The cake!"

"Oh no, Trent!" Aunt Patty mumbles, and concern fills me. Yes, for the cake, but also because Trent's long-awaited return isn't going to be a smooth welcome now.

In confusion, we walk to the kitchen. Morgan's attempting to shoo the dog. One of the servers stands still in shock with hands on her cheeks.

"Get this dog out of here!" Mom's command is louder than her clicking shoes as the Lab spins around, moving to the kitchen, seeming to look for something else to tear apart.

"Buster, no!" Trent emerges, dressed in a floral-print top, his long hair pulled back in a ponytail. He rushes to his dog. "Bad dog!"

"Well, that's not going to help us now, is it?" Her face red, Mom pivots to Trent, now holding his dog by the collar. "You didn't make reservations, and you show up with your rowdy dog—Where in the world am I supposed to get a wedding cake one day before the wedding?"

Trent winces, scanning all our faces. He waves at me and then Gavin. "Not the best reunion, is it?"

"We'll figure something out," I promise, being the best man, although I have no idea if a small-town bakery is capable of rescuing us on such short notice. Trent was never one to plan ahead, so I'm not surprised when I ask if he has a leash for his dog and discover he has none.

Gavin requests one of the workers to get the dog water as Trent vanishes with the Lab. "I'll keep him in the car for a while."

We'll need to figure out where the dog is going to stay the night. But I have other things to figure out first, like getting a leash.

My gaze flicks to the icing and sponge carpeting the floor. The room is silent, still, and I call Morgan as he pulls out the drawers. "You can make a cake right?"

"I'm no baker of wedding cakes." Morgan crosses his arms over the chef's coat, his brown skin glistening in the light. He doesn't need to take off his chef's hat for me to know his hair is more gray than black. He's been our chef most of my life. "Not to the standard Mrs. Kress expects for a wedding."

"I can bake the cake." Zuri steps up, looking at me with sincerity, and as my heart starts beating wildly, I almost forget what we're discussing until she speaks again. "I took a wedding-cake class once."

"This is a wedding cake we're talking about." Mom wrings her hands, shaking her head, disapproving.

"I want Zuri to make the cake." Hope clasps Zuri's hand, smiling. "The girls and I will help."

"As long as it's not a boxed cake." Mom yields, her gaze darting between me, the disaster, and Zuri.

"That's if you all have a grocery and hobby store. Point me there so I can get the supplies."

I nod. "I'll drive you."

"Can we go now?"

She's serious, so I glance at the stove. It's seven thirty. "The hobby store might be closed, but the grocery store is probably open."

"If I can get the cakes baked tonight, they'll have time to cool. Then tomorrow we can focus on frosting and decorating."

I block out everyone's words as I walk toward Zuri and catch the keys Gavin tosses me. Several voices shout out thanks to Zuri for the attempt. My mom, doubtful, claims she'll still try to call Delia's Bakery to see if they can make a cake on short notice. The bakery is thirty miles from Pleasant View, so I doubt her solution will work.

Zuri is our main plan—my whole plan.

In the hallway, I take her hand and stop walking. She halts. Her long maxi dress flows around her ankles with her movement and fits her trim figure in all the right places.

"I don't like when you ghost me." I use the words she used when I created a distance between us.

"I haven't ignored your calls." She looks at me with those guileless eyes that send my blood thrumming.

"I'm sorry if I said something to upset you." I tuck a loose strand of hair behind her ear, and she shivers. I have no idea what I'm even apologizing about.

"I'm sorry for getting upset for no reason." Her gaze flicks to my mouth before refocusing on my eyes, and I muster all my self-control not to pull her in my arms, snuggle her cuddly body, and kiss her. She rolls her eyes and resumes our walk. "I was a bit jealous. But I'm good now."

Does she mean she's good because she's moved back to our fake status or she's figured out that I like her? I settle for lifting our entwined hands and kissing her fingers. Whatever unfinished business is between us, we might have some time to resolve in the car or during this cake debacle now that she's finally talking to me.

CHAPTER 22

Zuri

My uneven breathing whispers into the silent kitchen as I lean in, my eyes narrowing. Morgan surrendered the kitchen to me—the fleeing chef likely feared repercussions from any association with my task. Now, it's just me and Serafina who flew in with Jeremy's boss this morning. She insisted on assisting, claiming kitchen-support experience from helping her best friend. I squeeze more blue icing from the piping bag.

"It's beautiful." Serafina sighs dreamily. "I can't believe how you're crafting the illusion of a waterfall cascading down the three-tiered cake." She nudges in a fondant rock at its base.

Am I succeeding? Since the two of us smoothly iced it with white fondant earlier, I'm now finishing the artistic aspects. The spacious kitchen island offers ample room for maneuvering as we add the final touches and edible decorations. An itch tampers with my concentration, demanding the use of my already busy hands.

I straighten, place the piping bag on the plate, then rub my wrist against the nagging sensation on my forehead.

Serafina steps away and rubs her back. "Hard to believe it's four twenty already."

"You should sit." I nod toward a stool without mentioning the obvious—the poor girl has been on her feet for hours, *and* she's pregnant. Still so much to do. My gaze sweeps the chaos strewn across the counters. Powdered sugar dusts one area. Bags of sugar, remnants of butter and marzipan, and bottles of vanilla and almond extracts stand among the various baking tools we'd bought. Three hand mixers each rest in their own unwashed mixing bowls, having done their duty crafting the separate frostings and fillings. I could have washed them in between, but I also wanted backup mixers should one of them break or for whatever reason not work.

"Go rest, Serafina. I'm almost done, and I'll clean the mess before the Kresses and their relatives return from the rehearsal dinner."

Last night, on our drive to the grocery market, I called Lexi to send me the video she recorded while I made a practice wedding cake after that class. I also had her text me the recipe from my Rolodex since I hadn't posted the cake or the video on my blog.

"I wish you'd made *my* wedding cake." Serafina slumps against the counter rather than leave. "You're an amazing chef. The Kresses are blessed to have you here, and it's been wonderful to see Jeremy as happy as he is around you."

Is that true? "We had fun last night." I smile at the memory. "Jeremy not only helped me shop but also stayed in the kitchen as we baked the three tiers. He even made me laugh in our rush to get the cakes made to perfection."

We finished the task well after midnight, and I slept in his childhood bedroom. Since Sonya's occupying Gavin's old bedroom, Jeremy slept in one of the vacant guest rooms. Her pursuit of Jeremy slowed since the ski area, which might have something to do with my little tantrum. Plus, Sara's been less invested in pushing them together. Perhaps she's just overshadowed by the wedding preparations, or maybe she fears making me mad before I finish the cake.

I grit my teeth against an itch under my hair cap, a necessary discomfort to prevent any stray hairs from marooning themselves in the cake. Earlier today, Hope and her friends helped acquire the decorations. But, while I had lots of helpers, I encouraged everyone not to miss the rehearsal dinner. I'm capable of managing this final task alone. Besides, part of me would have preferred to work solo at this phase, so if anything went wrong, I could fix it by myself. Of course, I wouldn't mention this to Jeremy's boss's wife, who's starting to feel like a friend. In truth, her presence has saved me hours. She's been incredibly supportive, and her energy and encouragement have really bolstered me.

I reach for the piping bag and lean in again to finish my waterfall before standing back to assess the cake. Moving from one side to the other, I survey the playful cascade accented with ripples and frosty edges to look like movement. My chest expands at the decent creation. "I'm no artist, but this turned out pretty good."

"As a kindergarten teacher, I can't promise I'm the best judge of art." Her laugh rings out. "But I'd say those hours you said you spent looking at the cake picture on Pinterest this morning paid off. It's stunning."

It kinda is. Impressed, I nod, but my eyes narrow. As much as I like the waterfall, should I add or remove something? Unless it's just me wanting perfection, I can't figure out what's amiss.

A shuffle in the hallway makes me jerk.

"They're back already?" I rush to the kitchen, needing to clean.

But rather than panic alongside me, Serafina smiles at someone over my shoulder. "Looks like I'm no longer needed here."

She gives me a little wave and scoots off as I spin around.

Jeremy emerges dressed in jeans and a V-neck navy sweater over a blue shirt. His mischievous smile sends my heart into hyperdrive.

I smile back. It's so hard to be mad at him, especially over my personal insecurities, really.

"As the best man, aren't you supposed to be at the rehearsal dinner?" I shouldn't want him to be anywhere near Sonya since she, too, went to the rehearsal dinner.

"Rehearsals are over, now it's dinner. I had to come and check on you." He stops in front of me. His hand lifts to my jaw, and his fingers brush off remnants of something, powdered sugar perhaps.

Struggling to breathe, I fight the urge to close my eyes.

"How's it going?" His hand drops to his side, and his gaze flicks to the island. "You—wow!"

His low whistle slides out. Amazement gleams in his blue eyes as he takes my hand and leads me to the island. "You made a waterfall cake? *How* did you do that?"

I shrug, my chest expanding as he assesses the cake. "Zee, you should be opening a cake shop instead of a café."

"Have you forgotten the pressure we were under last night?" Wedding-cake bakers, I'm sure, have to deal with deadlines and pressures from demanding clients like Sara, not to mention the women society has termed bridezillas.

"The waterfall is perfect." He points at the olive-green leaves and vines. "I like how they entwine the tiers. It adds a touch of organic detail."

"I hope it complements the watery motif."

"They'll like this better than Mom's original rose-themed cake. A waterfall is more meaningful to them."

"Hope told me to make whatever cake was easier, and I thought of that picture of them in Uganda in front of the waterfall."

"Exactly." He leans in, squinting as if studying something. He then ushers me over, and I move to crouch beside him. Our breaths unite as he points at the brown fondant-crafted stones.

"There's stones around the top tier and at the bottom tier around the waterfall's base. Is there any reason you didn't want to put the stones around the middle tier?"

I slap my forehead with the back of my gloved hand. "*That's* what's missing."

His detailed eye is always needed. It would look better if all tires matched.

I reach for the fondant from the container, the balls I'd rounded, and offer one to Jeremy.

"You should put it on."

His eyes widen. "You want *me* to mess up the cake?"

"You're meticulous. If anything, I'd be the one messing up."

He holds back his hands, and I point to the box of gloves. After he slides on a pair, I hand him the stone, then watch as he places the first stone. He then looks at the design on the other side when I hand him the next stone. While it takes forever, he lines the stones to match the other tiers. Then he steps back with a lopsided grin. "How did I do?"

I nod. "We make a great team."

He steps beside me as we admire the whimsical design.

"We definitely make a great team." He wraps his strong arms around my waist, drawing me in front of him. His smile wobbles, and his voice dips low. "Thank you... for saving me and making the cake on such short notice."

My heart is racing. The way he is looking at me with so much admiration... I part my lips to speak, but the words don't come out, especially when he leans in. Our lips meet, my fingers move to his jaw, and I savor the sensation of his stubble against my palm as he kisses me tenderly and sweetly. His breath of chocolate and something else has me melting into him, and his intoxicating scent makes me forget my tantrum yesterday.

But again, this is Jeremy, unpredictable where love is concerned. He's doubtful one day and confident the next.

We're panting and breathing hard when we pull back. My gloved hands still grip the edge of his shirt, and his arms remain curled around my back.

"You make me feel things"—his forehead rests against mine, and his gruff voice cracks—"things I hadn't in so long."

Is that an admission that he loves me? I dare not assume with Jeremy. I'm already terrified he'll hold onto his promise to end things after Gavin's wedding tomorrow.

"You're giving me mixed signals." I draw back enough to meet his gaze. I must make sure he's over his ex and wants us to make our pretend relationship real.

"I'm scared." His voice is hoarse, and vulnerability shadows his eyes.

"What are you scared of?" I hope not me.

"I really like you, Zee," he whispers, his eyes searching mine. "I just... haven't done relationships since—"

"Hello!"

We hear another voice, voices actually, and we tear apart. Heels click before Sara intrudes. My mind's awhirl. Was Jeremy suggesting he couldn't do relationships despite our chemistry? For a good communicator at company events, he has terrible communication skills in personal matters. I guess, sooner or later, I'll find out if I need to give back the ring. I like my ring though, and I'd hoped by now things would be clear between us.

"You want to help me put the cake topper on?" I nod toward its box. It should be presentable when his mother looks at it.

I don't consider myself emotional, but my chest squeezes as I take in the rustic barn and the hundred or so people seated in the decorative chairs. Perhaps it's the venue's vibe or me making a wedding cake yesterday, but either way, I'm longing for a real love story of my own.

Jeremy slides in next to his brother at the front with candles lining the aisle. His gaze finds mine, and my heart races the way it usually does. He's so handsome—yes, he wears suits all the time, but something about this navy suit and its white-and-yellow boutonniere with baby's breath... Well, it's formal in a way, and the others in the wedding party match him. To his left is Bryce, then Eric—with gray hair at his temples, he appears slightly older than Gavin and Jeremy. Bryce's wife, Liberty, and Eric's wife, Joy, stand on the other side in yellow dresses. In the front row in a fluttery pink dress, I'm seated with Chad and Tessa, also Hope's friends. Her stomach sticks out of her formal cream dress. She's almost six months pregnant. I met Tessa with all the girls two days ago. Then, yesterday, we connected as we shopped for the wedding-cake supplies. Serafina and Logan are seated in a group to our left.

Lights are strung across the lofty open-beamed ceiling and twine around the support posts. I don't have to step outside to know that it's crisp for April, but I don't expect sixty-degree temperatures when, through the window, I can still see snow covering the mountain peaks beneath the setting sun.

The string quartet begins, and we all stand. Hope emerges from a room on the side. Perhaps this is how their ceremony is slightly different? She's walking herself down the aisle, which is good because all eyes are turned to her. Her white gown glimmers under the twinkle lights. Her bouquet is so simple with white and yellow flowers that it's hard to imagine Sara helped select it. And her radiant smile is so vibrant it brings a rush of heat to my eyes as she trains her gaze on her prize—Gavin.

In the two weddings I've been to, the bride emerged from the outside or the back aisle, but it doesn't appear to matter to Gavin, who seems to struggle to keep his composure. His gaze is focused on Hope. Then he walks over to meet her, and they return to the altar together.

We all sit when the music stops and the pastor addresses the couple.

I find myself digging for a tissue from my handbag as the pastor talks about the three-strand cord that can't be broken. God is the gold cord between Gavin and Hope's marriage. "'Love is patient ….'" The pastor voices the familiar verse in 1 Corinthians 13, and now more than ever, it makes sense.

A tingling sensation heats my eyes, and my gaze flickers to the happy couple who have eyes only for each other. I think Jeremy has looked at me like that before, or was it all my imagination? Now, tears blur my vision as my gaze drags to Gavin's right, to Jeremy. He's looking at me right now.

Despite the heated looks and kisses we've shared, he's wishy-washy. I can't blame him. His ex didn't leave him much room for trust, and I'm the first woman he's sort of dated since Sonya, even if it's not for real. I twist the ring on my finger, a reminder of the bubble I've lived in for the last two and a half months or so. It's about to pop as soon as Hope and Gavin say I do. How am I supposed to get back to the real world?

I try to focus on the bride and the wedding party as the pastor announces them as a couple and grants Gavin permission to kiss his bride. I clap with everyone else.

Throughout the family and group photos, I compose myself and engage with the girls, including Serafina, who seems well acquainted with Hope and all their friends. My gaze keeps drifting to Sonya. Tall, poised, and chic, she's everything I'm not. Dressed in a stylish cream dress with her wavy hair cascading down her shoulders, she's as stunning as the models on magazine covers displayed at checkout stands. When she laughs, revealing her straight white teeth, she blends seamlessly into Jeremy's family and circle of friends. *She* belongs. And me? I'm his fake fiancée.

A chill tingles over me. I've been presumptuous in thinking Jeremy would choose someone like me to take Sonya's place. In terms of looks and wealth, I'm not in his league. So, unless he makes it clear he wants more from our façade, I can't assume he's fallen for me.

My melancholy takes residence as the night goes on. The photos taken, they bring in tables and rearrange the chairs, but I've lost my appetite. The bride and groom cut the cake and feed each other the first bites. As people eat cake, the girls and Jeremy compliment me. I attempt a taste to get an idea if I baked a decent cake. Yeah, it turned out pretty good.

Jeremy does a great job with his speech, and I tear up when his voice cracks as he praises his brother, his role model. "I'm confident

Gavin will be the perfect husband and Hope the perfect wife for him."

Several people blow their noses, me as well. Even Sara, seated at the corner table on the first row, dabs a tissue to her eyes. Gavin and Jeremy's dad nods, seeming proud of his sons.

If I didn't rely on a ride from Jeremy, I would've left before the dance, but of course, he offers a silent invitation to the dance floor. My heart races, and I grit my teeth. He has such an effect on me, yet tonight, our relationship ends.

I shiver when his palm rests on my waist, pulling me into an orbit of warmth and closeness. I feel so safe and secure in his embrace. My heart aches, and my arms wrap around him as if I can hold onto this moment, this memory.

"Is everything okay?" he whispers in my ear, causing me to stiffen. I refuse to showcase my emotional attachment. Jeremy dislikes clinginess, the kind Sonya has demonstrated these past few days.

"I think I need to catch up on sleep." I shudder against his shoulder. I'll be staying alone at Hope's house tonight. It's good because I can cry it out but also bad because my singleness will be the only thing consuming my mind.

"It's been a long week." His fingers caress my back, smoothing along the layers of my strapless pink dress. "As soon as the dance is over, I can drive you."

"Let's stay until the bride and groom leave." I whisper in his ear. I wouldn't want to take him away from his brother's ceremony.

He doesn't say much to me the rest of the night. He's probably sensed my withdrawal. We make a tunnel outside, and cold air seeps into my bare shoulders as we throw confetti over the bride and groom. Their smiles are broad beneath the fairy lights.

Then a coat drapes over me, and warmth embraces me as Jeremy whispers. "You need this more than I do."

"Thanks." Loud claps cover my response as the couple hurries into the limousine.

Minutes later, Jeremy and I are in the car as he drives me back to Hope's house.

"Are you sure you're okay?" he asks, his gaze on the winding road.

I ease off his coat, already missing the scent of him as I put it on the back of my seat. There's no need to wait any longer. So I also slide off the ring and tuck it in the console. "I'll leave your ring here."

"Oh!" Is he surprised? It's hard to see his face as we drive the mountain road. The headlights guiding our path only reveal his silhouette. "I bought the ring for you."

"But our agreement ends today." *Unless you want to change the terms?* I hold my breath, almost expecting him to say something. But he doesn't, and I won't be that girl clinging to him if he doesn't want me.

"If you say so."

He doesn't say anything else until he parks in the driveway and comes around the car. The ranch-style homes aren't far from each other. All are vibrant with light, save for the silence that indicates everyone is in bed.

He still opens the car door for me, but unlike the other times when he hovers closely, he steps far from the door as I step out this time.

"'Nite," he whispers, and I manage a thank you. As I walk toward the door, I sense him looking at me, but I don't look back. I punch in the code, and the beep signals.

As soon as I close the door, I toss my clutch bag and lean my head against the door. My heart thunders as fear invades me. I've made the worst decision to hand back the ring.

But I can't be clingy. Jeremy needs to use his words and not have me guessing whether he's in the mood to want me or not. I run a hand through my hair and groan. "What have I done God?"

If I'd asked God *before* I started playing this façade, would things be different now?

CHAPTER 23

Zuri

Squinting against the screen's glow, I reread the financial spreadsheets Jeremy crafted last month outlining my café's future. I don't have to scroll back to two months ago to look at the projections he'd made for the remodel, mostly taking down the wall. I had to pay the architect and laborers, expenses I hadn't expected I'd be responsible for given that I didn't own the building. But it wasn't on the company's agenda to change the appearance of my café, so that was fair. Good thing Jeremy invested in the café.

I skim the current list to the additional refrigerator for cold teas and calorie-free beverages, the artisan bakery supplies, and the employee start-up payments, all of which came to mind later when Jeremy brought it to my attention.

Then I read the four necessary insurances we added to the café's expenses. General liability, product liability, workers' comp, and business interruption. I hadn't anticipated any kind of insurance plan when I drafted what I needed for the business, but man, it's a must.

With the grand opening a week away, doubt gnaws at me. What was I thinking when I took on a huge business venture?

Tomorrow, I'll be meeting with the servers. Some are former employees of Carol's Café, who agreed to stay on and work for me. I had to persuade a couple of them with a slight increase in their hourly pay, especially since the prolonged reopening left them out of work for months. It only worked out for them to wait for me because one of them tutors international students at night, and the other works virtually as a telemarketer during the night shift.

I scroll with the mouse, reading the list, and smile as I remember that Jeremy insisted on buying two registers and a computer dedicated to online orders. We have another employee to man the website and focus on the online orders, which will come in handy once customers embrace online ordering.

I click at the top to open another tab for my blog. A blank page I'd opened intending to share the café's updates, but I don't feel like typing anything today.

Even with background music to lull the silence, the house feels emptier than before.

The computer displays four fifty-five. Damien and my friends should be back from work soon. I breathe out, staring at the blog's blank page, a mirror of the void I've been feeling since Jeremy and I returned to our lives. The whole façade is behind us, and I hope we are still friends because the café has Jeremy's fingerprints all over it.

It's been an entire week after our silent flight back when he worked on his laptop while I watched a movie. Flying first class should've been a great experience, but I couldn't enjoy it while seated next to Jeremy and acting like we were strangers.

I open another tab, now I have five of them open. Maybe it's time to share something on my Facebook page—I haven't posted a picture in ages.

I shift in the stool, having no desire to scroll through the folder to find what post to share.

The garage rumbles open. My friends must be home. And soon, they barrel into the house, chatting. Damien is arguing with Olivia about some financial thing I don't have the energy to try to understand.

"What are we cooking for dinner?" Lexi asks.

Damien glances my way, setting his computer bag on the nearby table.

"I haven't even thought about dinner." I close my laptop. "Let's order takeout."

He frowns. "We've had takeout for the last five days."

Olivia tosses her handbag on the island and wiggles onto a barstool. "I don't mind takeout."

"It adds up if we eat out all the time." Damien yanks his tucked-in shirt from his pants, follows Lexi to the pantry, and snatches a cereal box.

"We can cook pasta," Lexi says.

I shrug. "Cereal for dinner isn't bad." Yep, I've lost the desire to whip up meals. As odd as it seems, every time I cook, it brings back memories of Jeremy and our times in the kitchen. I slide my computer into its bag. I'm done working for the day too—not that I've accomplished anything. "How was work?"

"Where would you like me to start?" Lexi shakes Corn Flakes into a bowl. "Shall I rant about my boss or rave about the cool house I'll be house-sitting in two weeks?"

"As long as you're not house-sitting for six weeks this time." I slip my arm around her and rest my head against her shoulder. "I need all my friends around as I wallow for the next however many days."

"I got the Analyst of the Month," Olivia pipes up, and I congratulate her. 'The funniest part was getting to throw a pie in Jeremy's face. It's a tradition—for the annual pie war, the March analyst gets to throw a pie at the COO's face."

My mind rushes to Jeremy and our kitchen food wars. I fight the urge to ask how he's been doing this week. Has he missed me as much as I've missed him? I swallow all the questions and set the computer bag at my feet, slumping further onto the stool.

Damien pours two bowls of cereal, slides one to Olivia, then nudges me. "You want any?"

I shake my head.

A silence settles with the hum of the fridge as my friends pray, then resume eating.

"What happened between you and Jeremy?" Damien's question catches me off guard, and I blink.

"Did he say anything? Of course nothing."

His brows rise. "You'd better tell me what he did. Otherwise, I'm gonna confront him tomorrow."

"Damien!" I slap the island. "You can't fight my battles." My secret presses a heavy weight on me. "He didn't do nothing."

"You've been down ever since you came back from that stupid trip. Kress has been acting strange around me—guilty or something." He raises his hands. Then his gaze flicks to my ring finger. "You haven't been flaunting that ring around either. You're gonna tell me what happened?"

The girls are silent, acting almost guilty, and I clasp my hands together. It's long past time I come clean.

I blow out air as I'll need a deep inhale. "Jeremy and I had made an arrangement. He needed a fiancée..." The words fly out of my mouth fast as I focus on the ceiling, clearly needing divine intervention.

"You mean you two were faking it?" It's Damien's turn to slap the island.

I jolt, and the cereal bowls shake.

Olivia winces.

So Damien pivots to her. "You knew about this?"

She doesn't answer.

When he asks Lexi, she raises both hands. "Don't include me in sibling issues. I like you both, and I still need a place to stay... so."

"Yes, I told them not to tell you." The words are slow and painful as I drag them out of my mouth. "You didn't like Jeremy in the first place. I didn't think you'd be on board with it."

"You think I'm all for being lied to?" Damien's chest rises, then falls. The depth of disappointment as he looks at Olivia slices through my heart. He must be hurt that his best friend kept this from him.

"It's me you should blame," I say, but it doesn't make things any better.

He pushes back from the island, seeming not hungry anymore, leaving his cereal untouched as his sullen gaze sweeps over us. "You *all* decided to keep me in the dark?"

His pained voice makes me ache. I'm so disappointed in myself. Ugh, I'm such a terrible person. How does God put up with people like me?

"Jeremy told me to tell you, but..." I shake my head, needing to make sure he doesn't go attacking Jeremy over this.

"I can't believe this." He fists his hands into tight balls and walks to the dining table to grab his computer bag. "You could've told me you needed funds for your business."

He's forgetting he has looming college funds to pay for. Now isn't the time to remind him of that.

"You can't keep taking care of me. I didn't want you to know about my needs."

He shakes his head, then goes to the hall, and heads upstairs.

We stare at each other. Olivia's shoulders drop, and her gaze lowers to the cereal. "I should've told him."

"I know." I dragged everyone into my lies.

"He tells me everything, and I kept this big thing from him." Olivia plants a hand on her cheek.

Great. I've caused strife in their friendship.

We're sitting in silence, Lexi munching her cereal and Olivia staring at her bowl when Damien returns. Gone are his work clothes, exchanged for jeans and a black hoodie. He snatches the car keys from the counter.

"You're leaving?" Olivia hops up, wringing her hands.

"I'll be back at ten." He doesn't bother to look at us.

I know better than to attempt to talk to him when he's upset, so does Olivia. I'll reason with him after he cools down tonight.

The back door slams. Olivia pulls flour from the pantry, then swings open more cabinets. "Chocolate chip cookies are perfect for dinner."

Lexi lifts another spoonful to her mouth, then wags the empty spoon at our friend. "I get it—you and your bestie had a falling out. But cookies for dinner are not going to cut it."

Regardless, we end up settling for Olivia's cookies and cereal for dinner.

With Damien still mad at us the next day, he drives his car, leaving Olivia and Lexi to drive separately. Olivia is barely talking to me either. Until things work out with her and Damien, our friendship will be on edge.

I hold it together as I meet with my employees. Instead of the three I'd thought, Jeremy insisted I start with five and let one go later should I realize I don't need that much help. I've made that clear to the fifth hire. We go through our objectives and strategies for next week.

After the meeting, I linger in hopes Jeremy will show up. Of course, he doesn't.

The end of the day isn't much different at home, except it's worse when the girls return and we talk about dinner plans.

"Damien went on a date with Jessie." Olivia drags out the words, her hands resting on her chin. "Good for him."

I sip my kombucha, another memory of Jeremy now. "Damien's not listening to me here at home. I'll make his favorite meal at the café tomorrow and bring it to his office. Perhaps then he'll listen to me."

"This little fight gave him enough courage to ask her out." Olivia snatches celery from the plate Lexi just slid on the table. She then chomps. "Who cares."

Yep, she's upset about Damien's cold shoulder. Or is she more bothered about Jessie spending time with Damien today?

Olivia eyes the oven. "I feel like baking something."

"Why do you think I pulled out some healthy snacks?" Lexi smirks and bites into a carrot. "Okay, guys, we're all sad, but can we not eat cookies again for dinner?"

She then snatches her phone and scrolls through. "I'm ordering us salads and maybe we can have some ice cream after." As she takes command, we don't argue. "Now might be a good day to drag you both rock climbing with me."

"No rock climbing for me." Olivia rolls her eyes.

While I could learn rock climbing, I don't feel like it now. "I already had my adventures for the year." Skiing being one of them.

Lexi's dinner salad works out perfectly. Several minutes later, we've showered, changed into our jammies, and settled on the sofa to eat our salads in front of the TV. We're laughing as we watch one of our favorite office comedies, *The Dynamic*.

When we finish eating, I take everyone's plate to the kitchen and return with a tub of vanilla ice cream. Not wanting the cold to seep into my hand, I keep the container in a bowl to hold it since I'm seated between Olivia and Lexi.

"I can understand why Olivia has thrown herself into this wallowing frenzy." Lexi reaches for her spoon to scoop ice cream from the container, then shakes the spoon at me. "I still don't understand why you had to give Jeremy back the ring."

"Keeping a secret from your brother was all for nothing." Olivia scoops a glob of ice cream. "I'd hoped you and Jeremy weren't pretending anymore, and we wouldn't have anything to lie about."

"I thought so too." I barely have the energy to eat this frozen treat as I repeat what I told them days ago. "I need to hear the words from him. I can't keep getting caught up in this game of back and forth."

I scoop the ice cream, and the creamy concoction melts comforting sweetness into my tongue. My gaze remains on the screen at the boss as I assure Olivia that, before the end of tomorrow, she and Damien will reconcile their friendship.

"I finally found Cracker Jacks at a convenience store." Olivia mentions her apology offering to Damien, stirring an idea for me too. "I asked Nadia to help me leave them on his desk after he left. He should see it first thing in the morning."

"Tomorrow is Friday. He can't hold a grudge all weekend." A spark of optimism lights up my thoughts. Hmm... I know the perfect apology meal. "I'm going to give that new toaster a test run."

I jitter a bit, more from anticipation over tomorrow's culinary adventure than from the sugar rush. Still, I scoop up more ice cream, its coolness soothing on my tongue.

With my plan in motion at the café the next afternoon, I'm juggling several tasks while grilling the perfect loaded cheese sandwich. Then, just as perfection seems within reach, I burn it and set off the fire alarm. Its shrill blare ushers the entire building's employees into the parking lot—a less-than-ideal advertisement for my café to potential customers.

Not to mention this is the last way I want to face Jeremy again. He's probably glad to be rid of me—nothing more than a short jot in his ledgers. But I've got to get over this. I seldom had self-worth issues before his wishy-washy ways—talk about the perfect concoction for stewing a girl in doubt.

I stiffen my spine and grind my teeth. I'm done letting him or my past boyfriend or even my silly mistakes like today's debacle define who I am. I may have set off the fire alarm, but I'm a good chef and—as Olivia said—I am beautiful, confident, and me. Qualities no one else can claim. *Plus*, I'm about to realize my vocational dreams. What more can anyone ask for?

Sure, I'd love to know if he's part of my future recipe, but with or without him, I'm ready to cook up whatever comes my way.

CHAPTER 24

Jeremy

With the employee parking lot behind our glass building in a flurry, we await permission to return indoors. "I'd hoped to tackle some tasks before our meeting," the IT manager beside me comments. I offer her a sympathetic nod, but my focus shifts, propelled by whispers that Zuri is the catalyst for today's unplanned exodus.

Beneath the thick gray sky, I survey the displaced employees, searching for Zuri. There she is. Standing apart from the crowd, she's wearing a simple white blouse that makes her seem almost ethereal against the foggy backdrop. She wipes her hands on her dark jeans, head bowed, and engages in a discussion with a fireman stationed in front of the fire truck. Despite the distance, her apologetic posture tugs my heart.

Witnessing her in such a vulnerable state stirs a whirlwind of emotions. She must be grappling with embarrassment and regret after triggering a building-wide evacuation. With her culinary prowess, the toaster-oven mishap—as highlighted by one fireman—likely stemmed from an adventurous attempt at a new recipe, rather than the ones on the café's menu.

The impulse to cross the parking lot, wrap her in a comforting embrace, and reassure her that mistakes are part of life nearly overwhelms me. After all, no one was harmed, and no one is perfect.

That's not all I would like to tell her, though. Before she came into my life, I was content in my solitude, navigating life with a comfortable, predictable rhythm. Like a figure missing or added to a spreadsheet, her presence realigned the way I calculated my existence. Now, I'm not sure how I ever found satisfaction in my former normal.

If only I could've relayed how I felt before she handed the ring back to me.

"It's safe now." A firefighter by the fire truck blasts the megaphone announcement. "You can now get back into the building."

Zuri is one of the first people to disappear through the side door. Now, with the many people between us, I'm left battling how to get to her. I breathe in the midafternoon breeze as people return to the building.

When I return to my office, Jill is making her way to her desk, then instead rushes toward me. She waves a hand for me to keep walking as she trails me. "I'll follow you to your office. I know, once you get behind that seat, you won't want to talk about personal matters."

I stop inside and turn to Jill, now hovering at the entrance. "I'm already in my office." I'm also already aware of what she's going to say, so I raise my hand to stop her. But that doesn't ever stop this woman from speaking her mind if she believes it serves me right. Which I don't mind since she has my best interests at heart.

"This is my last time talking about Zuri." As her southern twang drawls, I have no choice but to listen when she grinds me about Zuri and why she hasn't come by lately. "If you didn't do anything to end things with her, why can't you do something to make her notice you?"

I drag out a breath, push up my sleeves, and stare at my persistent assistant. After three days without lunch deliveries from Zuri or her spontaneous pop-ins, Jill became suspicious by last Friday. While I see no need to tell her we were in a fake relationship, I explained we were taking a break. "I already said, she's busy launching her café. Next week is the grand opening."

She plants a hand on her hip, the button of her black blazer almost popping from the hole. "Don't tell me you plan to work on Monday when your fiancée has a grand opening."

I've entertained the idea of taking Monday off. Or would it be imposing on Zuri if I act too seriously about this whole relationship thing?

"I have a meeting to get ready for." I wave to Jill while internally acknowledging I have to do something, even if I'm not sure how to approach this delicate matter.

"The department heads won't blame you if you show up a few minutes late." She remains planted there as if saying what she's saying is more important. "Plus, that meeting is an hour away."

Right. If I want to end this lecture, I have to play along. So I thank her for the advice.

When she leaves, I sit on my desk chair. The refrigerator hum imitates my turmoil. My gaze drifts to the picture on my desk. Zuri and me when we met. I'm not ready to part with it yet. It's a snapshot of a moment that now feels like a lifetime ago. Her smile and the way we fit into each other's opposite worlds only deepens the somber mood that's taken hold of me since we decided to go our separate ways. Her absence invades every space in my office, even my penthouse, although she hasn't ever been at my house. She still dominates my mind when I close my eyes. I can almost smell her perfume on me constantly. Somehow, a huge hole has punctured my heart, the gap of her absence. Until now, I didn't realize I had quite an, um, active imagination, to say the least.

Work has always been my constant companion. It got me through my separation from Sonya. But this is *Zuri* we're talking about. My supposed future and not my past.

I open my drawer, and I pull out the velvet ring box again housing her ring. Funny, I still had the box from the day I proposed. After I slid the ring on her hand, the box stayed in my pocket.

As the diamond sparkles in the sunlight streaming through the windows, I smile. My chest swells at how accurately I picked out her ring. It fit her perfectly, and she didn't have to resize it. This ring belongs to her, and her alone.

After putting back the ring in my drawer, I reach for my phone. The selfie I took on our fake-engagement day stares at me, more real than the ruse I'd assumed we would carry on. I'd saved it as my background in case Mom somehow got ahold of my phone during our visit home. That part succeeded so well, and I think

Mom believed us. Sonya backed off, Zuri and I went our separate ways, and it all worked out as intended. Only, by then, I no longer wanted *the plan* to work—I wanted *us* to work.

Now, for reality, I need to take some crucial steps.

Zuri is as real to me now as she was the day I slid that ring on her finger.

It's been almost twenty minutes since the fire-drill fiasco. I have a legit excuse to text her. I need to know how she's feeling.

Jeremy: Rumor has it you burned down the café.

My phone dings a response so soon that my chest warms. Her name on the screen looks just right. I swipe to read her text.

Zuri: What a way to start a business. Does a business advisor carry some of the blame?

I smile. At least she still has her humor.

Jeremy: I just wanted to see if you're okay.

My thumb hovers. Should I add anything else? I've never been one to text long messages, and what I need to say to her is longer than any balance sheet. Soon, those promising three dots appear then vanish, then appear then vanish. This happens several times before the message arrives.

Zuri: I'm okay. Are you?

I scratch my jaw. Now how to answer that.

A knock on my door has me spinning toward it. Damien emerges, lurking at the door this time rather than storming in the way he usually does. He's probably decided to respond to my email in person rather than emailing me back.

"You got a minute?"

I nod and place my phone face down on the desk. Then I shift into my leather chair. "Have you decided whether to take that job or not?"

He doesn't need a week to think about it if he wants a promotion.

"While I don't think I'm qualified to take on the role of regional manager, I'm not here to discuss the job." His eyes hooded, he crosses his arms. "Thanks for thinking about me, but the position also involves you training me. So, first, we'd better settle our personal issues."

He can receive training from the previous manager, but if I train him myself, he'll know what I expect from him, rather than having to learn as he goes. "If you're interested, make sure to send your application to HR by next Friday. It's a competitive position."

He sucks in a breath before drawing it out. "I'm here to talk about Zuri."

A knot tightens my stomach, my defenses going up. "Damien—"

"Don't even start with me about your office not being the place for personal talk." He shakes his head and puts on that firm leadership persona he'll need should he be the regional manager.

I have no choice but to lean my hands on the desk and give him a few minutes of my time. "I have a meeting in"—I glance at my watch—"thirty minutes."

"Why did you do it?"

I can't pretend not to know what he's talking about.

"My sister is miserable, and if you were just acting around her, then you had no right to make her fall for the wrong guy."

I palm the back of my neck, my muscles tensing. "You said it yourself. I'm not the right person for your sister."

Perhaps I'm also seeking Damien's approval. Still, I can't look at him, so I face the window. The city is active now, near lunchtime.

"Do you like Zuri or not?"

At his question, my gaze jerks his way, unbidden. His nostrils flare, and his pain is a gut punch, forcing me to confront the situation.

"From the start, it was... complicated." I move my hand on the desktop, needing to stay busy, and reach for my pen beside the keyboard. "The day I slid the ring on her finger, everything clicked. I saw myself spending the rest of my life with her."

Emotion lodges in my throat, and I struggle to talk around it. So, I tap my pen on my chin, not daring to look at him and reveal how deep I'd fallen. I'm the boss here, and breaking down in front of my employee won't go in the books.

"At least, you asked her to tell me the truth." He smirks. "You know she almost burned down the building making me a reconciliation sandwich." Damien mentions the dispute he had with Zuri over the lie, and I feel responsible. However, his relaxed demeanor reassures me he's no longer mad at his sister. I can already picture her thoughtfulness in making things right with him—with everyone if she had her way.

"Zuri with her reconciliation meals." A chuckle escapes my lips. She'd brought me a meal to reconcile the day my mom showed up.

I miss those days when we had lunch together. My lunches lately have been hit or miss. Today, at least, I'll have lunch with the department heads as we review progress and discuss new objectives for the company strategies.

"What are you going to do about it?" His question draws my gaze to him. His expression softens, and that's a big deal. But I'm still not prepared for the hint of his smile that follows. "You're in love with my sister. But have you made it clear you love her, or are you waiting for her to come here and hand-feed you her feelings?"

His question hangs in the air, and I barely hear his farewell as he walks out. No doubt, what I feel for Zuri is love. With her, I experienced emotions I never experienced with anyone.

She's a chef with a loose schedule, and I'm the guy who always has a plan. But we make a great team. Our conversations flow. Even when we flew back in silence, I felt comfortable just because she was seated next to me. With her, I feel respected, understood, and valued.

My chest rises, and so do I as I pull to stand. I have a meeting soon, which I intend to make, but I need to see Zuri before she leaves. I step out of my office.

Jill tips her chin toward the conference table beyond the watercooler. "Marino got here early."

"Perfect." I walk over to where I usually meet with the department heads for in-person meetings. Perhaps Nico can lead the meeting until I get here. I call out as I near the table, and he looks up from his laptop. Frowning.

"Let me guess. You haven't talked to her yet." He trains his eyes on me, seeming disappointed after his and Wes's prep talk on Sunday. "I thought I had problems."

"I didn't realize you're so eager for the meeting." I stop him from talking about Zuri.

He leans back and drapes a hand over the back of his chair. "You'll never guess what I got myself into." He nods a few times. With that grin he's got going, I might be here for a while, but I still want to know.

"You decided to run for president?" I snicker. "Now that would be something for someone who wasn't born in America."

"This is even crazier." He emphasizes crazier. "I finally agreed to my rock-climbing instructors' plan for this blind date she's been nagging me about." He lifts his hands, shaking his head. "I didn't realize I was that optimistic, but seriously, do people still go on blind dates?"

"I was fake dating. Didn't know such a thing existed until I went for it." Now I'm in love, and I have to tell him about my plan. "I gotta go talk to Zuri. Can we talk about your blind date later?"

I then request he run the meeting until I return. Jill usually sends out the agenda to the team before the meeting.

"When's lunch delivered anyway?" Nico checks his laptop screen as if he hasn't heard my urgency and request. But he must've because he waves me off. "Go get the girl already!"

***

My palms sweat as I step into the café's open-air front room with tables arranged under the new overhead lights. Cheery artwork depicts people gathered around dining tables or laughing alongside displays of fresh fruit and vegetables. I navigate the rows between seating arrangements, my chest swelling, my pride not only for Zuri's realized dream but also for my small part in her journey.

But the unmistakable hint of burnt bread undermines the smell of new furniture and a faint smell of fresh paint. As I approach the kitchen door, trickling water boosts my hope. She's there. Not long ago, she guided me back there to prepare our dinner as we discussed our fake arrangement. Little did we both know her invitation into her world would unlock my heart.

Hesitation grips me at the threshold, and a battle between hope for the future and fear of the unknown anchors my feet.

Zuri stands by the sink, washing her hands, her gaze fixed on a to-do list on the nearby corkboard. The AC kicks on, and its breeze wafts in, tousles her short curls, and highlights the simple appeal of her maroon leggings and black top. Gone are her jeans and white top. The outfit effortlessly accentuates her hourglass form. She's breathtaking. My breath catches.

She turns off the faucet, and I clear my throat to make my presence known. Still, she jumps a bit, turning around. Her hands, dripping water, clutch at her heart as she gasps. "Jer!"

Warmth floods me at her familiar endearment. Jer. I've longed to hear it, to be near her. I should've brought her ring with me. I want it back on her finger where it belongs.

We both stand frozen, locked in each other's gaze, absorbing the sight of one another. If only looks could satisfy my longing as I take in her doe-brown eyes, so sweet and innocent.

My chest heaves with each breath, my mind racing yet blank—no prepared speech comes to mind. But perhaps, at this moment, words are unnecessary.

Still, I clear my throat. She's waited too long for me to voice my mind. "When you walked into my office three months ago with that apology meal, I was famished. The aroma alone distracted me from my wait for someone else, a different woman I'd planned to rope into being my fake fiancée for the wedding." How that other woman has faded into insignificance! "She's a distant memory now, and her face barely registers. But I had described to Jill the 'perfect woman' I expected that day."

A light laugh escapes as I recall the miraculous turn of events. "Jill sent the other woman away before you arrived, claiming she didn't fit the description I'd outlined. Then you showed up, the stunning woman I'd described. You, not her, were meant to walk through that door."

"I call it divine intervention." She shakes a finger at me, and her smile, so infectious and warm, lights up her features. "And to think, you weren't even supposed to be at that party. Remember how I practically slammed the door in your face?"

"Yet you invited me before you even knew me."

With a shrug that belies her kindness, she confesses. "Damien was skeptical you'd come. But I pushed for your invitation. I saw an opportunity for him—and perhaps for me—"

"To see a side of me hidden from the world." I take a slow step forward. "You always see the good in everyone, Zee. Despite any preconceptions Damien may have shared, you chose to see beyond them."

"Food gatherings have a way of breaking down walls."

But I'm letting her steer the conversation away from what I fear to say. I dare not do that again. A deep breath drags out my innermost confession.

"You shouldn't have given me the ring back." My voice lowers to a whisper as my trembling hands seek refuge in my pockets to stay concealed.

"But you mentioned after the wedding—"

"That was before I knew you, before I spent time with you and realized what I was missing." Before the pivotal moment in our relationship. "There were no rehearsed lines the day I proposed to you on the rooftop. Yet, looking into your eyes, brimming with hope and trust, I found myself envisioning our future together."

Why did I ever think this would be hard to say? The truth pours from me now.

"The calmness you instill in me overwhelms my senses, compelling my words to spill freely. Your faith and sincerity inspire me." I advance toward her, and the warmth emanating from her smile suffuses my being, a sensation that sends joy spiraling through me. My chest warms. "Whenever you're upset because of me, I feel lost and empty."

As I take another step, she mirrors my movement, closing the distance between us. With each step forward, my words flow more effortlessly, driven by the truth in my heart.

"I'm compelled to step away from my desk so I can spend time with you." I'm tempted to skip the upcoming meeting. "But more than anything, I like you so much—I can't imagine going back to a life without you in it."

She presses a hand to my cheek, closing the gap entirely. "The main reason I agreed to this fake arrangement was because I liked you from the start. I love you, Jeremy Kress."

I sweep her into my arms, lifting her off her feet.

"We're in luck, Zee." Breathing in her essence, I set her down and cup the softness of her chin. "Because I'm in love with you too, and this time, it's not just temporary."

At last—oh, at long last—I kiss her, investing all my pent-up emotion and excitement into the moment. She kisses me back, and relief washes over me—relief and gratitude for having found someone to love who loves me back. No doubt, Zuri is mine permanently.

EPILOGUE

Zuri

Abuzz with chatter and activity, the café is now as real as my engagement. I stand back, savoring the unreal sensation as people walk in or out, food bags in hand, my café logo displayed on the reusable bags.

Despite my reluctance to broadcast the opening on social media, the little I mentioned on my blog has drawn a surprising crowd, enough to escalate my heart rate as I weave between tables, ensuring every guest feels welcomed.

I steer clear of the cash register, given my desire to be everywhere at once, and instead, walk to a table close to the door where a middle-aged couple hovers by the entrance. In a navy pantsuit, she checks behind the door, perhaps reading the sign. They might be looking for an office in the building.

"Hello." I give a little wave, and they look at me. "Are you here to have lunch?"

The woman brandishes a flyer. "Is this Zuri's Daylight Café?"

"Yes, it is." Smiling, I introduce myself as the owner.

The man gestures toward the paper, then nudges his charcoal jacket aside to tuck his hands into the pockets of his tan pants. He rocks back on his heels as he cranes around. "My wife and I own Local Lens, a media company for small business owners."

The woman steps forward. "The COO of Stone Financial Enterprises dedicated his March financial advice column, which usually focuses on debt management and financial planning, to talk about this café instead. We'd like to schedule a time to talk about your café and your cookbook."

Stone Financial's COO. Jer. I grin.

"Jeremy Kress often leads free workshops and seminars on financial wellness. He's a great supporter of local entrepreneurs and innovators," she explains.

"Our media company wouldn't be in business if it weren't for him," the man chimes in.

"He supports small businesses?" This newfound aspect of the man I've grown so fond of further captivates me.

Listening to the couple recount the annual challenges and competitions Jeremy organizes in partnership with their media company—offering funding, mentorship, and publicity for entrepreneurs—astounds me. I always knew Jeremy was kind, but his humility kept this detail from me. As my respect and affection further deepen, my chest swells. All this time he's been silently supporting and rooting for me, even from behind the scenes.

"Thanks for coming." I welcome them inside and direct them toward the line to take orders. "Once you've placed your order and paid, feel free to find a spot to sit." I glance over the crowd, skeptical of finding an empty seat. "That's if you'd like to dine in."

As passionate as I still am about making the café a place for people like Damien and Jeremy to step away from their desks when it's mealtime, implementing online orders and designated pickup times has been a game-changer. It's allowed us to efficiently prepare and pack meals, so at least those people who can't—or won't—take time out for lunch will be getting good food, not skipping meals.

Thanks to the employees of Stone Financial and other nearby offices, the café has been bustling since ten thirty, even before our official opening time. Opting to open the doors thirty minutes early seemed a kindness rather than letting our eager patrons wait outside. Good thing I've planned our regular hours to start at seven a.m.

When I return to the kitchen, Jeremy's voice rings out, directing Lexi to the cash register. "We can't keep customers waiting. Use Zee's phone for the app to process payments."

"I'm mostly here to take pictures." Despite her protest, Lexi sets her camera aside on the counter's far corner and takes my phone from Jeremy to man the register.

Nico calls out for a server to pass him a disposable container, ladles pasta into it, and hands it over. "We have to move fast."

Wes flips sandwiches on the griddle, and Nina oversees quesadillas, while Damien and Olivia are tasked with the southwest rolls, packaging them as orders come in. Jill monitors the incoming online orders, relaying them as they're keyed in at the register.

Everyone is unified in their green aprons, adorned with cooking utensils and the café's name—a thoughtful gift from Jeremy just two days prior.

I search for where I might be of use, but everyone has their responsibilities well in hand.

"Is it slowing down out there?" Smiling, Jeremy passes covered containers toward the counter.

"I heard you're the reason for the crowd today." I refer to the couple from Local Lens.

"Don't believe all the rumors." He winks, sending a flutter through me.

"It looks like I'll need to hire two more people." I whisper to Jeremy, struggling to hide my awe over the café's popularity.

"You're not wrong." Nico calls out from the stove, always alert and observant. "We can't play hooky and skip work every day."

"Thank you so much, everyone." I raise my voice above the clamor, my gratitude enveloping each team member.

"Jeremy left us no choice," Wes interjects. "But he promised us two hours off early tomorrow for working late tonight."

Damien, my friends, and Jeremy all took today off to support the café's bustling opening. Jeremy's dedication is particularly palpable. He he even stayed late last night to assist with the final preparations.

"Let's hustle, let's hustle." He claps his hands and moves around as if born for this role. I assist him in passing the food to the counter as orders flood in, maintaining our rhythm until the pace begins to slow.

We keep moving. I flit between the kitchen and dining area, expressing my gratitude to customers and reminding them to check out coupons on my blog. When the crowd thins and the lunch rush concludes, I breathe out my relief.

Back in the kitchen, I find Lexi tearing open a bag of flour and Olivia fetching a mixer while others clear the counters.

"What's the flour for?" I arch my brows. "Aren't you all too tired for more cooking?"

Olivia shrugs. "Jeremy wants us to celebrate the day's end by making shortbread cookies."

My gaze shifts to Jeremy, and he presents me with an apron, mirroring those worn by everyone else. I slip the apron over my head and secure it behind me. "Baking it is."

"No one makes shortbread cookies without you taking charge." Jeremy guides me toward Lexi and Olivia, who have readied the supplies and mixer. "You and I will mix the ingredients together."

"We'll take over once the batter's ready," Olivia says while Lexi mentions she'll capture the moment in photos.

The kitchen's still abuzz—dishes headed for the sink, trash being discarded, and leftovers being saved and raided. Jeremy and I fall into an easy rhythm, cutting the butter into the sugar and creaming them before combining them with the other ingredients.

"After everyone eats the cookies, maybe we could treat them to dinner this evening? My treat, as a thank you for their help."

I like how he uses "we" in his sentence. "I could cook dinner at the house instead."

"I'm not letting you anywhere near a kitchen once we leave the café." He grins and flicks flour onto my apron.

Memories of our first time in this kitchen flood back, and I smirk at him. "You know you just put flour on my apron."

"And what are you going to do about it, Miss Blackwood?" His tone warms all my insides. He then scoops up more flour into his palm and blows it onto my face. That smirk and mischievous glint in his eye gives away his intent.

"What's making cookies without a little food fight?" His smile widens, and I beam back, the excitement infectious.

"Oh, it's on, Mr. Kress." Adrenaline mixes with anticipation as I scoop a handful of flour from the mixer and aim for him, but he's quick to shower me with more flour.

I manage to scatter some onto his sleek hair, laughing as I look for an escape, but with the kitchen bustling, I resort to circling around. And he catches me easily, spinning me into his arms and gazing down at me. His hand caresses my cheek, and my heart starts racing as he tucks a stray curl behind my ear. The kitchen falls into a hushed silence, and I sense all focus on us. But my gaze remains on my prize—Jeremy.

"In this very kitchen, I first fell in love with you." His voice goes husky, and a deep seriousness replaces his playful demeanor. "You looked beyond the façade I put up and invited me into your world without fear. You saw the real me, beneath my stern exterior. Remember when you covered me in flour during our so-called food wars?"

I nod, my heart thumping in my chest.

"You make the best shortbread cookies there are."

"You'd better like her cooking now that you're in love with her!" Jill calls out from the background, but Jeremy's intense gaze holds mine, making everything else fade away.

"Food is just one of your many passions I admire. But more than that, I admire your confidence and your faith in God." His confession earnest and his gaze intent, he grips my hands. The vulnerability in his blue eyes touches something deep inside me. "I want to know everything about you, Zee. I want to grow old with you and share in that faith. Maybe you can help me understand God better."

I nod, tears brimming at his heartfelt words, and my heart thuds. Who could imagine this moment, so sincere and full of love, in this very kitchen where our "fake" romance began?

"I know we've done this before." He releases me to create some space between us, then thrusts his hand into his pants pockets, and pulls something out.

I catch the sparkle of diamonds under the kitchen light, even before it's fully revealed. This time, it isn't nestled within a box.

"I could have bought you another ring, but this one—this was always meant for you." His voice carries a weight of tinged emotions. "Despite my never measuring your ring size, it fits you perfectly. Just like you seamlessly fit into my life... my world."

His eyes, shimmering under the fluorescent glow, probe mine, and emotions tighten my throat, so raw and sharp it feels like I've swallowed shards of glass. Around us, people express their awe with soft oohs and aahs as Jeremy articulates his declaration of love, each word coated with the depth of his feelings.

"Being with you creates a sanctuary of peace, a sense of safety, that makes me feel at home."

"Oh, Jer." I manage, my voice trembling. "You better never entertain any doubts about us again. You're literally my latest obsession. You complete me."

A smile breaks across his face, his lips parting, perhaps in readiness to echo my sentiment.

"With you, I can share my deepest fears, my highest hopes, and my wildest dreams." His gaze is tender, his words sincere.

"You make me feel safe," I add, recalling our initial encounters and how openly I shared my café struggles with him, something I'd never done with anyone else.

"Traitor!" Damien's playful accusation slices through the thick emotional atmosphere.

Then Jeremy lowers himself to one knee, a posture that heats up the anticipation already sizzling through my body. "Zuri Blackwood, will you marry me for real this time?"

"Yes, Jer, yes." I breathe out, and tears stream down my face as he slides the ring onto my finger.

The kitchen erupts in applause and laughter.

"How many times do you have to propose to her?" Jill's voice rises above the celebration, eliciting chuckles from all of us.

"Each time they find something to bicker about," Nico quips, reminding us of the ups and downs that flavored our relationship, any relationship. "But let's not forget, you're the one who brought them together."

Jeremy stands and draws me into his embrace—warm and comforting as he casts a grateful glance toward our friends. Then he seals our promise with a kiss so tender and profound it gives full testament to the depth of our love. Surrounded by friends in Zuri's Daylight Café, my heart swells. Here we are. I'm his for keeps, not temporarily, and we get to celebrate a dream achieved through my passion for cooking.

The party I threw to test my recipes brought a recipe for a new future into my life, sprinkling ingredients of love, hope, and uncertainty to season the mix of my daily routine. Had it not been for this passion, I wouldn't have organized the party nor had a reason to invite Jeremy. Yes, food has the power to unite people, creating bonds that bake into everlasting love.

It's not just the shared meals. The love and commitment between Jeremy and me also seals our connection. While food can draw people together, love's the ingredient that ensures they remain a part of each other's lives forever.

Join my Insider group and download the exclusive Recipe Collection from Yours Temporarily. You will receive weekly updates, sneak peeks and Work In Progress.

YOURS BLINDLY IS NEXT IN THE SERIES

Visit my website at www.rosefresquezbooks.com

Listen to my books for free on YOUTUBE

Connect with me in my reader group on Facebook

Follow me on Goodreads and Book Bub.

OTHER BOOKS BY ROSE

THE BUCHANAN SERIES

1. *First Site*
2. *Something right*
3. *Bright Side*
4. *Short Sighted*
5. *New Light (A Christmas Novella)*

ROMANCE IN THE ROCKIES SERIES

1. *Complex*
2. *Choices*

3. *Beyond Repair*
4. *Stand Out*
5. *Crystal Clear*

THE CAREGIVER SERIES

1. *The Doctor's Nanny*
2. *The Entrepreneur's Nurse*
3. *The Physician's Helper*
4. *The CEO's Companion*
5. *The Investor's Wife*
6. *The Soldier's Trainer*
7. *The Realtor's Attendant*

THE BILLIONAIRE REUNION SERIES

1. *A legitimate Date*
2. *A Sudden Romance*
3. *A Necessary Compromise*
4. *A Genuine Disguise*

5. *A Convenient Marriage*

THE OFFICE HEARTTHROBS SERIES

1. *Yours Temporarily*

2. *Yours Blindly*

3. *Yours Forever*

4. *Yours Faithfully*

You can also send me an email at rjfresquez@gmail.com

www.ingramcontent.com/pod-product-compliance
Lightning Source LLC
LaVergne TN
LVHW091116080826
845145LV00008B/1934

* 9 7 8 1 9 6 1 1 5 9 2 0 4 *